# TIDES OF FATE
## BOOK 3 OF THE CHRONICLES OF TALAHM
### COLLEEN MITCHELL

COLLEEN MITCHELL WRITES, LLC

Edited by Halie Fewkes Damewood, Lauren Loftis, & Shanna Lowe
Cover Art by Angelique Modin
Interior Illustration by LeighAnn Lopez

First paperback printing July 2025.
Kalispell, MT

Library of Congress Control Number: 2025912632
Paperback ISBN: 979-8-9850548-5-9
eBook ISBN: 979-8-9850548-4-2

For the best friends in my life whose
unmatched encouragement buoys me
through the harder, trying days.


A cord of three strands is not easily broken.


**Tim**
*A man* who makes me laugh
like no one else, who loves the LORD,
is a wizard in the kitchen, and lifts me
up when stormy seas strike.


&


**Jeannie**
*A woman* with relentless drive
to do good and honor God,
and who wasn't shy to ignore Mr. Pearce
during choir so we could write.


The only way to live is to risk living.

Silent Fields
Korad
Helcari Isles
Erusa
Stedrov
Borna
Sifnova
Zima
Fjords of Ferluna
Bearsmouth
The Sleeping Sea
Skypoint
Camelot
Petra
Riker's Rest
Valona
N
W
E
S
TALAHM

Northern Reaches
Skoye
Perga's Scepter
Sapphire Falls
Doltev
Nevari
Port Benga
Avon
Pevek
Starlight Canyon
Ekranom
Keldvaar
The Glass Channel
Ida
Whitehall
Set'ra
Dragonspring

# WHAT HAPPENED IN THE PROPHET'S RUIN

Portals began opening on their own across Earth and Talahm, and Julie vanished through one. During a Kraken attack, Argent lost his enchanted journal, cutting him off from Emma.

While Luke led rescue and disaster efforts across Renova, King Aragon refused to send a coven to search for Julie. Emma and Bethany returned to Camelot, shocked to find the walls still in ruins. Bethany joined the Royal Coven, but she couldn't make contact with the missing covens in Ralador. Luke, haunted by a Vision of a woman in purple strangling Argent, became convinced she was an ally—and that Argent was working to bring Septim back.

When Lord Knight Elijah Cade arrived asking for help in the Trident, Emma and Luke traveled west with him, leaving Bethany behind to integrate with her new battle sisters. Luke's animosity toward Argent caused a rift between him and Emma, which only deepened when she spotted Argent in the Trident and later reunited with him.

Argent told her what happened to the journal, and they kissed.

Luke schemed to lure Argent into the cathedral, hoping the woman from his Vision would appear and kill Argent before Emma could interfere. But the woman never came. Instead, they found Magdalin, Sargateth's long-missing wife, who revealed she'd been trapped on Langoth, a world of darkness and crushing gravity that Emma realized was orbiting a black hole.

On the journey back, direwolves hunted them. During an attack, Luke's shield failed, and a wolf injured Argent. Then Bethany's final message arrived: something was picking off her coven. Luke, shaken, sent William back to the Trident to sail south while the rest of them raced back to Camelot.

King Aragon refused to let them leave again. But Argent, Emma, and Luke escaped to Arthur's Grove. To get past the final magical barrier into the grove, Argent sacrificed Septim's memory of the day he died. Later, on their way into Ralador through the lava tubes, they faced a magical trap that forced them to relive their worst memories, but Emma broke them out. Argent revealed his was Septim receiving his powers from a woman in purple—the same woman from Luke's Vision.

Luke realized too late that she wasn't an ally. She was the enemy.

In Valona, they found Igraine Pendragon—King Arthur's mother—alive and holding ropes tied to nooses around Bethany's and Julie's necks. Emma freed them, but in the fight that followed, none of their magic worked against her. Igraine tried to strangle Argent—but Emma stopped her with a bolt of lightning. Mountains Crumble Beneath His Claws, Magdalin's Olis twin and Igraine's captive, opened a portal to Langoth, and Luke forced Igraine toward it with his shield. She fell through, but used a golden whip of magic to drag Bethany in with her.

Luke returned to Camelot via dragon with Mountains, who was too weak to open another portal. Onboard *The Sea Wolf*, Emma purged Septim from Argent's mind. When they returned to Camelot, Julie reunited with Tomás, and Argent had Emma destroy the ring Igraine had used to control King Aragon. Aragon admitted his failures as a father and regent. Luke, burdened by guilt, confessed that chasing his Vision had cost them Bethany.

Then Tomás, after years without a single glimpse of the future, had a Vision at last: Igraine would return. And destroy Talahm.

# PRONUNCIATION GUIDE

**Agamemnon** – Ag-uh-MEM-non

**Amity** – AM-itty

**Aragon** – AIR-a-gone

**Argent** – ARRG-ent

**Artair** – ARR-tare

**Catigern** – CAT-ih-ghern

**Cara** – CARR-uh

**Coventra** – Coe-VEN-truh

**Davan** – Duh-VON

**Ebe** – Ebby or Ebbie

**Elvara** – El-VARR-uh

**Hela** – HELL-uh

**Helcari** – Hell-CAR-ee

**Igraine** – EE-grain

**Keldvaar** – KELLD-var

**Khozek** – COE-zekk

**Langoth** – LAN-goth

**Le Fay** – Leh-FAY

**Magdalin** – MAG-duh-lin

**Nimüe** – NIM-you

**Olii** – OH-lie (plural of Olis)

**Olis** – OH-liss

**Petra** – PET-ruh

**Ralador** – RAL-uh-door

**Raphael** – RAFF-ay-el

**Renault** – Rehn-ALT

**Renova** – Reh-NOV-uh

**Reva** – REE-vuh

**Rhakmar** – RACK-marr

**Rishon** – Ree-SHAWN

**Sargateth** – SAR-guh-teth

**Septim** – SEP-tim

**Severna** – Sev-AIR-nuh

**Talahm** – Ta-LAW-m

**Tomás** – Toe-MOSS

**Valon** – VAL-un

**Valona** – VA-lone-uh

# CONTENTS

## CHAPTER ONE

# A WITCH OF RENOVA

**B**ethany Hawkins woke to the freezing cold and furious whispers of women she thought dead.

The last thing she remembered was a golden whip of magic shooting out of the portal Igraine Pendragon had fallen through. Then it had been only pain, darkness, and screaming, but she couldn't remember if the screams had been hers or Igraine's.

Now, lying flat on her back, she felt like she'd been hit by a bus. With magnificent effort, Bethany opened her eyes. A single glass-housed lantern hung from crisscrossed wicker poles. The structure looked too flimsy to be of solid construction, and after a moment, the ceiling rippled like cloth. Struggling to turn her head, she saw a small table by her bed with a pile of clothing on top, including a tattered leather cuirass, ripped battle skirts, and burned deerskin leggings.

Someone had found her. Someone had given her softer clothes and removed her broken coven armor. She tried bringing her hands to her face to wipe away the sleep, but someone had also bound her right arm securely to her chest....

And snapped a heavy manacle around her left wrist.

The manacle clanked loudly, instantly cutting off the whispers.

"Bethany?" A familiar dark-skinned face materialized over hers, slowly swimming into focus. Rissy Clement, their emergency healer and dervish with air magic, was alive. "Can you hear me?"

Bethany tried to talk, but her tongue stuck to the roof of her mouth.

Rissy helped Bethany sit up. Her head swam as Rissy twisted away and grabbed a waterskin, holding it to Bethany's lips. "You've been unconscious for five days."

Greedily sucking down what felt like enough water to fill an Olympic swimming pool, Bethany coughed. "Where are we? Is this a tent? What happened to—"

"This is what passes for a medical tent here," Rissy answered, pressing her fingertips into Bethany's bound arm. "They call it Langoth."

"That hurts," Bethany hissed through clenched teeth as a hazy projection of her broken bone flickered to life. What she wouldn't give for Luke to be her doctor right now.

Rissy sighed, deep worry lines etched into her forehead. "I did what I could when you arrived, but fixing this is above my skill level. A better healer than I will need to re-break your bone to set it properly. It's already knitting back together."

Bethany stared at Rissy's hands as the healer stood. "You're not shackled."

"We didn't kill anybody when we got here." Hela Tanberg, Bethany's Coventra, came into view. Her wild red hair and scratchy voice further disproved Igraine's claims she'd burned the rest of Bethany's coven.

"I'm sorry, *what*?" Bethany bent her head down to her shackled hand and cleared the wax from her ear, because surely she misheard. A strand of blonde hair Bethany desperately wanted to wash fell into her face, and it resisted her attempts to blow it out of the way. She swung her legs over the edge of the cot. Her bare feet hit frigid dirt, and she immediately drew them back onto the thin mattress. "And why is it so *cold*?"

Hela sifted through the clothes on the table and handed Bethany a pair of soft boots, one torn down to the ankle. "I didn't see it happen, but when you and that harlot Igraine got here, one of you killed the settlement leader's apprentice witch."

Bethany's brain latched onto a single word as she tugged on the boots one-handed. "Where's Igraine?"

Hela grimaced. She glanced over her shoulder at Rissy, who crouched between a man and woman on sick beds. "She did a runner. Harlow and I went after her, but she hid herself from all our tracking spells."

Bethany's breath stuck to her throat. "She's gone?"

Hela offered her a measly bread roll. "We're *all* stuck here, Firewhip. Including Igraine. It's Langoth. The home of the Fifth Travelers. *Nobody* gets off this planet."

Bethany stuffed the food into her mouth. Although that news threatened to send her into a tailspin, Bethany remembered how she and Igraine had ended up here. How Igraine couldn't shut up about how she'd forced *Mountains Crumble Beneath His Claws* to build her an army of creatures... from Langoth. She took another swig from the waterskin to wash down the dry, bland bread. "I wonder if that claw necklace Igraine wears could be our ticket off this rock."

Hela's eyebrows raised, and her coven tattoo jumped with the pulse at her throat. "What do you mean?"

"She hacked it off the Olis she had captive. They can create portals. What if their claws are like the gauntlet Rowan uses to open the portals to Earth?"

"She had an *Olis* captive?"

Bethany paused. "I guess you missed a lot." She got to her feet, her shoulders sagging. The only other time she'd felt this heavy had been on one of those amusement park rides that shot its riders into the air so fast it created G-forces on the body, but Bethany stood perfectly still. "Why do I feel like I gained a hundred pounds?"

Hela pinched the bridge of her nose, clearly exasperated, and helped Bethany into the rest of her ruined armor. "Go back to the part about the claw. Do you really think it would work?"

Bethany tried to crack her back, but her broken arm made it hard to get any leverage. "Even if it doesn't, it's not like there are any other options. I'll just have to track down that royally selfish cow and steal it."

Hela gestured to the restraints. "I can't break you free. We tried the first night, but it's enchanted like the Archmage's work."

Bethany stared at the manacle. Dim runes were etched around its circumference.

Magic-suppressing cuffs. Like the ones Mountains had worn in captivity beneath Valona.

"Hela," Rissy called out, and the Coventra left Bethany alone with her thoughts. Their angry whispering resumed at the end of the other sick beds.

Bethany couldn't walk far, her manacle connected to a chain secured to an iron peg pounded into the dirt. "What's up with them?"

Rissy shot Hela a look that Bethany had learned meant something like 'stop being stupid.'

But before Hela could explain, a bitter burst of cold froze them all. The tent flap pushed open, and a tall, broad-shouldered woman entered, her dark eyes glittering in the light she held in her palm. Shoulder-length, salt-and-pepper hair fluttered in the breeze.

"I ought to execute you for what you did to my apprentice," she said in an accent that sounded vaguely Russian. "You better hope you have the power to help me stop the next wave. It's the worst one I've ever seen, and it will be here in less than twenty minutes."

Hela blanched, her already pasty skin whiter than Bethany thought possible.

"Are you talking to me?" Bethany asked with a sinking feeling, pointing at herself.

A striking half-moon tattoo covered the left side of the woman's face. She zeroed in on Bethany with hawk-like precision, taking two steps forward. "Yes, I am talking to you, O witch who murdered the only help I had to keep my people alive."

Hela stepped next to Bethany. "I can vouch for her. This is Bethany, my Firewhip, but she is skilled in all of the branches of magic."

Bethany opened her mouth to add more, but the hard line of Hela's tightened jaw stopped her.

"I am Kenna, chief of the Fifth Travelers," the woman said, fishing an iron key from a leather pouch at her waist.

Agony flared through Bethany's broken arm, and she gritted her teeth.

Kenna's eyes shifted, glancing past Hela. "Clement, numb her arm. She won't be of use to me with pain distracting her."

Rissy hurried over and wrapped both hands around Bethany's bicep, squeezing gently. A moment later, the discomfort dulled to a soft ache.

Kenna grabbed Bethany's manacled wrist and unlocked it. Almost as soon as the cuff fell to the ground, Bethany called flames to her hand, the warmth of magic spreading to the tips of her toes.

"Keep that fire lit," Kenna commanded. She ducked back through the tent opening, Hela right behind her.

Bethany looked for the rest of her things, finding them in an unceremonious bundle by the entrance. Striding over, Bethany let the flames trail up her arm and sorted through the pile.

She unearthed two daggers near the bottom.

Bethany deftly slid them into the sheaths built into her skirt, tucking the ruined cuirass over them before joining the others outside the tent.

She shivered despite her magic. They stood on the edge of a tight circular courtyard surrounded by brown tents, all interconnected. Tall poles topped with lanterns provided light in the dark, though an odd red hue covered everything.

Nothing seemed out of the ordinary until Bethany looked up.

Neither night nor day, an oblong red disk streaked the sky, an enormous, pitch-black ball at its center.

The increased weight, the bitter cold....

"A black hole," Bethany croaked, unable to take her eyes off the monstrosity. "Langoth is orbiting a black hole."

"Quickly now," Kenna snapped, hurrying across the courtyard. "I haven't the time to explain the danger to someone dimwitted enough to dawdle when we have *less than eighteen minutes*."

Neither battle witch had adjusted to Langoth's increased gravity, so they struggled to keep up. By the time they made it to the center of the settlement, Kenna was speaking with a short, heavyset man who leaned on a staff without a gemstone.

"The tidal wave's peak will fully crest the cliff again," the man said as they approached. "This one is higher than the others." Like Kenna, he had a phase of the moon inked on his skin. He looked afraid.

A chill worked its way down Bethany's neck.

"Misha, gather what earthwitches we have and pack dirt outside the stakes," Kenna commanded. She turned to Hela. "You are a waterwitch. Stay here and divert what flooding you can. Rustle up your other witch and station her at the sick tent. I'll not have any more deaths in my village. Pray this whelp can do what you claim."

Hela pressed her fingers to her throat, and Bethany felt her use the Coven Mark to tell Harlow Barnes to report.

"You." Kenna pointed at Bethany. "Follow me." Without waiting for a response, she headed toward a thin gap in the courtyard lined with two rows of stones.

Leaving the confines of the tents, Bethany's limbs dragged against the increased gravity. Along the path, poles with lanterns extended far into the darkness.

Another prickle raised the hairs on the back of Bethany's neck. *Are there more of the creatures Igraine captured here? And what didn't she snag?*

She heard the scuff of Kenna's shoes, the only sound ahead of her, but the feeling didn't go away.

A whisper brushed past Bethany's hair.

*Bethie*, it crooned in a voice Bethany never wanted to hear again.

Bethany almost stopped walking, but dread forced her forward. She strained to see past the lights and into the darkness, but she couldn't make out a thing.

*Bethany Hawkins... I have something you want....*

Bethany tried to shut the voice out. "One emergency at a time," she muttered.

"An apt saying," Kenna said, coming to an abrupt halt. She threw out her arm, stopping Bethany at the edge of a vast, sheer cliff. "It's hard to see each wave without a sun."

Her heart palpitating uncontrollably, Bethany backed away from the drop-off. The red velvet donut in the sky drew her eyes up, but its light did little to prepare her for the dark mass obscuring part of the horizon. "Why don't you just move to higher ground?"

Kenna's voice was thin and weary. "We *are* on the highest ground. My people live here because we must if we want to survive. But now I have no hope but you."

Bethany swallowed, squaring her shoulders. "If I'm the one who's responsible for your apprentice, I'm sorry. And if it was Igraine, I'm still sorry."

Kenna didn't seem to accept the apology. "The last wave was four days ago. Your Coventra could barely help, and my power is far from its former strength. Keeping the village safe nearly killed me." Her eyes narrowed. "You will obey my every instruction if you wish to get out of this alive. Is that clear?"

Bethany nodded, trying to squash her panic. "Crystal."

# CHAPTER TWO
# DUALITY

The cold, hard stones of Camelot's infirmary dug into Emma's knees, but she barely noticed. Her father, Tomás, the elder Prophet of Camlaan, held her hand in a death grip as he sat on the edge of the infirmary bed. He'd just spoken his first prophecy in almost three years.

Her father's mismatched green and gold eyes fluttered open and focused on hers. "I Saw utter failure—death and destruction beyond belief."

Stunned, she rocked backward, but her dad's hand tightened, keeping her in place. Emma's eyes flickered to her mother, Julie, who sat on her father's right, looking just as startled. Julie reached out as if to brush away the hair that had tumbled over her husband's eyes, but she drew her fingers back at the last second.

"That's not what I just Saw," Luke said from behind her.

"What?" Emma glanced over her shoulder at Luke, her studious but stressed-out brother, who was also a Prophet. He hadn't moved from his seat on the bed, his chin-length black hair mussed from running his fingers through it.

Luke swallowed, slowly unclenching from the bedspread. "I had almost the same Vision, but I Saw victory. Our victory."

"That's never happened before." Renault Le Fay, the commander of Camelot's soldiers and half-Olis son of Morgan Le Fay, sat at Tomás's left, disbelief etched on his scruffy face. Focusing, his beady eyes darkened. "Two Prophets with different Visions of the same event?"

Emma didn't care about this development. She brought them back to the only thing that mattered. "Did either of you see Bethany?"

She watched as father and son stared at each other.

"Wherever this battle happens, was Bethany there?" Emma's chest tightened, her heart hammering in anticipation.

Her father shook his head.

Luke squeezed his eyes shut, as if replaying the Vision. His brows drew together, and Emma knew before he opened his eyes that he also hadn't Seen Bethany on the battlefield.

"Not Seeing her in the Vision doesn't mean she won't be there," her father said, though he didn't sound convincing. "It was chaos."

Emma wrenched her hand from her father's and scrambled to her feet. "There has to be a way to save her right now. If you both Saw Igraine, that means there's a way off Langoth."

A measure of hope replaced some of the dread on Luke's face.

With her best friend's life literally on the line, Emma didn't want everyone to get distracted by the novelty of two versions of the same Vision.

Emma narrowed her eyes at her least favorite Olis. *Mountains Crumble Beneath His Claws* had said moments before her father's prophecy that he couldn't open a portal without Camelot getting sucked into the dying lands. Now, she wasn't sure if she believed him. If conflicting prophecies were possible, what else could be?

Familiar magic built in her chest—the kind she'd felt when she'd made precipitate prophecies. The first time, she'd inadvertently doomed her high school bully to a life of regret, and the second had saved her father's life from an arrow to the heart. By sheer chance, Bethany had bumped into a miserable Chad Halliwell in college. And Emma had watched the second unfold before her eyes during the last moments before Septim's curse broke, freeing the city.

"I'm getting Bethany back today."

"No, you're not," Mountains said in a singsong voice that sent a deep tremor of anger through her.

She stared Mountains down, blue-black energy crackling around her palms. "Bethany is my best friend, you overgrown rat. I'll do whatever it takes to get her back, whether you like it or not!"

"Emma—"

She ignored Renault's interruption and squeezed her eyes shut, focusing her attention on the magic building in her chest and hands. "Bethany will walk through those doors now!" With the final word, she stared confidently at the infirmary doors, but they didn't budge.

From the corner of her eye, she saw Prince Argent step around the foot of her father's bed, the infirmary lights highlighting the scar on his cheek. He smiled encouragingly.

Luke stood behind her and placed both of his palms on her shoulders. Warmth spread down her arms as Luke's magic joined with hers, together as Sorceress and Sentinel.

Clinging to the connection, Emma reached up and laid her hands on top of her brother's. "Bethany will come home right now!"

She heard nothing but the gentle swish of Mountains' tail over his sickbed.

Her heart in her throat, she tried again, squeezing Luke's clenched fingers. "Mountains will open a portal for us right now!" Her magic fizzled, then faded entirely. She hadn't felt the same rooting she had when she'd made the precipitate prophecies about Chad and her father. "Why won't it *work* this time?"

Mountains gave an infuriating guffaw. "I already told you. Even if I *could* open one, I wouldn't do it here. Your quaint little castle would implode."

Emma wanted to punch Mountains in his smarmy face, but Luke held her in place.

"Magic cannot solve everything," Sargateth Rishon, Archmage of Camelot and firstborn of the Olii, said, speaking quietly from where he leaned against the infirmary windows. Magdalin Skyheart, his wife and Mountains' twin, stood tucked into his side with her arms wrapped around his middle. "We've been given a gift. This is the first time we have the opportunity to make a difference in how a Vision comes to pass. We have a way out."

"A way out of what?" Julie interrupted. "And what exactly is Perga's Scepter? A thing we need to get?"

Mountains made a noise of disgust. "A way out of certain defeat. Don't you know anything about prophecies? They always come true, and if these two are actually at odds, then only one can triumph. And Perga's Scepter is a *place*, you uneducated buffoon. It's home to the Jade Temple and the Titan Obelisk, which is the oldest and most stable gateway between the worlds. If Igraine *can* escape Langoth, it would be at the Titan."

"Don't insult my wife," Tomás rebuked sharply. He tried to stand, but he'd been paralyzed by the Tears of Nightshade and needed assistance. His enchanted exoskeleton, broken by his sudden thrust into the Vision, weighed down his legs even more.

"I'm not giving up on Bethany," Emma insisted. In the back of her mind, she could still feel the magical connection she'd created with her best friend during the fight beneath Ralador's capital city. The connection had survived Bethany's trip to another world, even if they couldn't directly communicate across such a vast distance.

Flanked by Argent's comforting presence, Luke came around to her side, draping one arm across her shoulders. He met her gaze, and the fiery determination in them matched her own.

"Both of us have only used three of the four trips between here and Earth," Luke said. "What's stopping us from going back to Earth and immediately taking a fifth trip? We'd land on Langoth with Bethany and the Fifth Travelers. Sargateth can come with us and open a portal to bring us all back!"

Emma's heart sped up. "That's perfect!"

"No!" Magdalin let go of Sargateth, rushing over as if they planned to execute this new strategy right away. "I was there, remember? The survivors were the lucky ones." Magdalin's soft voice forced everyone in the infirmary to quiet. Wind whistled through the spider cracks in the window broken earlier by Renault's angry magic. "Not every scout who went through a fifth time arrived on Langoth. Kenna, their leader, told me that many people ended up going missing in transition."

Morgan Le Fay, twin to Sargateth, stamped her amethyst staff on the flagstones. A chair materialized beneath her, and she sagged into it, looking like all the weight of her millennia rested upon her shoulders. Her black hair, cut to a bob just below her ears, framed her face, her dark eyes glittering. "Until you saved Magdalin's life in the Trident, we did not know about Langoth. We had never suspected a third world and counted the Fifth Travelers as not just lost but dead. For months, Sargateth feared Magdalin was on Earth, but we used our passages to their end. If we had gone after her, we would have been trapped on this Langoth or lost to the universe."

The last thing Emma wanted was to die in the vacuum of space because they unraveled magic by crossing too many times between worlds.

"It's not worth the risk," Magdalin finished.

Anger reared its ugly head again, but Luke beat Emma to the punch. "Stop telling us what is or isn't worth Bethany's life!"

"Like I said," Mountains interjected dryly. "She'll stay lost for now."

Emma skirted around Magdalin, stalking over to Mountains' bed. She pointed at him with one long, accusing finger. "If you can't open a portal here, go out to the Ogwen Plains and open one there. Pull her through like you did for all the animals and *people* we saved from those cages in Valona. Do *something* useful!"

Mountains bared his fangs, snarling. "I'm the one who saved your sorry hides from Igraine in the bowels of her fortress. *I'm* the one who opened the gate to Langoth when you failed to defeat her. *I'm* the one who made it possible for you to push her through it at all! And I've yet to hear a thank you!"

Emma glared at him, her hands curling into fists. They tingled as her magic sparked again, flowing down her birthmarked arms. She hated everything about him—his crusty fur, the stump of the claw Igraine had cut off at the knuckle, his mangled wing. Even in his state of utter dependence, he still wormed his way under everyone's skin. "Open a portal."

Sargateth darted between them and forced her to take a step back. "Don't antagonize him," he whispered. His kind green eyes, normally bright and mischievous, had dulled, strain pulling at the corners. Light brown hair fell midway down his neck, feather-soft but mussed.

"The only place I'd be willing to even attempt one is on Perga's Scepter with the Titan Obelisk to anchor it, and that's quite a long journey from here," Mountains snapped, shifting to the edge of his large infirmary bed so both paws hung over the edge. "The universe has destabilized, you dull moron, and portals require *stability*. I'd tell you to ask Firstborn why rogue ones are still popping up, but he just talks around his answers."

Emma narrowed her eyes. First at Mountains, then at Sargateth, who shifted uncomfortably but said nothing.

"As I thought," Mountains said with an exaggerated sigh. "He probably left this out of your history books, but the Olii harmonize with Earth. And, apparently, Langoth.

We four have long been absent from Skypoint, haven't we? It puts far too much strain on the others in their seasons of residence."

King Aragon, who had remained stoic and silent for a long time, finally spoke. "This is getting us nowhere. We must prepare a party to leave for Perga's Scepter. But before that," he pointed at Luke and then down at Emma's father, "you two need to determine the difference between winning and losing. Both prophecies cannot be true."

Emma desperately wanted to keep the focus on Bethany, but she didn't know what else to try if their best hope of saving her was in Perga's Scepter.

"Twelve Olii in the air," Tomás began tentatively, but Luke shook his head, walking over to the beds.

"I Saw only ten flying. Sargateth, Morgan, and Mountains were on the ground in battle."

"I Saw them present at the temple as well."

Luke patted his pockets and fished out a notebook and pen. His shoulders rounded as he wrote. "Fifteen Olii if we fail. Thirteen if we win."

Julie got up and peered over Luke. "Why would there be more Olii in the scenario where we lose?"

Mountains snorted. "Some of my kin would gladly watch puny humans die. Pray that you end up with ten who do not have that disposition."

Luke scribbled some more, pausing to bite the end of his pen. "We'll need to find them and tell them what's coming—and make sure the right ones end up at the Scepter."

"You'd have better luck turning back time. The Olis Council does not treat with humans," Mountains said.

"Too bad," Luke sniped, making another note. "I need to look at their faces to match them to my Vision."

Tomás drummed his fingers against the tops of his thighs. "The King and the Prince are present, amidst many other men whom I did not recognize."

Emma's heart flip-flopped. She reached out and grasped Argent's hand, savoring the warmth of his fingers as they curled around hers. They moved closer to Luke.

"Who could the unfamiliar men be? Our forces consist of coven witches. Did you See if they fought with us or against us?" King Aragon questioned.

Tomás and Luke both shrugged. "I couldn't discern any identifying armor or marks," Tomás said. "Much of the Vision was a haze—a quick succession of images and events. It's difficult to say whose side they are on."

King Aragon made a noise of acknowledgment, but his brow remained furrowed in thought.

Renault got to his feet, crossed his beefy arms, and moved like an over-sized hawk to the end of the bed. "Was

I there?" he asked. While he sounded suspiciously neutral, his eyes gave away his hunger for battle.

Tomás and Luke shook their heads.

King Aragon began pacing, waving Queen Amity away when she tried to stop him. "Camelot is now home to two dragons. At first blush, this quest seems like it might benefit greatly from such an asset, but I would not leave Renault to protect the city without them."

Luke answered the King's unspoken question first. "No dragons helped in the version where we win."

"Neither is their absence the reason we might fail."

Luke sat in the spot Renault had vacated. "Did you see Argent's bow? It didn't look like the one he has in the armory."

Emma tensed, her mind immediately thrown back to watching an arrow pierce her father's chest.

Tomás frowned, pressing his palms against the tops of his deadened legs. "No... Argent carried a sword in mine. Not a bow."

"Draw it," Renault said, his eyes slowly bleeding to purple as he stared at Luke.

Luke flipped to a new page and furiously started sketching. Emma came over, watching her brother draw glyphs up and down the wood as the bow took shape. "It was almost as tall as Argent, and it glowed."

"Uncle," Renault said, gesturing for Sargateth to move closer. "Is that what I think it is?"

Luke held the drawing out for the Archmage. Sargateth's face lost the rest of its color. "I killed Atlas with that bow!"

"Who's Atlas?" Julie asked, putting both hands on her hips.

"You don't want to know," Mountains said quietly.

Sargateth kept silent, returning to his spot by the wall with a funny look on his face. Magdalin leaned back into him, her arms wrapping around his waist, and rested her head against his chest.

"The Elvara Bow is powerful enough to kill Igraine with a single shot," Renault said, tone low. "But it's been locked up in Skypoint for millennia. Only the Olis Council has the authority to release it."

Argent's hand felt clammy against Emma's. She didn't blame him. He hadn't picked up a bow since Septim forced him to shoot her father.

King Aragon drew their attention. "Sargateth, leave with Morgan at once for Skypoint. Retrieve the Elvara Bow and rendezvous with us on the road to Elidon. We leave tomorrow for Perga's Scepter."

"Sire," Luke said, spinning on his heel. "Dad and I have to go with them to identify the Olii who shouldn't come—otherwise, we risk failure."

King Aragon raised an eyebrow. "Sargateth can command ten to go. It does not matter to me which ten."

But Sargateth shook his head reluctantly. "Prophecy is imprecise, but it would help our chances of success to know which Olii should remain behind. I agree that Luke and Tomás should come with us."

"It won't be easy," Mountains piped up. "They'll insist on Catigern. Proper ceremony, you know."

Sargateth sighed in defeat. "He's right. We'll all need to go to Skypoint first."

King Aragon frowned. "Very well. But go ahead with Morgan to... soften them up. I won't have us inviting displeasure by surprising them with a host of humans at their door."

## CHAPTER THREE

# AN INKLING

Luke tried to sleep, but every time he nodded off, his guilt and fear for Bethany yanked him awake.

He sat against the cold stone of the library's tower stair and stared at the door, not truly seeing it. After Sargateth and Morgan had left for Skypoint, taking Magdalin with them, Luke hadn't wanted to be around anyone.

He doubted Emma could sleep, either. He'd watched as she and Argent had left the infirmary together, envious that she could turn to him for support when Luke's support was trapped on Langoth.

Maybe none of them would sleep tonight.

The events of the last weeks replayed in his mind as he tried to figure out how he could have done things differently and what difference it might have made.

Could he have saved Bethany from Langoth?

He wrestled with what he knew of prophecies. They could not be changed any more than the past could. But now they had the chance to choose the outcome. To influence whether his came true or his father's did.

Luke tilted his head back and rested it against the smooth stones of the wall. The cold soaked into his scalp, distracting him from the yawning hole in the center of his chest, where his heart had been yanked out when Igraine pulled Bethany through the portal.

*Lord, protect her. It's all my fault. If I hadn't....*

There were so many things he should have never done. Would any of this have happened if he'd not suspected Argent? The Prince would eventually be his king. If it had been Aragon.... Luke cringed, remembering that he *had* accused the King of being controlled. It didn't make him feel any better that he'd been right. Igraine's claws had been deep in the Pendragon dynasty for centuries without any of them knowing.

Now he understood some secrets were poisonous. His secrets, paired with the cursed sleeping aid, had only increased his paranoia. Paranoia that drove him to keep even more secrets, and, worse, to lie about them.

When he'd faced the painful reality of what he'd done, Luke had to stomach the fact that he'd nearly gotten Argent Pendragon, heir to the throne, killed.

And what would King Aragon have done? Blinded by his suspicions and egged on by Igraine, Luke had never once considered what the ruler of Renova might do to him for causing the Pendragon line to end.

If Luke had succeeded, he would have been guilty of regicide.

The blood drained from his face, and the lights from the sconces swam in his vision.

*I would be dead now.*

And for what? If Igraine had successfully strangled Argent—if she'd left him broken and lifeless on the stone floor of that chamber—would she still have dragged Bethany through the portal to Langoth? Or would he have killed his Prince only for the love of his life to watch him die a traitor's death?

Igraine would have won.

Sick to his stomach, Luke hugged himself and tried to stop the dizziness from pulling him under. He ignored the extremely small part of his brain that reminded him that *none of that ever happened.*

Luke didn't know he'd forgotten to set a privacy charm until Queen Amity quietly adjusted her skirts and sat on the floor next to him. Her warmth seeped between them, but his dread and guilt kept him from looking at her.

"It wasn't your—"

"Please don't," Luke interrupted, his voice ragged.

"Why not?" the Queen replied, not missing a beat. "Are you so determined to bear the guilt alone when doing so would only hurt you more? It does none of us any good, least of all you."

Amity's warmth chased away the cold, leaving Luke stiff and uncomfortable. "I never meant—"

"Of course you didn't," Amity said. She cupped his cheek and turned his face toward her, forcing him to meet her kind, forgiving gaze. "If you had meant any of it with your true heart, you wouldn't be sitting here intent on suffering for it." Without waiting for his permission, Amity tucked her arm over his shoulders, and he leaned against her like he had often leaned against his mother on Earth. The parallel made him want to cry.

"I'm sorry," Luke whispered, his cheekbone pressed against the Queen's bony shoulder.

Amity gave him a gentle squeeze. "You know," she said after a beat of silence. "It's a pity you forgot about that interesting object at the base of the Titan Obelisk in your Vision, isn't it?"

Confused, Luke's breath caught in his lungs. "What?"

The Queen tightened her arm, holding him still with startling strength. "Such a pity. You could have saved Bethany with it." Amity's free hand came up, clenched around the hilt of a long, sharp dagger that caught the light from the sconce.

She plunged it into his heart.

Pain radiated through his whole body, and Luke strained to draw breath.

"At last," Amity breathed. Luke blinked at her through the haze of pain, and her features melted away, revealing Igraine Pendragon in her place. "Victory shall be mine."

Luke's head fell forward. Just as his chin met his chest, he jerked awake.

Amity—or, rather, Igraine—no longer sat beside him. Luke sucked in a deep, cleansing breath. He scrabbled his hands across his chest for the wound but found nothing. His heart thundered, the adrenaline of the vivid nightmare pumping wildly through his veins.

The light above him flickered again, casting shadows across the still-closed door to the library.

No one had come to find him.

Luke scrubbed at his face, the days-old growth of beard scratchy against his palms. His heart clenched, and a sob escaped his throat before he could stop it.

*Had* he forgotten about something about the obelisk? He pressed his palms against his eyes, replaying what he'd Seen in his head. The Olii in flight. The seething mass of fighting on the temple grounds. Prince Argent shooting an arrow from that glowing bow into the throng.... And, sure enough, a football-sized black rock with blocky cobalt blue threads perched at the Titan Obelisk's base.

How had he missed that?

And how had his nightmare known?

The door clicked open, and soft lights from the library illuminated Queen Amity's golden tresses.

Luke shied back, his muscles tense as he pressed against the wall. *Was that a Vision?* "What are you doing here?" he asked, unable to keep his wariness buried.

The Queen frowned and stepped into the tower, leaving the library door open behind her.

Luke scrambled away, knocking his knee against the stone. He wanted to keep some distance between them, but he also didn't want to fall down the stairs and break his neck.

"Luke.... I know what you want to say."

"I really doubt that," he replied, still edging down the tower stairs. It didn't seem in Amity's character to assassinate him, but that dagger had felt so real in his chest. Instead, he brought one hand up and cast a shield that immediately flared to life between them.

The surprise on Queen Amity's face almost made him waver, but before he could give in, he turned away and fled, the shield at his back.

The castle would rouse soon, and Luke made a beeline for the Artair Apartments to talk to Emma.

He'd barely had time to apologize to her for his poor decisions about Argent. Anxiety wound in his stomach. Even though he had no idea what the nightmare-vision meant, he worried Emma would dismiss his concerns without listening.

He quietly closed the door behind him, pressing a hand against the wood to shield the entrance from intruders.

One *specific* intruder.

He paused, letting his eyes adjust to the large common room. A fire crackled low in the hearth, because no matter the season, castles were always cold. Emma's room, normally shared with Bethany, was on the right. Luke passed his own room and knocked lightly on Emma's door.

He heard a quiet rustle of bedsheets and whispers. *Who else is in there?*

The door creaked open, showing Emma's tired face. "Luke? What's wrong? You woke Mom up."

"I—sorry," he apologized, momentarily thrown by the fact that his mother was sleeping in Bethany's bed. But with the consequences of secrets still fresh in his mind, Luke took a deep breath. "Can I talk to you? It's important."

Emma's pale face relaxed. "Yeah, let me get dressed."

Luke swallowed, nodding in agreement. She clicked the door closed, and Luke spun on his heel, hastily deciding to change his own clothes. In the silence of his room, he put on what would be his traveling pants and shoved his feet into his deerskin boots.

On the bedside table, the sleeping stone Igraine had used to influence him sat innocently by his lamp. He froze, staring at it.

Could she still be using it against him? A pit of dread opened in his stomach. He considered smashing the stone against the floor but suspected it might be enchanted not to break. He snatched it off the table. The faster Emma could destroy it, the better.

Emma waited for him in the common room with their mother.

"Morning, kids," Julie greeted quietly, looking far more awake than either of her children. "It's been a long time since I could say that to you both." She pulled Luke into a hug that made him want to melt, then kissed his forehead. "I'll head down to help prep for leaving."

As Julie made for the door, Luke remembered the shield he'd placed over it. "Hold on, let me get that for you," he said, jumping to press his hand against the wood. The lock clicked, and he pulled it open.

Their mother slipped through, leaving them alone.

"Was that a shield?" Emma asked curiously.

Luke didn't answer, instead holding out the star-shaped sleeping stone.

Emma's face fell. "You didn't use it again, did you?"

"No!" Luke exclaimed louder than he meant to. "No. I want you to destroy it."

"Gladly, but not up here." She slid the stone into her pocket. "Let's go down to the courtyard."

Luke hesitated. He didn't want to run into their mother when he told Emma about his nightmare and the strange object atop the Titan Obelisk.

"What's going on with you?" Her genuineness loosened his reluctance.

Luke took a deep breath. "I'll tell you on the way."

Luke waited until they were halfway down the long hallway that connected the residential side of the keep to the library before saying anything else. "I saw something last night, but I couldn't tell if it was a Vision." He opened the door to the tower stairs and gestured for Emma to go ahead.

But she didn't. Instead, she stopped in her tracks on the rich carpet covering the stone floor. "What was it?"

Paranoid and exasperated, he wove a privacy charm around them and gently pushed her to keep walking. As they descended, he told her the rest, his eyes fixed on the back of her head. He tried not to read too much into it when she tensed and looked back at him, almost missing a step. He snatched her arm to save her from stumbling.

"Are you sure it wasn't just your overactive imagination? Or this thing?" She touched her pocket with the sleeping stone in it.

"I don't know. In my Visions, it's like I'm actually there, and my senses work like in reality. That knife to the heart felt exactly like I'd imagine it would in real life. But there's no way Igraine is here, let alone impersonating the Queen. And it's not like me to forget an important part of a Vision." He fell silent, unsure if he should continue. But he didn't want his secrets to come between them again. "It made me wonder if it's a warning. Like one of the Pendragons might betray us."

Emma stopped, slowly facing him despite her precarious position on the steps. "Argent would never betray me."

Luke held up his hands in a placating gesture. "I didn't say he would. I don't know what to make of that dream or nightmare or whatever it was—I just know it felt like my Visions, even if it didn't have all the same elements the others do."

Emma scrutinized him, her brows furrowed. She pressed her thumb into the palm of her right hand, where her white tesseract birthmark rooted the black-and-blue tendrils covering most of her skin. "I trust Argent."

"And I trust *you*. I haven't quite worked back up to trusting anyone but family yet. I don't even know how to tell the others I forgot about the thing at the Titan Obelisk."

Emma reached back into her pocket and withdrew the sleeping stone, eyeing it with both venom and curiosity. "Could this have... *given* you your Vision of us winning?"

"I don't know," Luke answered with a pained whisper. "But we can't take that as a reason to not try to make that Vision come true."

"Agreed," Emma replied without hesitation, and her shoulders relaxed. "Let's get rid of this."

She stalked down the stairs and Luke followed, canceling his charm when they emerged in the southwestern corridor leading to Pendragon Hall. They continued down a wide staircase into the keep's courtyard and crossed the magical barrier that kept the first-floor corridor open but protected from the weather.

To their left, a wide, sturdy carriage rested on its tongue. In the predawn dark, Luke barely recognized his mother moving around it.

Arrows thwacked against training targets, echoing across the courtyard. Argent steadily drew the weapons from a quiver at his waist, sending them into the straw dummies with his personal bow from the armory. The arrows struck the dummies with alarming precision.

A hawk screeched, and it took Luke a moment to find the bird zipping toward the entrance to Pendragon Hall, a scroll clutched in its talons. At least the main form of communication in this world came back after they'd freed the hawks from Igraine's traps in Valona.

"If that's from Sargateth, it's probably not good news," Luke mused darkly.

Emma set Luke's erstwhile sleeping aid on a large paving stone and conjured a small shield around it. She cupped her hands together and flexed as if squeezing a ball. Inside the barrier, the device rattled faster and faster until it exploded, vaporizing. Releasing the shield, she brushed her hand over the stone, sending the dust away in a whirlwind.

"Earth magic?"

"Don't tell the architect."

Luke tried to smile but couldn't.

"Nifty stuff." Their mom's voice startled him, and he jumped, despite knowing she was nearby.

"What were you doing over there?" Luke asked, peering at the monstrous carriage, now more visible as the sun rose.

Julie pressed her lips together in a thin line. "Mountains can't fly, can't walk very well, and refuses to take human form to ride a horse. So that's going to be his transport. We'll have to figure out what to do with him when we reach Skypoint—or even the Scepter—on the way."

"Artairs!"

They looked up to see Renault coming toward them, a sheet of parchment crinkled in one hand and the hawk perched on his shoulder.

Argent stopped training, unstringing the bow as he strode across the courtyard to join them. Emma kissed him on the cheek.

"Mountains was right." Renault handed Luke the missive.

Luke scanned the letter, annoyance building with each word. "The Olii are in an uproar over the 'return of the traitors.' They're refusing to hand over the bow until Mountains is returned unharmed, and they hear from the 'witnesses.'" He glanced up at Renault. "I assume this has to do with whatever Catigern is? Who are the witnesses?"

"Catigern is the Olis Council's courtroom. As victims of Igraine, Mountains, Julie, and the Prince must testify and make the case for why the Olii should give us the Elvara Bow."

Julie cleared her throat. "I have to testify about what now?"

"The atrocities you suffered while Igraine held you captive."

"Great, as if I wanted to relive that," Julie muttered and turned away, beginning to pace.

Luke sighed, running a hand through his hair. He met Renault's piercing gaze. *Could he know what that object is?* The back of Luke's neck prickled. He glanced toward Emma, and she nodded, seeming to read his mind. It was a show of his trust in her that he didn't ask Argent to leave.

"Renault, I remembered something else about my Vision." He took out his notebook again and quickly sketched the football-shaped stone. Holding it out to Renault, he braced himself for disappointment. "Is this here in Camelot?"

Renault's frown deepened. "No.... But there's a book in the library that might help. Wait here." He turned on his heel and strode away. The hawk squawked in protest, taking flight.

When Renault returned, he held a fat leather-bound tome. He handed it to Luke.

Luke accepted the book and read the title, raising his eyebrows. "*A Brief History of Severna?* This must be over a thousand pages!"

Renault scowled at him. "If that sketch of yours is accurate, you're going to have to make a detour to Severna." He dropped his voice. "And if the Elvara Bow is involved.... Atlas was the Nephilim King before the Olii formed Severna. Read that book on your way. You'll need it."

# CHAPTER FOUR
# IT'S WET OUT

Bethany forced herself to slow her breathing. Adjusting to the red-tinted light from the black hole's luminous disk, the tower of water that loomed on the horizon took shape. "I may have missed a physics class or two, but doesn't water move faster than that?"

Kenna ignored the question and turned away from the cliff, marching to a raised, elongated pile of dirt. "This is the foundation of our defense. Danya—" her voice caught on the name, "—my apprentice was responsible for fortifying the breadth of the cliff."

Bethany's stomach twisted at the witch's name. On one hand, she wished she could remember what happened during the fall through the universe, but on the other.... She peered into the dark punctured by the path of lanterns. The black hole sucked the light from them even at a distance. "How far are we from the village?"

"Five hundred paces, which is a quarter of a mile for those of you with newer measurement systems." Kenna glanced up at the approaching wave and scowled. "This is the highest wave since they began cresting almost a year ago," she muttered. "Come here."

Bethany obeyed, taking the opportunity to cast several orbs of light. The illumination made Kenna blink and shy away, but she showed no sign of surprise at Bethany's ability. Looking around, Bethany guessed that a pointed section in the dirt foundation was meant to cut the force of a wave, but the pile only came up to her waist. Off to the side, she saw a gap they had walked through without her even noticing the dirt on either side.

"This is the center of the berm, and it extends at angles for five hundred paces on each side. This directs the water away from the camp. Raise the earth along the entire barrier until it reaches two heads above yourself."

Bethany frowned, glancing again at the approaching wave. "Is there enough dirt here to—" She cut herself off at

Kenna's raised eyebrow. "Yes, ma'am." Bethany crouched, planting her good hand on the frozen ground. She closed her eyes and connected with the earth. Much like when she used her Coven Mark, she could visualize the entire berm that stretched across the cliff's edge and curved on either end to direct the water away from the tents. She also sensed that the dirt had been used many times. Though solid where she stood, she felt plenty of loose and 'ready' dirt to raise the slope another four and a half feet.

"Now, Bethany," Kenna commanded, her voice edged with fear.

Standing, Bethany concentrated and brought her hand parallel to the left edge of the berm. Her muscles strained with effort, but the earth obeyed. As soon as it reached the right height, Kenna sent a concussive force at the wall to pack the dirt, shaping it from the top down. She ran the full length of the barrier, and Bethany breathed hard, raising the dirt on the right.

*Bethany, you're such a powerful, obedient young witch....*

"One emergency at a time!" Bethany yelled, hoping that if Igraine was close enough to send her creepy whispers, she was also close enough to see that Bethany was trying to help save the entire settlement from destruction. "Help or shut up!"

A deep humming began, as if it had risen from the ground, and Kenna sped past. Wild-eyed, Bethany looked at Kenna, who pointed toward the ocean.

Their berm was almost done, but simple packed dirt against a gigantic tidal wave? It would crumble the instant the water hit, and it would take both of them to hold it up with magic... magic that Kenna perhaps didn't have if she'd almost died four days ago.

Kenna raced back to Bethany. "Hold the line with as much power as you have left for as long as you can. Do you understand?"

Bethany longed for the use of her right arm but gave a curt nod. "Let's do it," she said over the growing hum. The ground began to vibrate, and she channeled more energy into holding the berm from end to end.

"Brace yourself!" Kenna cried out.

The wave's roar deafened Bethany, and her teeth clattered in her skull the moment the tower of water sheared over the edge of the cliff. Thunder swept through the ground and would have crumbled her berm without the magic holding it together.

Despite the noise, Bethany heard Kenna chant in a language that sounded familiar yet unnatural to her human ears. The magic charge it caused sank into the ground and dirt barrier—and Bethany felt the earth change.

The soil beneath her fingers electrified, and Bethany watched it transmute into basalt, shocked. Hoping the chant affected the entire berm, Bethany closed her eyes and shoved her shoulder against the new hard, smooth surface, whispering a prayer to Luke's God that this would save them.

She smelled the tangy saltwater the instant before it slammed against the point of their barrier, the deafening noise drowning out her scream as the magic struggled to hold against the pressure of the wave.

*Oh, what power you have—*

"Shut *up!*" If Bethany survived this and found Igraine, she would slap the old witch for trying to distract her at such a crucial moment.

Kenna's impressive magic withstood the initial impact, but as more water crashed against the barrier, it began to crumble. The wave flowed over the forward point, creating a rough edge for the water to catch and pull at the stone. Through her magic, Bethany felt the basalt wash away in the water, and panic filled her throat even though the water never rose above them. The wave swept to either side, but still came—ever coming.

Next to her, Kenna's eyes were shut, both of her hands pressed against the smooth stone. Her half-moon tattoo glowed with magic.

Finally, the water broke through, tearing little bits of rock off the inner edge like a failing dam. High-pressure jets of water soaked Bethany, chunks of basalt nicking her skin.

Kenna doubled down, chanting more. Her tattoo glistened with sweat and water, her limbs trembling with the effort.

And then... it all stopped.

The water that poured through the cracks diminished, the roar faded, and only the rush of the diverted water remained.

Bethany cut off her flow of magic, sagging in relief. The saltwater ran down her hair, stinging the cuts on her face. Kenna collapsed like a ragdoll and fell into the muddy dirt at their feet. Her magic dissipated, apparently only effective while actively held.

"Kenna!" Bethany wobbled over, dropping to her knees. The numbing charm on her arm had begun to wear off, and a sharp pain ricocheted through her shoulder. "Kenna—" With her good hand, Bethany cupped the older woman's cheek, her tattoo hot under her touch. Wet, stringy hair clung to Kenna's face, but her eyes remained closed. Bethany's fingers moved to Kenna's neck, searching for a pulse.

A weak heartbeat pushed against Bethany's fingers, and a wave of relief swept through her. *Not dead. That's good.*

Bethany lifted Kenna's head from the mud, maneuvering so that she could rest Kenna's head on her legs. Despite the water, the frozen ground hadn't thawed, and Bethany was both stuck in the mud and pressed against the earth's hard surface.

Kenna's hand twitched, coming up to grasp Bethany's good wrist. She opened her eyes, her irises a brilliant shade of purple that, within seconds, faded to a dark green. Bethany opened her mouth to comment, but Kenna cut her off.

"I will not survive the next one."

Bethany couldn't argue. If she could steal Igraine's claw back... she could take Kenna and the Fifth Travelers with her when they escaped.

Kenna coughed, and Bethany helped her sit up. Weak, she sagged against Bethany, whether she wanted to or not.

"I might know a way we can all get back to Talahm," Bethany said, her voice loud now that the awful hum of the wave had ceased.

Kenna fumbled for the leather pouch on her waist. Trembling, she tugged out a small hand-stitched notebook, its pressed paper rough with fibers. She touched her forefinger to the last page, and words flowed across the surface like water, forming a message. She tore it out and held it up like an offering. The paper folded itself into a tiny bird and zoomed off toward the village.

"Neat trick," Bethany said, wondering why Kenna hadn't reacted to what she'd said.

Kenna took a few more labored breaths. "There is no way back to Talahm, silly girl," she wheezed. "We have nowhere to go if the portals do not open themselves, and we cannot predict when they will open or to which world they will lead."

*I can give you that way out,* Igraine's sibilant voice whispered, and this time Bethany realized it wasn't auditory.

It was in her head.

*Come find me, Bethie dear.... I need to speak with you alone.*

Footsteps sounded behind them, the squelch of mud loud in the deep silence that had fallen after the wave spent its strength.

"Thank the living stars!" Misha exclaimed as he sloshed through the debris, using his staff to clear a path. The folded paper message sat perched on his shoulder. A woman dogged his heels.

"Firewhip!" Rissy exclaimed, shoving past Misha. "Are you hurt?" Their designated coven healer squatted beside Bethany, quickly casting a healing projection.

"Besides the still-broken arm, I'm fine. Numb it again and check Kenna. I think she used too much magic."

Rissy glanced at Bethany with narrowed eyes. With a single touch, she masked Bethany's pain and switched the projection to hover over Kenna. "Hela's with Harlow."

"Is the camp okay? Did anyone get hurt? Did anything flood?"

"No, no one's hurt—not any more than they already were. Putting you on the berm worked this time. Four days ago was a different story." Rissy squinted at the projection. "Misha, your leader is exhausted. I'm not sure what kind of witch she is, but she did too much."

"I will carry her back," Misha said, his face betraying his doubt that he could lift her.

Rissy raised an eyebrow and looked at Bethany. "Can you levitate her instead?"

Bethany tested her magic on one of the larger rocks that formed the spine of their berm. It made a thick, slopping sound, and mud and water dripped from its bottom when Bethany lifted it three feet into the air. "Yeah." Struggling to her feet, she took a moment to steady herself before levitating Kenna.

Rissy, still maintaining the projection, took a closer look and paled. "Quickly. She's deteriorating fast."

Bethany hoofed it back toward the village, desperately hoping that she would not be the cause of this woman's death too.

# CHAPTER FIVE

# THIRTY YEARS

Julie snapped the long, thick leather reins attached to the carriage. A team of four black horses pulled them down the overgrown road heading east toward the Cumbrian Mountains. The River Nimüe flowed to their left, the waters rushing toward Lake Ogwen, now three days behind them.

The others rode horses with heavy saddlebags, and Mountains begrudgingly shared the carriage with supplies. Taking the lead, King Aragon trotted in front. Luke and Emma rode with Prince Argent between them, strapped with his personal bow, and two witches from the Royal

Coven, Evie Watson and Dakota Pack, flanked the coach. They, along with the King, planned to take the horses and carriage to the northern side of Skypoint and meet the rest of the group after the Olis Council concluded.

Compared to the mass of people rescued from Valona, their party of nine now seemed tiny.

The road had given Julie time to think, even though Tom sat with her on the driver's bench. She'd barely talked to him, even when he made comments about their children as if he'd helped raise them. Twenty years later, he still knew all the little buttons to push—humming her favorite tunes and lullabies they'd sung to the kids at bedtime. She struggled, wanting both to kiss him senseless and to stew over how he'd left her a single mother.

She'd known he was alive for two months, but it had done nothing to prepare her for his presence.

Mountains, meanwhile, had made himself a nest inside the carriage, and she wondered if the Olii were part bird.

It had been so long since she'd been on any kind of adventure—so long, in fact, that she could barely remember where she'd gone or what she'd done. Falling through that portal had been the best thing to ever happen to her, even though it led to torture and pain.

It reignited her thirst for the unknown.

Before this, the closest she'd ever gotten to royalty was during her six-month stint as the youngest CEO ever hired to head a Fortune 50 company. She'd done all the hard work to earn the position, only to face patronizing boardroom politics not worth her salary—or sanity.

Now, in the presence of real royalty, she marveled at the respect the Pendragons commanded. She was still impressed with how Argent had handled Cordelia Roque on the voyage back from Valona.

While packing, Julie had swiped a map from the library to study this strange new world. Tom spent their first day on the road attempting to help, pointing out where they were headed.

Skypoint. Bearsmouth.

Perga's Scepter.

The names, foreign to the mouths of anyone on Earth, stirred a deep yearning within her to know more about their cultures, people, and secrets.

But asking Tom about any of them meant letting him back in.

So, instead of asking the questions she wanted to ask about this world, she stoically made notes to herself. She knew her silence frustrated Tom, that he wanted her to dig into the history of his homeland, but she wouldn't give him the satisfaction.

Maybe she could ask Mountains instead.

The deep green of the forest reminded her of south-central Europe, one of the many places she'd explored in her youth.

Before she'd met Tom, and her life completely changed.

"I feel like I'm in a movie, hunting vampires."

"I don't remember any of those," Tom replied, massaging the tops of his knees. He'd told her that he knew when they were stiff, even if he couldn't feel anything below his waist. That poison had done a number on him.

Julie thought about how long she'd been alone on Earth. Tried not to let it bleed into her words. "My favorite one didn't come out until a few years after...." She didn't know how to say it. If she wanted to say it. *You abandoned us? Faked your death? Lied to me?* She'd had him back in the flesh all of a scant few days, and it still didn't seem quite real.

The carriage bounced, and she wished she'd brought a seat cushion. A wheel hit a divot in the road, and she bumped against his shoulder, sliding away when she felt his warmth.

"You can say it," Tom said. "It's the truth."

Julie clenched her jaw and refused to look at him.

"I can still take your anger."

A hot flush spread from her face down her chest, but she kept her mouth shut. Her parents had once told her that Tom Jackman was the only man who could handle her temper, and she wanted to throw his old police baton at his head right now.

Though he'd probably just snatch it from the air like he'd done countless times before.

She pointedly stopped her thoughts from speeding toward what had often happened *after* those fights.

The further east they rode, the thicker the trees closed in. While King Aragon remained at the vanguard, Luke pulled ahead of Argent and Emma when the road narrowed. It looked like the River Road leading away from Trident Bay, but this path felt more imposing.

Above the trees, impossibly tall mountains disappeared into the clouds, their steep faces cloaked in snow, with patches of pine dotting the summit like the bristles on a toothbrush.

One of them was Skypoint.

"It's been a joy to see them all grown up," Tom said, now coming at her from a different angle.

She couldn't believe his gall. When she glanced at him from the corner of her eye, he wasn't looking at her, his gaze fixed on their children. She could see the pride on his face, but he hadn't raised them. He hadn't borne seven-year-old Luke's wild grief going to a funeral without a body because everyone thought Tom had burned up in the car crash.

He hadn't tended to Emma's heart, long fractured from not having her dad when she needed him most.

"How dare you," she seethed through clenched teeth. "You didn't raise them, you coward. *I* raised them. *I* organized their birthday parties. *I* read bedtime stories to them, took them to church, and held them when they cried because they didn't have their dad anymore." She breathed hard through her nose, suppressing the lump that had risen in her throat. If she laid eyes on him, she'd scream. "Imagine what it's like for me to find out that the husband I buried is actually alive and well on a different *planet*, living a life he told me *nothing* about during the nine years we were married."

He stayed quiet, and she recognized his silence as one of his many tactics to draw out her fury like venom from a snake bite.

It worked. It always worked.

*So much for keeping my mouth shut—*

"You may work for royalty, but you made royally stupid decisions." The words escaped her mouth before she knew she'd thought them, but it didn't make them any less true. She kept her eyes on the rhythmic movement of the horses' rumps in front of her. "It should have been a decision we made together. When Emma told me the whole story...."

"Emma doesn't know the whole story," Tom said when she trailed off. "I admit there are many things I should have done differently—"

"Don't you dare say 'but,' Tom Jackman. Or Tomás Artair. Or whatever you call yourself here," Julie hissed, finally looking at him. His annoyingly handsome face relaxed, clearly satisfied she'd taken the bait after days of emotional stonewalling. "You left to fight a war I didn't even know about! Military wives know more about their husbands' deployments than I did about where you're *from*. And what do you even *mean* that Emma doesn't know the whole story? She's been talking to you for four entire years through that fancy journal!" She took a breath, glancing furtively around to check for eavesdroppers. Both Dakota and Evie stared straight ahead, though Dakota's cheeks looked suspiciously red.

"Would you have believed me?" Tom interrupted.

The question slowed her roll enough that she heard the rush of the river barely visible through the trees. The steady clop of the horses and the rattle of the carriage seemed loud in comparison.

"Look me in the eye and tell me you wouldn't have called me a liar."

It irked her that he was still unafraid to match her energy. She met his gaze, his green-gold heterochromia as striking now as it had been when she'd first seen him singing outside that church in Edinburgh. "Of course I would have called you a liar! I would have tried to get you committed to the loony bin, too! And then you would have talked me down, apologized for your fabulously stupid secrets, and done magic to prove you are who you say you are. We would have made a plan and figured it out because *we were a team.*"

Regret flashed across his face.

"Instead, you faked your death and turned me into a single mother. You wrote letters to your children but not to your *wife.* In what world does that make sense?"

"The one where you forgot Olii have sensitive hearing, and there's a delightful window between your feet to let me see which way we're heading," Mountains said. "Did you really keep your ancestry quiet while on Earth, Tomás Artair? You lived a double life and faked your death to escape it?"

Julie's heart thudded as she clammed up, anger swirling around her stomach. She was sure that if she'd been born with Talahmi blood, everything would be on fire right about now.

"The logic of men is far below that of the Olii. Shouldn't you be groveling for her eternal mercy and forgiveness?" Mountains made a noise like a chortle. "Bah. Your spat is the most entertainment I've had in about a century. Please, continue."

Julie handed Tom the reins and crouched, slamming the window shut. When she sat back down, she whispered, "Can you make it so he can't hear anything from in there?"

Tom frowned and snapped his fingers, cutting off Mountains' roaring laughter.

"Is everything all right, Prophet Artair?" Evie Watson asked from her horse, a look of concern on her almond-shaped face.

"Yes, Mage Watson," Tom said, his voice clipped. "This was not our first fight."

Julie's face burned, and she hoped that Mountains' interruption had knocked some sense into her estranged spouse. She had never thought of him as her ex, and she didn't want to start now, even if he did a superb job of riling up her anger. "You have thirty years of lies to make up for. Make this stupid bench less painful."

"As you wish," he whispered, and a moment later she sat on thick pillows instead.

CHAPTER SIX

# RENAULT CALLS HIMSELF A HISTORIAN?

As the sun set on the sixth day, long shadows crept across the small clearing where they'd decided to make camp. Argent dismounted and stretched. Next to him, his father started unsaddling the horses, and Luke walked the edge of the glade, weaving a giant shield as Evie and Dakota trailed him, setting traps and staking lanterns.

As Argent heaved off his saddle, Julie stopped the carriage in the middle of the clearing. He watched, persistently curious, as Julie hopped down from the driver's bench and unbuckled the draft horses. She ignored her still-seated husband, who didn't appear particularly bothered by the cold shoulder.

Argent's horse nudged him from behind.

"Yes, sorry," he said, setting down the saddle and pivoting to lift the heavy saddlebags. The decision to resume his morning target practice was already paying off, both in terms of his strength and in shooting game for dinner.

Though he and Luke had stuffed their luggage with as many library books as they dared, they'd been reading Renault's parting gift by the light of their evening fires. So far, they hadn't found anything about Atlas or the Elvara Bow, but they were less than a quarter of the way through the beefy history book.

Argent slung the bags over one shoulder and retrieved Luke's collection, leaving his father to brush down the horses. The straps dug into his skin as he carried them over to where Emma had started the fire pit, not far from the carriage, but far enough away from the trees that a watch could alert them to attacks.

"Is this... normal for your parents?" He set the bags down and glanced at Julie, still working with the horses. "Every night she leaves him there to struggle off by himself or wait for Luke or my father to help him."

Emma looked up from the fresh dirt she'd overturned to protect the clearing from a wildfire. "I mean—" she hesitated, dropping her voice to a whisper. "Dad lied to her for ten years, abandoned us to fight in the Valon War, and basically told both Luke and me to keep it all secret in the letters he left for us. Until the portals started going haywire and leaving monsters on Earth, he was convinced she'd never accept the truth. *I* had to beg him to let me tell her."

Argent raised his eyebrows. He hadn't known all the details despite writing Emma for four years through their paired journals. "That seems extreme."

Emma sighed and stood, brushing off her hands. "As much as I hate to say it, he wasn't wrong. Mom's dealt with a lot in the last couple of months, beyond learning he's alive." She paused, her eyes flickering toward him and then quickly away. "I try to see it from both of their perspectives. If I were in her shoes, I wouldn't be very forgiving. But if I were him.... The war was so bad. You know. You lived through it."

"It was not so much living as surviving. And even that did not end well." Argent tried not to think about those days. He reached up and scratched the back of his head, the top of his forearm bumping against the hunting bow strapped to his back. He felt awkward now for asking about Emma's parents.

The sound of wood dragging across grass made him look up. Luke had finished shielding the clearing and was pulling a log over to the fire. Behind him, Dakota hauled a second log with her earth magic.

"Can you guys get firewood?" Emma asked, sounding as eager as Argent to end their conversation.

Luke grunted as he dropped the end of the log in front of the saddlebags. He caught Argent's eye, and an unspoken understanding passed between them. They nodded at each other, and Emma rolled her eyes.

It was nice to be on good, or better, terms with Luke.

As they speed-walked toward the forest, Argent breathed in the earthy springtime, chilled by the approaching night. It brought back memories of playing in Arthur's Grove as a child with his brother, Prince Adam, before the Valon War started.

They crossed the threshold of Luke's shield and the noise from the clearing vanished.

"I still can't believe Renault didn't include a table of contents, chapter divisions, or an index in his so-called history book," Luke grumbled, bending over to collect dead branches from the forest floor. "I'd skim forward if I wasn't sure we'd miss something considering how disorganized he is."

"It must be one of his earliest works," Argent answered, gathering his own fuel for the fire. "I've read some of his other books and they're not nearly as hard to get through as this monstrosity."

Luke harrumphed, shaking his head. He'd tied his hair back in the same style as Argent, and the white patches at his temples stood out in the approaching darkness.

Argent retrieved another stick. He'd been stewing over Luke's prophecy for days, but he didn't know how to tactfully ask all his questions. He decided to follow in Emma's footsteps and try being direct instead.

"In your Vision... did you see who I'll shoot with the Elvara Bow?"

Luke shook his head. "There were moments when I Saw things from the middle of the fray itself, and other times like I was hovering over it all. But I never Saw who will take the arrow." His voice tightened. "It may be more than one."

Argent appreciated Luke's discomfort, but he couldn't let it deter him. He scanned the trees, wondering if any game might make an appearance tonight. Nothing moved except the soft whisper of wind through the branches. "More than one arrow, or more than one person?"

Luke shrugged, almost dislodging his kindling. "Both?"

The sky had darkened, and Argent strained to see the forest floor. They wouldn't stay here much longer, especially out of sight of the clearing. He picked up a short but chunky log. "What happens if we gain the bow, but not the item in your sketchbook? Would one element of victory be enough to prevent your father's version from coming to pass?"

Luke stopped walking and stared at him. "We can't take that risk."

Argent studied Luke's face and kept silent, sensing he had more to say.

Luke sighed, glancing over his shoulder toward their camp. "Maybe Mountains knows what that artifact is. If we need the Olii's help, we're running out of time to read the rest of the book before we get to Skypoint."

Argent raised both eyebrows. "You're joking, right? Mountains?"

A ghost of a smile crossed Luke's face. "Stranger things have happened."

Argent and Luke returned to the clearing as twilight slipped away. Emma stood by the fire pit with a ball of flame in one hand.

"About time," Mountains grumbled from his nest between the two logs.

Luke arranged the kindling pile for his sister, and Argent laid his armful of wood off to the side.

Someone had helped Tomás down from the carriage. He now sat at the end of a log constructing what looked like another pair of journals, a small enchanting kit unfolded on his lap. King Aragon sat across from him on the other log with Julie, Evie, and Dakota, who was carving a stone with her earth magic.

Argent took a seat on the other end of Tomás's log, where his saddlebag still rested in the knotty grass. He heaved out *A Brief History of Severna*. Opening it to where they'd left off the night before, Argent sighed. He hated the way young Renault had approached historical research.

Mountains, just a few feet away, twitched his ears.

The fire flared as Emma's magic took hold. Luke brushed his hands off on his legs and sat next to Argent, who passed him half of the book. Emma took Luke's other side.

For a few minutes, only the crackle of the fire, the gentle chirps of night insects, and the crinkle of parchment pierced the air.

Then Luke closed the book and pushed it back onto Argent's lap. "This is getting us nowhere," he said with a tinge of frustration. He extracted his sketchbook from his jerkin and found the drawing. "How on earth are we going to find this—” He stabbed the oblong object with his index finger and gestured toward the tome. “—in here?”

King Aragon frowned. “What are you looking for?”

Luke walked past Mountains and handed the King his sketchbook.

The Olis tracked Luke with narrowed eyes, his ears pricked.

“I’ve never seen this before,” King Aragon said, glancing up.

Argent met his father’s gaze and let the right corner of his mouth curl up.

The King looked back at Luke. “Where did you see this?”

Luke rubbed his temples with both hands. “From a part of my Vision I initially forgot. I asked Renault about it before we left, but instead of giving me a straight answer—”

Mountains snickered.

“—he gave me this behemoth to read through and said something about Nephilim and Severna. But we haven’t found anything about it in his so-called ‘brief history.’ I don’t even know what a Nephilim is.”

Argent watched the resident Olis’s golden eyes widen, and his heart sped up.

“Tomás, you didn’t see this in your Vision, did you?” King Aragon asked.

Luke took the book back and handed it to his father, who furrowed his brows as he studied the drawing.

Argent was surprised that neither Luke nor Emma had informed their father of the missing piece until now.

"I Saw nothing placed atop the Titan Obelisk. But if this is part of what helps us triumph over Igraine, we must identify it."

Mountains' arrogant tones contained a hint of glee. "Renault calls himself a historian, yet he is just as secretive as his dear mother and uncle. Bring me the drawing."

Argent fought to suppress his excitement that Luke's plan had worked.

Luke cautiously approached the Olis and held out the sketchbook.

"As I suspected," Mountains said with far too much smugness. He picked between his fangs with an intact claw, though there was nothing to dislodge. "This is called the Khozek. The amplifier, the strengthener. You know how magic feeds on emotions and intent? The Khozek amplifies magic funneled through it. And the key to this ingenious device is guarded by the Olis Council."

Argent drummed his fingers against the book's cover as he started putting the pieces together. "If its key is at Skypoint, where is the Khozek itself?"

Mountains grinned, exposing his fangs in the firelight. "I assume dear Ren–Ren's dry attempt at history will tell you it lies beneath Severna's crystal waves. But the real story is that Firstborn moved it into the bowels of the Shadow Star when the greedy, arrogant humans finished building Keldvaar."

Luke made a strangled sound. "The great library in the capital?"

"The very same," Mountains confirmed.

Luke sat back down, passing his sketchbook around for everyone to take a look. He ran both of his hands through his hair.

Argent flipped through Renault's book, looking for any hint of the word *Khozek*. "My teachers always said Severna is cursed land."

"I didn't know that," Julie interrupted, raising her hand. She pointedly did not look at Tomás. "And I'd bet my kids didn't either."

"Typical Earthlings," Mountains said with clear disdain. "You also probably don't know that the Nephilim *are* the curse—and the only thing keeping Keldvaar, and the rest of this world, safe is the shield the Khozek sustains around Severna's entire border."

Julie cleared her throat. "As my son already said, some of us have no clue what a Nephilim is."

Mountains gritted his teeth and rolled his eyes. "Then let me dumb it down for you. They are the spirits of the giants who perished in your world's great flood. You didn't think portals only let physical beings through, did you?"

Dread bubbled in Argent's stomach. Since Emma had freed him from Septim, most of his nightmares concerned becoming possessed again. "So if we take the Khozek, the Nephilim get out?"

Mountains shrugged. "Only if it's not replaced with something else to power the shield. But that's simple enough to procure from the Sal Dorhana of Skypoint."

The only thing Argent knew about the Sal Dorhana was that it was the Olis name for the Impossible Room beneath Camelot. He had no idea other such places existed, let alone in Skypoint.

"The Olis Council will outright reject your appeal if any of *you* request the key to the Khozek," Mountains continued with a beady look in his eyes. "But I will have no such issues. If this artifact is part of the formula to your winning Prophecy, it will provide you with a way to retrieve your precious Bethany. And, perhaps, even thwart the prophecies entirely by trapping Igraine on Langoth forever. Thus avoiding a battle at all."

Silence filled the clearing as they waited for Mountains to continue, but he licked his maligned paw instead.

Argent caught his father's equally stunned expression. If they could lock Igraine on Langoth, it would solve their biggest problem.

"So there *is* a way to save Bethany!" Emma said. Standing, she planted both hands on her hips. "I knew you were lying—"

"Shut up, you stupid girl," Mountains thundered, causing a flock of birds to flee the trees behind them. "I haven't told you a single lie, and I won't tolerate your unfathomable disrespect. My kind are supreme creatures, created for stewardship over Talahm and balance between the worlds, and all you want to do is tear apart the fabric of the universe for your friend. The Khozek *could* save her *if* it's used at the Titan Obelisk. But if you open your mouth at all in Skypoint's hallowed halls, I won't so much as utter its name, and you will lose your only chance to thwart prophecy."

## CHAPTER SEVEN

# CATIGERN

By the time their party—now six—reached the mountain entrance to Skypoint, Luke wished he had a wider range of magic. Sargateth, Morgan, and Magdalin had gotten the best deal by flying there days earlier.

Bitter winds whipped around the rickety wooden platform they'd cobbled together from trees harvested over three and a half miles below. Emma, the only one capable of expending the energy, lifted the blasted thing up, and Tomás and Luke kept the air breathable. It was hard not to feel resentful that Mountains couldn't help.

A snow-encrusted, double-paneled stone door loomed in front of them. As Emma shook like a leaf under the magical strain, Mountains reared up, pressing both paws against the doors. They swung open at his touch, and he leaped into a dark hallway, magical torches flaring to life as he crossed the threshold. The rest of them hurried in, Emma last of all. When she landed inside, the hastily constructed platform disintegrated, tumbling thousands of feet before exploding into splinters.

Emma fell to her knees, and Prince Argent quickly knelt beside her, holding her steady. He kissed her temple, smoothing back her hair with one hand. She leaned into him, eyes closed, her trust in him obvious.

Luke's heart twisted at the sight of his sister and the Prince. Each moment of intimacy between them made him long to hold Bethie again—to laugh at her jokes and protect her like he should have in Valona.

The warmth of the tunnels caused the ice crusting the men's beards to melt. Luke lowered his hood and wiped his facial hair dry with one hand, leaving a splatter of water on the dull gray floor.

Behind them, Mountains slammed the doors shut with his paws, whispering a quiet word of magic to seal it against the wind. After what it took to get this high, Luke knew that no other humans could make it here without an Olis to guide them.

Emma sucked in a deep breath and coughed. She opened her mouth to say something, but snapped it shut again when Mountains peered at her.

Satisfied that Emma wouldn't risk the Khozek, Mountains tried to extend his wings. One unfurled with no a problem, but the other seemed stuck, and he winced.

Luke stumbled over to the far wall, his legs shaking as he leaned next to his father. Tomás's enchanted exoskeleton had held up surprisingly well. Luke watched out of the corner of his eye as his mother slipped her arm around his father's waist and tucked her shoulder under his armpit.

Luke smirked, and Tomás looked down at her with clear surprise. "I can—"

"Shut up," Julie muttered deadpan.

Luke had to clap one hand over his mouth to stop a chuckle from escaping. But then he thought of Bethie again, and his mirth evaporated.

He looked around to distract himself. The smooth tunnels stretched wide enough for an Olis to walk through with both wings fully extended. Movement caught Luke's attention, and his mood soared at the sight of Morgan Le Fay hurrying toward them.

"Oh, thank the Lord you're here!" Morgan gripped her amethyst-capped staff with white fingers.

"Are they ready for us?" Argent asked, helping Emma stand. She leaned against him, her eyelids drooping.

"They are muttering about insubordination and the consequences for ignoring a banishment. Sargateth has been tied up trying to prevent any of them from leaving, but he's been unsuccessful in acquiring the Elvara Bow. If they didn't have to follow the rules...." Morgan weaved forward and laid a hand on Emma's shoulder. At the contact, her cheeks gained color, and her eyes snapped open, the cobalt blue shining brighter than it had moments before.

"What was that?" Luke asked in amazement.

Morgan smiled, touching Luke's arm a second later. Energy flared in his veins, and he felt ready to run a marathon.

"That was the healing power of Skypoint, channeled directly into your magic. Come. The council will hear us whether they want to or not."

Morgan led them through winding halls, and Luke mapped the twists and turns in his head. Finally, they arrived at a pair of massive stone doors he could only assume hid the Olis throne room. The sconces on either side of the hallway cast shadows across carvings that looked suspiciously like the ones on the doors to Pendragon Hall.

Luke glanced over his shoulder at Mountains, who stubbornly remained at the rear of their party in his Olis form. Since arriving a short time ago, Mountains' appearance had improved. This was his home, his birthplace—he and Magdalin were the Skypoint Twins.

Lowering his voice so only Morgan could hear, he said, "How is it that twenty-one Olii ganged up on and banished the three who made oaths to humans? It doesn't make sense."

"My kind are the most stubborn of the Lord's creations. And it was eighteen, actually," Morgan corrected. "Three abstained."

"Three?" Luke whispered. "Which pair split?"

"Riker's Rest. *Sprawled on Scattered Crystal Sands* and the twins from Silent Fields chose not to vote."

Morgan shifted into an enormous cat, her wings tucked neatly against her sides. A lock clicked, and Morgan gave them all a significant look before rearing up to plant both paws on the double doors, using her weight to push them open.

Sunlight blinded them.

After a moment, Luke's eyes adjusted to the sudden change. Twenty-four low but massive marble benches swallowed most of the room, arranged in a semicircle before them. Behind the thrones, wide, open windows exposed the panorama of Petra, the air clean and cool. Luke narrowed his eyes, catching sight of the slight shimmer of magic across the stone openings.

Olii occupied twenty of the thrones, either lying down as sphinxes or sitting on their haunches. Most had opulent carpets or pelts draped over their chairs, presumably so the cold stone didn't irritate them.

The Olii's fur ranged the full spectrum of brown, from light beige to almost black, but they all sat too far away for Luke to spot the differences in their markings.

Luke pulled his bag to one side and rummaged inside to retrieve his notebook, where he'd sketched the faces he remembered from his Vision.

Sargateth sat on his haunches in the open area before the thrones, his wings fully extended. They trembled, as though he'd been there a long time. His chocolate fur sported circular black markings like an ocelot, though he was much larger.

Luke could feel magic pouring from the eldest of the Olii, and he hung back with his father.

"Do you recognize any of them?" he whispered, thumbing through his notebook.

Tomás hesitated. "Not from back here. Unless we see them up close...."

Luke showed his father his sketches. "Let's hope they'll let us get close enough. These are the ones from my Vision."

In a show of strength, several Olii extended their wings, including one who stepped off its throne to approach the newcomers, wings quivering.

"The Firstborn returned to demand the Elvara Bow, dared to lock us here, and now you allow mere humans to enter our hallowed halls? We called for *Mountains Crumble Beneath His Claws*, not for an invasion!" the Olis spat, his deep, accented voice filling the entire chamber.

Luke suspected this Olis had led the charge to banish his kin so long ago.

Sargateth reared up, flapping his wings mightily at the apparent leader of the Olis Council. "Back to your seat, *Eternal Winds Obey His Call*. You are the one who demanded witnesses, and so witnesses have come."

Eternal Winds bared his fangs at Sargateth, but folded his wings and returned to his throne, lounging on it as though he ruled the entire world from that perch.

Luke peered closer at the thrones. The one that Eternal Winds returned to had carvings in the four corners of the bench's backrest: a lemniscate, a crown, four lines emanating from a single point, and the image of an Olis's head in mid-roar. Scanning the rest of the thrones, including the four empty ones, Luke saw symbols signaling each Olis's name on their assigned thrones.

As quietly as he could, he pointed it out to his father.

"Now that everyone is present, I *officially* invoke Catigern. Take your seats, brethren," Sargateth commanded, his voice biting.

Mountains remained where he was, somewhat shielded from view, and Luke hoped it wouldn't take him the entire proceeding to bring up the Khozek.

Magdalin walked into the room, causing an outbreak of mutters. With both shoulders back, she headed straight to her throne. Its corners showed another lemniscate, an anatomic heart, three lines of wind, and the depiction of the sun against a horizon.

"You insult us with this inferior form," Eternal Winds snarled, gesturing with one massive paw to Sargateth's wife.

The Archmage spoke, his voice low and dangerous. "Has your complacency stretched so far that you no longer watch the turns of time? *Heart Who Breathes Eternal Sky* lost a wing in the Valon War. My wife can no longer abide her true form thanks to the atrocities she suffered under Agamemnon Septim's reign of terror. I will thank you to hold your tongues on the matter."

Eternal Winds did not respond, instead glaring at Sargateth. Energy crackled, the high emotion of the Olii charging the room.

Sargateth took several steps forward, entering the semicircle. "You have no excuse for being unprepared. Humans enter these halls because Catigern requires witnesses—and you lot insisted we hold Catigern rather than simply handing over the Elvara Bow."

Luke fought a grin, still trying to identify the Olii he'd seen in his Vision. Now that he understood the connection between the throne symbols and their names, he focused on their visual markings and compared them against his sketches. One of the lighter brown drawings had a large blotchy spot below the right eye and a black left ear. He wrote 'Eternal Winds' underneath the picture.

Only nine to go.

"Insolence!" cried another Olis. Her throne showed a sunrise, a breath of wind, three trees in a cluster, and the scales of justice.

Sargateth snarled. "If *Fairest Breeze Between the Trees*—or any other members of this assembly—cannot follow the rules, I will hold you all in contempt."

Luke didn't know what that meant, but the threat quelled the commotion. The sneers didn't fade, but the one called Fairest Breeze backed down. Her face matched one of his sketches, and he jotted her name down next.

"As I said when I first came to you *nine* days ago, two competing prophecies lay before us. In one, twelve of you confront Igraine Pendragon, but she triumphs. In the other, ten are chosen to face her, and she is defeated. The only other discernible difference between these Visions of success or failure is the presence of the Elvara Bow."

Sargateth paused, giving the assembly an opportunity to speak, but no one took the bait.

"Witnesses you desired, and so witnesses I have brought. They'll speak their testimonies of victimhood wrought by Igraine Pendragon, the witch who captured and imprisoned *Mountains Crumble Beneath His Claws* for at least the past one hundred years!"

His words were met with an uproar. Every Olis reared on their thrones, their snarls and growls filling the relatively small chamber.

Yelling over them, the eldest Olis detailed the atrocities committed by Igraine against not only the Pendragon dynasty, but also the rest of the world. Her meddling with magic had weakened the fabric between worlds to such a point that even the Olii had ceased to restore stability.

For over seven hundred years, neither of Camelot's Sal Dorhana twins had been allowed to fulfill their duties. And for a hundred of those, the Skypoint twins had been unable to fulfill theirs either.

"You called for Mountains Crumble!" Sargateth yelled. "And so we have brought him!"

Mountains struggled to the front of the assembly, each step clearly painful, even if he looked better than a few days ago.

"I am a wanderer," Mountains began, staring down each of the assembled Catigern. "Igraine Pendragon interrupted my wanderings by tricking me into her influence and then subjecting me to the whims of her quest for power." He weaved a gripping narrative of his imprisonment and how the Night's Empress had forced him to open portals, not just to Earth, but to Langoth. And once Igraine found out what kinds of monsters lived there, she focused all Mountains' efforts on stealing creatures—then people—from their homes on that dark world. The longer Mountains talked, the more thunderous the rest of the Olii appeared.

"Let the first witness approach," the Olis called *Sprawled on Scattered Crystal Sands* commanded, startling Luke enough to break his concentration. His mother stepped into the limelight.

Luke frowned. *Why didn't Mountains ask for the Khozek?*

"Speak," Crystal Sands continued.

Julie stared each of them down, letting silence percolate until even Luke wondered when she was going to talk.

"I am Julie Houston Jackman, wife of the Prophet who witnessed failure and mother of the Prophet who saw victory. I'm also the mother of your prophesied Seventh Sorceress." Even though Mountains had neglected to tell them anything about how to properly address this gathering of haughty creatures, she spoke with confidence. "I was captured, tortured, and promised death by Igraine Pendragon."

Tomás, who had hooked one arm through Luke's to keep his balance, tensed at Julie's use of her married name. Luke breathed a tiny sigh of relief that she'd called herself Tomás's wife, even if their reunion seemed to have suffered several setbacks.

"You do not have magic," another Olis interrupted. She leaned forward, sniffing at Julie. "I cannot smell Talahmi blood in you."

"Firstborn!" Eternal Winds roared, stamping his paws on the stone floor. "Not only do you bring humans, but you bring humans from Earth? This one has no magic!"

Tomás winced, muttering, "You shouldn't have said that."

"Is that contempt, Eternal Winds?" Sargateth asked with the barest hint of his fangs. "Every human here descended from an Earthly forebear."

Julie rested one hand on the grip of her holstered gun. "It doesn't matter that I can't control the elements like my daughter or create shields and heal like my son. What matters is that magic or not, I survived captivity, and you all demanded eyewitness testimony. So here I am."

Eternal Winds snorted, but the one who had smelled her lack of magic sat back in her throne.

Julie detailed everything that had happened from the moment the portal ripped her from Earth until Mountains had forcefully closed the portal to Langoth behind Igraine—and Bethany.

Then it was Argent's turn. He rattled off his titles as fast as he could, but Luke could hear anger bleeding into his words. "You keep insulting the firstborn of your entire race, not only by 'banishing' him and his family for their personal decisions, but for decisions they believed necessary to survive Igraine's return. Because she is returning."

Silence filled the chamber again.

Argent continued his testimony, beginning from the moment Septim's shade entered his body to what Luke figured was a highly censored description of Emma purifying his mind.

Argent had barely finished when a hard female voice interrupted.

"I see no reason to relinquish the Elvara Bow into your hands." The delegation turned as one to look at the speaker. The four corners of her throne showed sand dunes, a lock and key, and two temples. "Such a relic does not belong in the hands of humans convinced that murder is the solution."

Mountains snarled so loud everyone looked at him. "Igraine cannot be held captive. She's too powerful and depraved to let loose on any population, even the humans. If you don't hand over the Bow, she will slaughter you all."

A round of chuckles echoed through the room. "Let her try," the female Olis said with clear disdain.

"You're afraid of her even now, *Secrets Buried Beneath the Dunes*," Tomás said without warning. Aided by his exoskeleton, he took a step forward. Luke hastily moved with him, keeping his balance as he finished jotting 'Secrets Buried' by another sketch. "You, who deliberated over whether to send us an envoy to inquire about Mountains' disappearance, and chose to leave him to his fate?"

A ripple of restlessness swept over the Olii.

"Who are you?" *Secrets Buried Beneath the Dunes* demanded.

"Tomás Artair, Prophet of Camlaan. I Saw you choose to abandon one of your own."

His father's hand tensed over Luke's arm, and Luke readjusted his grip on the notebook.

Mountains stepped down from his throne, anger burning on his furry face. "You could have gotten me out years ago? You left me there to suffer, close enough to death that I now owe my life to a *human!*"

Luke felt a wave of satisfaction that he held something over the cranky beast.

The sense of restlessness increased, and Eternal Winds spoke. "We could not guarantee an ambassador's safety—"

"Liar!" Mountains roared. "Cowards! None of you have been as near death as I have, and I have no one to thank for that but Igraine—and you sorry excuses for the Olis race." He took several more steps into Eternal Winds' personal space, ruffling his good wing. This was his first show of genuine solidarity with the people of Camelot, and Luke watched with bated breath. Mountains tried to fully extend both wings, and only one of them made it. "You see what's been done to me?"

Eternal Winds was speechless as he stared at Mountains' wing. "A human did this!" he exclaimed, only to be batted across the face as Mountains reared up.

Luke openly smirked at the rebuke.

"Fool! A consequence of what the human *forced me to do.* And what she will force *all* of you to do in her service if you sit on your whitewashed thrones and do not listen to the mouths of Prophets."

Luke's heart sped up.

"The Elvara Bow is not the only thing we need to defeat Igraine Pendragon," Mountains continued, his voice calm but deadlier. "When we leave, we must take the key to the Khozek as well."

After a microsecond of silence, pandemonium erupted.

It took a full minute for the chaos to subside enough for Luke to discern words amidst the yelling.

"Traitors, all of you!" Secrets Buried wailed. "Bushéd bogadim!"

"You would release our oldest enemy?" Eternal Winds thundered. "The Khozek holds back a much greater threat than a puny witch!"

"That puny witch held me captive for a century!" Mountains snapped, having returned to his throne to rest. Luke suspected he would never make it back to full strength—and perhaps would never be able to fly again. "Do you think I haven't tried to kill her? You think I suffered all those injuries without trying to put her down myself? What *arrogance* to assume otherwise."

"I see nothing but arrogance in this room," Tomás interrupted again, sounding sad. "You have all fallen so far from what you were made to be."

A renewed cacophony answered his bold words, but he never cowered, calm in the face of anger.

Sargateth stepped forward, his wings unfurling again. "He's right, you know," the firstborn of the Olii said softly. "We were made to be the stewards of this world, and yet here we are, in a chamber inaccessible to the vast domain the Lord created for us, above those who look at us as gods." Disgust marred his features as he bared his fangs and spat at Eternal Winds' front paws. "Julie Jackman is a woman, not a witch, because the Lord willed it. The inhabitants of this world, those we call Talahmi, are here because *the Lord willed it*. And who are we, his creations, to question why he made us different? Of us all, who alone ventured into the sands of Earth during the same years he did?" Sargateth said in a low, dangerous voice. Searching the group's gaze without reply, he sat on his haunches. "That's right, none of you. *I'm* the one who watched our Lord die a criminal's death and then rise three days later. Nothing is more humbling, and before me today, I see the consequences of the rest of you not meeting our Creator face-to-face."

Several of the Olii shifted on their thrones, avoiding Sargateth's sharp eyes.

"All have transgressed, including us. All fall short of his glory. *Especially us.* We do not deserve the reverence afforded to us by the peoples of this world, and we certainly do not deserve to glorify ourselves."

The wind whistled past the high windows, and Luke's hand tightened over the journal.

"We are at a nexus, my brothers and sisters," Sargateth announced. "Our world's fate balances on the knife's edge between two competing prophecies, and the first step to securing victory is—"

An Olis with a much lighter coloring ventured forth, his approach cutting off whatever Sargateth had been about to say next. "I am *Sharpest Edge of Diamond Skies*, for those of you who haven't heard of me. Firstborn, you have spoken at length of these so-called conflicting Visions, and yet the men responsible for them have yet to tell us with their own mouths what they Saw."

All eyes turned toward Luke and his father, and Luke panicked.

"Sargateth and Mountains have already provided what details we know," Tomás said smoothly. "It is clear that our victory relies on obtaining the Elvara Bow and the key to the Khozek, as well as identifying the ten of you present in my son's Vision."

Luke held up his notebook. "I sketched the faces of those who will help us win. I've identified five of you who must be there—Eternal Winds, Secrets Buried, Diamond Skies,

Fairest Breeze, and Crystal Sands." He took a step forward. "I need to take a closer look at the rest of you to figure out the others."

Angry hisses filled the air, sending chills across Luke's skin.

"Give it to me," Sargateth said.

Before Luke could, Fairest Breeze shouldered forward and batted the notebook from Luke's hand. One of her claws caught the edge of his thumb, dragging across his palm.

Blood welled, and the wound seared with pain. He clutched his hand to his chest.

"What are you doing?" Sargateth's voice burned with anger, sparks lighting around them.

"Protesting," Fairest Breeze replied, tearing the pages.

Luke watched through tears of agony as Fairest Breeze ripped the notebook to shreds—not just the sketches, but everything he'd recorded for the last several months. Prophecies, exoskeleton designs, enchanting ideas, even a rudimentary dam to introduce electricity to this world. He couldn't believe that they needed this Olis in order to win.

Emma materialized next to him, her face betraying her fury. Their father began fussing over his hand, but Luke couldn't help the tremors of fear that worked through him at the sight of Sargateth's full power.

Camelot's Archmage reared onto his hind legs, wings slowly flapping to keep his balance. His front paws came together with a muffled clap, and when they pulled apart, two beams of bright white light caught Fairest Breeze by the neck. The magic lifted her up, and she struggled, her rear paws scrabbling at the floor. The pages of the destroyed notebook fluttered in the updraft caused by Sargateth's wings. "By my authority as Firstborn of the Olii, and as Protector and Emissary of Talahm, I charge you, *Fairest Breeze Between the Trees*, with the highest contempt of this court. You are hereby banned from departing Skypoint without special authority."

"Sarg," Luke said, distracted by the fact that his father's magic hadn't done squat to heal the wound, "She has to be there. She's one of the ten."

Sargateth snarled at the interruption but amended his sentencing. "The only such special authority granted will be to fulfill the Prophecy at Perga's Scepter. If you put one claw out of line, I will bind your magic until the Lord's return."

The white beams disappeared, and Fairest Breeze collapsed to the floor, chest heaving. Another Olis slinked forward and shepherded her away. Luke's vision was too blurry, and the pain in his hand too great, for him to know whether he recognized the figure.

"I should've shot her the moment she got too close," Julie muttered, startling Luke. He hadn't seen her come up behind him in the commotion. Her hand on his back, though comforting, didn't help.

"Now we can't identify the last five," Luke whispered, his heart in his throat.

Emma stomped over to the wrecked notebook, gathering the scattered pages. She stuck her middle finger in the air at Fairest Breeze before coming back to their family circle. She placed the leather binding and the pages into Julie's hands and started piecing them back together.

"I will grant you the bow and the key," came the now-subdued voice of Eternal Winds. "But before you leave, you must draw a replacement from the Sal Dorhana."

"Obviously," Sargateth replied. He turned away from the thrones and padded over to Luke. "How badly did she get you?"

Luke held out his hand, and blood dripped to the floor. Sargateth's wince made his stomach sink.

"It won't close," Tomás whispered urgently.

"Since the wound is from an Olis claw, it won't close without Olis magic," Sargateth replied quietly. "I can heal this, but you will have a scar for the rest of your life."

"Like I have a choice?" Luke seethed between gritted teeth.

Sargateth healed him faster than Luke could even comprehend. In a blink, his palm was whole, but for a ropy white scar where the cut had been. The pain dissipated with each beat of his heart.

A moment later, Emma handed him his notebook.

His *fixed* notebook.

Luke stared at it. He slowly opened it to the sketches, good as new.

Out of the corner of his eye, Luke caught Sargateth doing a double-take. Then the Archmage's eyes narrowed, and he turned to face the thrones once more.

"I hereby impart my authority as Firstborn upon *Heart Who Breathes Eternal Sky*. She will remain here and, with the help of Luke Artair's drawings, identify the rest of those required for the Vision of triumph. She will send you when it is time to fly."

# CHAPTER EIGHT
# THE HAWK

The seaport at Bearsmouth was three times larger than the Trident, but the only ship anchored at the docks was *The Sea Wolf*. A cool spring breeze blew in from the sea, bringing the salty scent Argent had grown fond of while sailing through the Helcari Isles.

Argent felt conflicted about returning to this ship. He'd spent most of his time aboard running from lies and accusations, only to find worse behind the wheel.

His best memories on Cordelia's brigantine were of Emma. Argent dismounted his horse at the port stables, and caught her eye through the throng of activity. They smiled at each other, and some of Argent's anxiety melted away. Having her here in the flesh was so much better than writing through the journals.

The Elvara Bow was strapped across his back, its heavy enchanted wood both comforting and foreboding. Sargateth had made sure he'd kept the twelve special arrows separate from the ones he normally used and warned him not to touch them until they arrived at Perga's Scepter.

These arrows were not for defense.

He kept trying not to think about Luke's Vision, but he knew he'd eventually need to face the fact that he might need to take more lives.

"Not one extra moment of healing," Mountains muttered as he leaped from the carriage and stretched like a tomcat. He had not stopped complaining from the moment Diamond Skies and *Nightbows Sweep Past Timeless Stars*, the twins from Silent Fields, had ferried him from Skypoint to the carriage below. "While my *sister* gets to stay and soak it all in, the traitorous—"

"Careful how you talk about my wife," Sargateth warned, unloading the supplies from the carriage. He dumped the first heavy bundle into Argent's arms without so much as a warning. "Or I might do to you what I did to Fairest Breeze."

Argent turned on his heel to escape the tension and almost knocked over Tomás. Julie had actually helped him down from the driver's seat this time. Dakota and Evie, the witches from Renova's Royal Coven, hurried past carrying a large trunk between them.

"Sorry," Argent apologized, regaining his balance.

"No harm done," Tomás said with a wide smile. "That looks like the extra swords, so be careful loading those."

Argent adjusted his hold around the heavy bundle and gave a curt nod. The Prophet hobbled away, and Argent scoured the docks for the King.

His father had already boarded *The Sea Wolf* and was on the ship's main deck in a heated discussion with William Pendragon. William was the ship's first mate and also the King's uncle, making him Argent's great-uncle... and only supporter during Argent's year-long voyage.

"I got your bags," Luke said, coming up beside him. He started to slide the strap off his shoulder, but then his eyes landed on the swords. "Never mind."

"Follow me. I'll show you where to put them." Argent made a beeline for the gangplank.

As they approached, the King left William alone on the main deck, walking with Morgan Le Fay to the forecastle. When Argent and Luke boarded, William effortlessly snatched the swords from Argent's arms and stuck out a rough hand for him to shake. "Good to see you again, lad," said the man who could have been King.

Argent took his bag from Luke. "Uncle William, you remember Luke Artair, son of Tomás." William had made part of the journey from the Trident to Camelot with them when they'd found Magdalin, but he turned back once they realized Bethany had been captured.

William shook Luke's hand. "I trust your last quest ended well?"

Luke hesitated before shaking his head. "Not exactly." He looked around the deck. "How long will it take us to reach Perga's Scepter?"

William frowned beneath his bushy beard. "From here, it's a straight shot across the Sleeping Sea and would take about two months. Maybe less if we have good winds. But with a Kraken out there.... Not worth the risk. Besides, the King just told me that we're making a stop in Severna."

Argent sighed but said nothing. That must have been what they were arguing about.

William frowned. "What's in Keldvaar except the Shadow Star and a bunch of stuck-up scholars who think they're smarter than the rest of the world?"

Luke shifted uncomfortably, either because he didn't want to talk about Bethany or because of the strain from carrying the bags. "We just have to go there," he said, looking disgruntled at William's disparagement of scholars.

"I see," William said, an edge in his voice. "Matters of state. I may have abdicated the throne, but I didn't abdicate my name." He turned to Argent again, his face softening. "Don't bully the captain too much, please? She's been a menace since you mutinied on the jaunt from Valona."

Argent peered around William's broad shoulders to where Captain Cordelia Roque stood on the sterncastle, studying a map. The long feather in her hat ruffled in the breeze. "She won't be an issue."

She glanced up, and her eyes narrowed. Argent lifted his middle finger, imitating Emma's angry gesture to Fairest Breeze. Cordelia sneered, then bent back over her table.

A tickle of amusement lifted Argent's mood.

"Portal to port!" came Emma's cry from the crow's nest as the sun dipped toward the horizon on their second day sailing east.

The ship made a hard tilt starboard. Argent braced himself on one of the main deck's benches, where he'd been reading *A Brief History of Severna* while Emma was on airwitch duty.

But not everyone reacted as quickly.

Dakota, an earthwitch with little exposure to the ocean, lost her balance and scraped her knee, and Argent winced. As they skirted by the portal, Argent rushed to the railing for a better look. Almost close enough to touch, Argent felt drawn toward it, just like he had with the portal beneath Valona. This too must be connected to Langoth.

A deep shiver caressed his spine.

His eyes stayed locked on the inky blackness even as the ship drew away, and he watched as the portal zipped itself back up, disappearing as if it had never existed.

Emma landed in a crouch next to him, and he jumped. He hadn't heard her come down from her perch.

"That was close."

"Too close," Argent agreed. He didn't want to think about what would happen if the ship collided with a portal.

"There's a hawk incoming, too," Emma said, lowering her voice. Shielding against the sun with her hand, her eyes tracked the bird across the horizon, and she pointed. "There."

Following her gaze, Argent found the small hawk speeding toward the ship. The bird flapped its wings hard, slowing down to land on a barrel in front of King Aragon on the poop deck.

The King offered the hawk his forearm. It flapped up, and he extracted the letter from the bird's harness, but he didn't open it. Instead, he turned the envelope over and frowned at the back.

"That's odd," Argent said, furrowing his brow.

"What is?" Emma asked and sidled closer.

Argent welcomed her proximity. He tucked his book under one arm and grabbed Emma's hand. "If the letter is to him, why not open it right there? No one's with him."

The King descended to the sterncastle and entered the navigation room.

Argent trotted across the deck, pulling Emma along behind him.

"What are we doing?" she asked in a whisper, glancing around to see if they'd attracted the attention of the crew still putting the ship to rights after the hasty detour around the portal.

Argent capitalized on the distraction. While they were all occupied, he and Emma slipped up the stairs, and he led her to a nook he'd discovered on the voyage to Helcari.

"Eavesdropping," he whispered breathlessly, placing the book on the deck. He tucked himself into the tight space that butted up to the thin planks lining the navigation room.

A look of delight blossomed across Emma's face, and she wasted no time joining him. She waved her hand, and Argent felt her magic protect them from discovery.

They both quieted, though her closeness increased Argent's heart rate. He wound his arms around her and pressed his ear against the wood.

"It's for you," King Aragon said, his voice tight.

The hardened wax of the envelope's seal cracked, and they heard parchment.

The few seconds of silence stretched, and then—

"Read it for us," the King said.

*Us? Who else is in there?* Emma's thoughts projected into his head.

Argent shrugged, but he didn't open his thoughts to her, too focused on the conversation.

Then, Sargateth spoke, sounding as tense as the King. "'Uncle, the last scout has returned, mission complete. Davan Ender brought two from Earth: Jack and Audrey Hawkins. Bethany's parents. Earth is in an unprecedented state of turmoil. Portals, creatures, and quakes like the ones here have ravaged their world. Jack and Audrey were on the last airplane from America to Scotland before international airspace shut down. This must end, and it must end soon.'"

At least it was short. Renault's brevity left nothing to the imagination.

Emma had frozen at the mention of the Hawkinses.

"Bethany's parents I can understand," said Tomás, answering the question of who else was present. "But the 'last scout'? I thought *I* was our last scout."

Sargateth sounded deeply uncomfortable. "You were the last to leave. Not the last to return."

Argent was stunned. Emma had written of her suspicions about her history professor before he'd lost his journal in the Kraken attack, but to hear confirmation of another—secret—scout, straight from the Archmage?

The slosh of the sea against the ship punctured the following silence. Then, Tomás spoke, sounding angry. "Why didn't I know about this? You're telling me there was a man I could have trusted to watch over my family instead of spending eleven years regretting coming back?"

Argent glanced down at Emma and saw his own astonishment reflected back at him.

"There was nothing Davan could have done for them," King Aragon said. "Your family was not his mission."

"Then what *was*?" Tomás pressed.

"Tell him," the King said, clearly frustrated.

Sargateth sighed, and the truth came out. "We sent him to carry out two tasks. First, to watch for signs of Lancelot's Prophecy, and second... we thought there might be descendants of Arthur still living on Earth. Descendants who could try to claim the Pendragon throne."

"Davan says his mission is complete," Aragon said, the paper crinkling again. "Are the Hawkinses going to try to wrest the kingdom from me while I'm gone? My instructions were to find Arthur's descendants and take care of them. Not to bring them here and expose them to a world they know nothing about."

Argent suddenly felt very glad he could stop himself from projecting his thoughts to Emma. He'd never considered the existence of other Pendragons, whether they went by that surname or not. If there were others, even if not the Hawkins family, would his family be safe?

"This is ridiculous," Tomás said.

"A hundred percent ridiculous," Emma whispered, sounding betrayed. Her fingers dug into Argent's chest, but he barely felt them.

"There's not a drop of royal blood in Jack or Audrey," Tomás continued, his exoskeleton squeaking.

"Davan did not return with anyone else," Aragon replied coolly. "His mission was to protect the kingdom."

Emma suddenly wriggled out of his embrace and escaped the hidden nook, and Argent startled. She started pacing just out of his reach.

"He's wrong—he has to be wrong," she muttered, pressing her left thumb deep into the tesseract on her right palm. "There's no way Bethany is a Pendragon. And even if she is—oh no. Argent, what if he tries to stop us from saving her?"

Grateful for Emma's concealment spell, he grasped her shoulders and made her look up at him. "I'll get to the bottom of this, I swear. Everything will be fine."

A sinking feeling filled his gut, but so did determination. Argent would talk to his father alone, because if it was true... it could change everything.

Later that evening, Argent slipped below decks, seeking his father out. Finding solitude on a brigantine stuffed with people was harder than he'd imagined.

He hadn't been alone with his father since he and Emma had destroyed the eagle ring, and even then, she'd been with him.

As he descended the stairs to the crew's quarters, trepidation clung to him like a wet blanket. Everyone but the King tended to things above deck while *The Sea Wolf* carved east through the dark blue waters.

"Father," he said, wincing when Aragon jumped to his feet. He'd been sitting on a small wooden stool by a hammock, elbows on his knees, the letter crumpled in his fist.

"Argent," King Aragon replied, his voice weary. "What do you need?"

"The truth."

His father stared at him, brows furrowed, and confusion clouded his face. On this voyage, the King dressed like everyone else—no grand robes, no crown, no sign of royalty but for the etching of a dragon on his leather jerkin.

"It's just us down here," Argent continued, gesturing to the empty quarters. His heart pounded. "Did you send Davan to kill your potential rivals?"

Even though their relationship had improved since the incident with the eagle ring, he expected dismissal, deflection, and what Emma called 'pulling rank'. But to Argent's surprise, his father seemed relieved.

"*Our* rivals, Argent. I won't ask how you found out because I was going to tell you regardless. I sent Davan to ensure the Pendragon throne would remain within our family. To find Arthur's earthly heirs and to *take care of them.* Ensure they never find Talahm. Never learn their ancestry. None of it."

"If they survived at all," Argent interjected, his mind now going a mile a minute. "Do you truly believe it's Bethany and her parents?"

"It does not matter what I believe about the Hawkins family," Aragon sighed. "I've heard the conversations about using the Khozek to rescue Bethany. If Igraine gains the upper hand, we would face an even worse fate than we already do."

Argent frowned. "What do you mean?"

"We've been presented with three possibilities. In the first, we face Igraine and lose. In the second, we face Igraine and likely sustain heavy losses, perhaps including one of us. And in the third, we use the Khozek to save Bethany, at the same time giving Igraine the chance to escape." He crossed his arms. "The safest option is to not risk Igraine escaping Langoth at all."

"This isn't about Bethany possibly being a contender to our throne?" Argent asked, still suspicious. He mirrored his father, crossing his arms. He leaned against one of the pillars supporting the deck.

The King shook his head.

"If it was Emma locked on Langoth—"

"But she isn't. If it were Emma, this would be an entirely different discussion." His father took a step closer.

"Because Emma is important enough to save, and Bethany isn't?" Argent pushed away from the column.

His father's jaw tightened. "Bethany is not the fated Seventh Sorceress. I cannot risk this entire world's future on whether the Khozek can rescue Bethany before Igraine claws her way through."

Argent stayed silent. He turned his father's words over in his head, trying to find fault with them. Finally, he said, "Any citizen, including Bethany, deserves as much right to life as Emma does."

"This is about more than one person's life—and about more than Renova," his father continued, crushing the letter further. "The entire world is at risk if Igraine escapes. All of Petra, Helcari, Korad, and Ekranom will lose their freedom if Igraine returns."

Argent frowned and opened his mouth to respond, but his father kept going.

"Listen to me, Argent, Igraine will not stop at the ends of this world. She was born on Earth. What makes you think she would not attempt to subjugate them as well? Our greatest strength is the oaths made to Arthur. The fealty Sargateth Rishon, Morgan Le Fay, and Magdalin Skyheart owe our crown. If Igraine usurps the oath, more than Renova's future could crumble."

Argent understood instantly. Despite the fact that Renova's army had once been the largest on Petra and the Pendragon kings had sailed full naval fleets, the Ancients had been at the vanguard of every war.

The worlds *would* fold if Igraine forced them to do her bidding.

"Release them from their oath. We lose nothing by letting them serve out of love instead of force."

A flinty look entered his father's gray eyes. "It's not that simple. They made the choice freely. And all three made it to the throne. To undo their oath would take great magic, without coercion, in Camelot. I cannot simply say 'be free' and they become free."

"So you've considered it," Argent said with some measure of relief.

"If we fail in our quest and doing so would prevent Igraine from gaining indescribable power? Absolutely. But we lost that option the moment I sent them to Skypoint."

For so long, his father had obsessed about protecting only their kingdom—only Renova. But now, with two worlds teetering between peace and destruction....

"Argent, no single person outweighs the needs of the many."

The creak and sway of the ship were loud in the silence that followed.

"Would you sacrifice *Mother* to save the kingdom?" Argent asked, aghast at the thought.

A spasm of discomfort flitted across his father's olive complexion. "Your mother and I have spoken at length about what we would do in such a situation, and under very specific, very *improbable* circumstances, yes. We would sacrifice each other if it meant saving a greater number of lives. Bethany Hawkins is not worth sacrificing the entire universe on Igraine's altar."

Argent felt cold. "I refuse to believe you would let my mother, your *wife*, perish if she was in Bethany's place."

Aragon straightened, his eyes narrowing. "I am a King, Argent, and it is my responsibility to make difficult, sometimes heart-wrenching decisions. Life or death is never an easy decision. What is more important? Risking Igraine's freedom for one woman, or sacrificing one woman to protect the lives of all the citizens of Talahm? Of Earth? If we don't stop Igraine from coming back, there will be death. But if the Khozek can let us block off *all* of Langoth without taking any chances, I will take that opportunity." His father sighed, sitting back down on the tiny stool. "One day you will be King, Argent, and you will discover the heavy burden of choosing between what you want and what you believe is right for the kingdom." He held out the crumpled letter.

Argent hesitated before taking the parchment, carefully smoothing it out. He recognized Renault's narrow, choppy penmanship that hadn't improved even after 400 years. He scanned through the words he'd overheard with Emma, but his heart skipped a beat at the last line.

*Does the King know his wife is with child?*

Mouth dry, Argent stared at his father. "Did you know?"

The King shook his head. He drew in a deep, ragged breath, and glanced up, clear pain in his eyes. "Your mother carries the next Pendragon heir. If either or both of us die, that child will be Igraine's next target. We cannot give her the chance to erase us all. Because if she does, nothing stands in her way of usurping the Ancients' oath of fealty to the throne. She'd be unstoppable."

## CHAPTER NINE

# A RISKY DEAL

"Clear a bed!" Rissy Clement shouted as they entered the courtyard.

Harlow stuck her head out of the infirmary tent where Bethany had woken up, then disappeared back inside.

Bethany's magic felt weaker, depleted, but she couldn't tell if it was from holding back the tidal wave or something more sinister. Kenna, levitating in Bethany's net of magic, had fallen unconscious on the short journey from the cliff.

Rissy held back the tent flap as Bethany maneuvered her floating cargo into the dimly lit infirmary. Harlow had just finished clearing off the bed Bethany had occupied earlier.

"Set her down gently," Rissy instructed, and Bethany did what she could, her strength waning. Once she moved the older woman to the thin, straw-stuffed mattress, she almost collapsed on the bed behind her. Drained, she didn't think she could stand, even if she wanted to.

Rissy tossed up the medical projection and started working feverishly, snapping instructions to Misha, who had followed them inside. A few minutes later, Kenna's eyes flickered open, conscious even if she didn't seem strong enough to do anything but blink.

A hand clamped over Bethany's shoulder, and Hela thrust a hot cup into her good hand. "Drink. It's the only thing on this forsaken rock that will counteract the effects of the sky monster."

"Black hole," Bethany corrected under her breath, sniffing the cup's contents. Steam coiled off the surface of the dark brown liquid that did a great job masquerading as hot chocolate. It even *smelled* like her favorite winter beverage. She took a sip and nearly coughed it back out. "How the heck did they figure out how to get *hot chocolate* here?" She frantically blew on it to ease the heat. As she drank, it filled her with warmth and her magic stabilized.

"It's hard to make," Hela whispered as Harlow set another steaming cup on Kenna's bedside table. Rissy continued her work, then tilted Kenna's head forward to help her take a drink. "I saw how much the last wave took from Kenna. If anyone needs this right now, it's you two."

Bethany thought about what she planned to do. "Listen. Igraine is still out there. She was whispering to me inside my head the whole time I was helping Kenna with the berm." She hesitated saying the next part, but trust between battle witches was paramount. "She offered me a way out. A way home. I think she can't escape by herself and needs help to do it."

Hela's hand tightened over her shoulder. "You plan to hunt her down?"

Bethany nodded.

"I will go with you."

Shocked, Bethany looked up at her Coventra so fast she almost cricked her neck. "I appreciate the offer, but I think it can only be me."

Hela arched her brow in challenge. "With a broken arm and exhausted from the wave? She will smash you like a spider."

Bethany couldn't disagree that it was a possibility. "Maybe. But she wouldn't have stuck around as long as she has if she could open a portal by herself. She whispered to me, not any of you. I want to figure out why she can't use the claw on her own."

"And to steal it?"

Bethany shrugged the shoulder Hela held. The prolonged touch felt comforting in this cold world. "At this point, anything goes. I'd rather not get sucked into a black hole, thank you very much."

"Did you say black hole?" a weak male voice said from behind them.

Bethany stood on shaky legs, leaving Hela behind with Rissy as she navigated through the tight quarters to the beds with the unknown man and woman on them. She took another sip of her hot chocolate, wondering whether either of these people had gotten such a treat.

The man struggled to sit up, pushing himself against the bed's headboard until he could look at Bethany without straining his neck. His dark eyes met hers through the gloom despite his long hair falling in front of them. Dirt marred his cheekbones, and a thick bandage was wrapped around his chest. A wild beard obscured the bottom half of his face, but she had heard that voice and seen those eyes before.

"Why do I know you?" Bethany murmured, staring at the stranger's face. She pointedly ignored that he wasn't wearing a shirt. The only bare chest she cared about was Luke's.

"I told you they would plaster our faces all over the newspapers," the woman muttered from the other bed, sounding much weaker than the man.

"And I told you they wouldn't admit anything to the international press—" The man fell silent when the woman coughed.

Bethany shook her head, frowning. "It wasn't in the newspaper." She gestured at the man with her cup. "I've seen you in person. I've *met* you." The memory slipped from her grasp given the chaos of the last few weeks. "You're from Earth."

The man brought his knees up to his chest, still watching her with interest. "Isn't everyone?"

Bethany ignored the question. "What did you do?"

A moment of hesitation.

She was surprised he didn't ask about the black hole. "What did you do for a living?" she clarified, exasperated.

"I spoke at universities."

"About?"

The pause in the man's breath made it clear that he did not want to share that information. But apparently it did not matter, regardless of what his neighbor thought. "Astrophysics."

A lightbulb clicked in Bethany's brain. She almost laughed at the absurdity. Of course this dude would pick up on space language. "When I was in high school, my best friend dragged me to your talk at a nearby college. She followed your work for years after that. You're Lincoln Emry, aren't you?"

The man's head fell backward, his eyes dead. "Prisoner 23566."

"Is that a Les Misérables joke?" Bethany scrunched her nose.

The woman, who had yet to identify herself, rolled onto her side. "Don't you have a number yet? I thought they gave them to all of us."

Bethany cocked her head. "This isn't a prison camp. What did you think this is, Siberia?" She chuckled at her own joke, but it shriveled in her chest when she saw the despondent looks on their faces. "Seriously?"

"Lincoln and Penelope Emry," the woman exaggerated her English accent as if quoting from the newspaper's society pages. "The disgraced children of the Baron and Baroness, sentenced to life in the gulag. What a tragedy."

"Quiet, Penny," the man—Lincoln—whispered. "She said *black hole*. Those don't exist near Earth."

"That would be infinitely more exciting." Penelope threw an arm over her face.

Bethany gave a pained sort of giggle. "If you can walk, I can show you."

A spark filled Lincoln's eyes, bringing him back to life. "You're not lying? There is truly a black hole out there?"

Instead of answering, Bethany smiled, meandering back to the tent flap. Hela raised her eyebrow but said nothing as Lincoln and Penelope fumbled with their bedsheets. Lincoln was the stronger of the two and helped his sister shuffle over, their bare feet and ragged clothing making them look like they'd come out of a prison.

"You didn't gain a hundred pounds," Bethany said as she ducked into the courtyard and cast a quick warming charm at them as they made their way outside. "You're just on Langoth, the dying world."

The astrophysicist collapsed to his knees, his head turned toward the sky, his mouth open in wretched awe. Penelope clenched his shoulder.

"How—"

"It's proof, brother," Penelope whispered. Her delight contrasted sharply with her brother's despair. "Earth is not alone."

Lincoln reached up and grasped his sister's hand, their fingers white with the pressure. "This is not the kind of vindication I wanted, Penny. The time dilation alone could mean they're all dead before I even get the chance to clear our names."

Bethany's brain short-circuited. "Time dilation?"

"Black holes slow down time," Lincoln said, struggling to his feet. His eyes were still glued on the dull red accretion disk looming over the planet. "Each day here could be years on Earth. There's no way to know for sure."

Bethany's heart raced. She'd forgotten what else black holes affected. Did this mean time on Talahm was passing a lot faster than she realized? What if she got home only to find that Luke had aged a decade and moved on with his life?

"I have a way off this rock," Bethany said quietly, returning to the elephant in the room, trying to suppress the panic rising in her chest. "But it's not to Earth. Even if you wanted to go back...." She trailed off, letting the unfinished end of her sentence speak for itself.

"There's nothing left on Earth for us."

"Then I hope you're okay with medieval society. Because that's what's waiting for us on Talahm."

Penelope rubbed her hands together. "Brilliant. I've always loved Renaissance fairs." She ducked under her brother's arm, and they helped each other back inside. Lincoln took furtive glances over his shoulder at the monstrosity above them.

Hela chose that moment to exit the tent, giving the Emrys a sidelong glance. "Firewhip, if you are going after

Igraine alone, take this." She held out a second cup of hot chocolate with a sealed lid.

Bethany accepted it, putting it into the purse-pouch at her waist. "Here goes nothing," she said, giving a jaunty mock-salute to her Coventra. Deflating, she quickly explained what black holes did to their perception of time. "I don't know how long I'll be gone."

"If it takes longer than what we think is four days, we're dead anyway," Hela answered. "If you need backup, we're all one call away with the Mark."

Bethany touched the Coven Mark on her throat, one of the only vestiges in her possession that hinted at her allegiance. Everything else had been torn or burned. She had no comeback except gratitude, so she nodded and turned away to begin her hunt.

The light of the inner courtyard did not extend past the tents. It would have been sheer, complete darkness if not for the red hue cast by the matter spiraling into the black hole above them.

*Emma would know what that red donut is actually called.*

Igraine may not have a Coven Mark, but she'd been in Bethany's mind long enough for her to know how to find the old hag's magical presence.

She sank back into that feeling, immediately sensing Hela's bright blue presence beside her. In the tent, Rissy and

Harlow glowed white and orange. The rest of the settlers, the Fifth Travelers, were muted in color, some of them brighter than others. Someone with a soft purple aura lay by Rissy and Harlow—Kenna. Even Lincoln and Penelope had a dull brown glow to them.

Casting her mind's eye out further, she expected to find evidence of Igraine but sensed nothing. No tracks, no aura, no evidence that the woman had ever been near the settlement. When Bethany came back to herself, she shook her head, clearing the lingering fog from her effort.

"I couldn't find her. It felt like the block that kept me from seeing the witches in Valona when I first got my Mark."

"How will you track her, then?" Hela asked, sounding like a high school teacher trying to coax the right answer out of a particularly difficult student.

Bethany recalled her years reading fantasy books and watching movies with tracker and ranger characters. She gave Hela what she hoped was a deranged grin. "Like an animal."

Bethany spent what felt like hours slowly moving around the perimeter of the camp, looking for signs of Igraine's non-magical presence. She hit paydirt near the berm, where a set of sloppy bare footprints trailed off into the darkness parallel to the cliff. She followed the prints until the ground dried up and the trail all but disappeared.

The increased gravity made every second feel like minutes, each tick of the clock in her head a signal that the next wave was coming—the one they wouldn't be able to stop. Their only hope now was Mountains' claw, even if they had to work with Igraine Pendragon to use it.

The area outside the Fifth Travelers' settlement was as wild and terrifying as one would expect on a doomed world. Ground vegetation was sparse, and the trees were short and fat, their trunks compressed by the magnificent pressure.

Bethany glanced over her shoulder, panicking when she couldn't find the lights of the settlement. She wasn't far, but the black hole sucked all the light away.

A low snarl tore her attention away from the invisible settlement, and she produced a ball of fire in her good hand. At the same time, she formed a thin but stable shield along her forearm. It wasn't enough to stop something truly deadly, but it calmed her racing nerves. She'd rather be ready for an attack than avoid her magic in the name of stealth.

Behind a gathering of squat trees with droopy needles like an evergreen on steroids, a corgi-sized rat with matted gray fur and long, sinuous whiskers crept closer.

Igraine, the old hag, had captured countless creatures like the one before her, but this one didn't look *too* threatening. Bethany straightened. The motion jostled her arm, and she cursed herself for not asking Rissy to secure and numb it before she left.

The oversized rodent squealed, launching itself at Bethany's face with a speed that seemed unnatural on Langoth.

She brought up her shield, and the wild monster smashed against it, its red eyes gleaming. The impact sent her stumbling back, and only through sheer luck did she not fall down. Pain ricocheted through her arm. Not a second later, the now familiar ripping sound reverberated through the air, and a portal without any distinctive coloration tore open beside her and the beast. The rat clearly knew the implications because its attention diverted immediately to the portal.

The center, normally dark with the void of space, flickered twice before showing people in medieval peasant clothing milling around a small country village. In the few seconds it took Bethany to comprehend what she saw, one of the people waved their hands, and the rest of them began running away—from the creature, which had jumped through.

Bethany scrambled backward in horror, breathing hard as the portal zipped itself up.

She'd never been able to see the *other side* before. Without the amber or purple to clue her in on a portal's destination, she couldn't tell if this one had connected to Talahm or to a really good reenactment festival on Earth.

But no matter where these portals went, she couldn't let another monster escape.

*If this world is going into a black hole, things like that should go with it.*

It took her another minute to recover her heart rate. In the scuffle, she'd lost her bearings and had to cast a tight dome of lights to find the footprints again. They hadn't disappeared. Out here, on the frozen ground, they were much more subtle than in the muddy waste from the tidal wave's runoff. But it was only a few paces later that the tracks vanished again. Without being able to track Igraine's magical aura, Bethany was at a loss for how to continue. But going back to the settlement empty-handed was not an option.

For all she knew, Igraine could have set her own traps—traps she'd fallen for before.

So she set out again, leaving a trail of magic to find her way back to camp and hoped she was going in the right direction.

*This is a bad idea*, the rational part of her brain said in a voice that sounded like Luke. *You should have accepted Hela's help.*

"No, we can totally do this," she replied. Her stubbornness usually won.

*And what, ask her nicely to help you and not eviscerate the entire population? She wiped the floor with you all in Valona, and you had a full coven then. Even Emma couldn't scratch her, and she's the Seventh Sorceress.*

Bethany grimaced at her own logic. "She's the one who wanted me to come find her, you know."

*How do you know that was her and not your imagination? And those footprints could've been anyone's, not just Igraine's. She's long gone, Bethie dear. You're on a wild goose chase.*

A sinking pit of dread opened in her stomach. What if she *had* imagined Igraine's whispers? What if they were well and truly stranded here? Without the claw.... Forget the black hole. They'd all die in the next tidal wave. She stopped walking and physically shook her head. "Shut up," she said firmly. "I wasn't imagining it. She's still here."

But she didn't actually have a plan. Finding Igraine was one thing, but navigating the old crone's offer of help without ending up a prisoner was another thing entirely.

If her rational brain had been a person, it would have audibly sighed. *She caught us by surprise the first time. And you know, it's just as dark here as it was in her tunnels.*

There were a lot of "yeah, buts" on the tip of Bethany's mental tongue when she heard the telltale rip of the universe again. She hadn't realized just how often the rogue portals had been opening. Something must be unraveling to have this kind of effect on the nature of magic.

The portal opened, flickering like a TV screen. Once the image manifested, Bethany's heart dropped like a stone.

She saw Goatfell—obelisk and all.

And not only that... those were *her parents!*

A slightly older man with short-cropped white hair stood behind them with an awfully large suitcase.

*That must be Professor Ender!*

The snuffling of another corgi-rat filled Bethany's ears, and she raced toward the portal, not sure if she planned to leap through it or head off the monster.

"Mom! Dad!" The words escaped her lips before she could stop them.

But she never saw if they heard her. A blast of magic lit the space between her and the portal, and the corgi-rat was flung away from the image as portal zipped itself closed.

"No!" Bethany skidded to a halt, breathing hard. She searched for the source of magic. It had to be Igraine. No one else from the Fifth Travelers would be out this far. Alert, she turned in a circle, keeping her shield at the ready.

Another group of trees came into view as she blinked away the residual light and her eyes adjusted to the darkness once more.

"Come, pet, am I really that hard to find?" came Igraine's sultry voice.

Bethany whirled toward the copse. "As a matter of fact, yeah. You are."

Coming into full view, Igraine pouted. Without her glamour, she looked like the husk of a human. Bethany had heard enough of Igraine's gloating and accusations during their battle to know that King Arthur's mother had somehow cheated death for over seven hundred years. Igraine's hair, still gray, had lost its smoothness and shine. Now, it resembled the hair of a teenage girl experimenting with her mother's straightener—dry, brittle, and liable to snap like a twig. Deep wrinkles marred her forehead and cheeks. Her audacious, deep purple dress was ripped and burned from the fight in Valona and her chaotic fall through Mountains' portal.

Her left arm was held stiffly against her chest with a wide strip of purple cloth torn from the bottom of her dress. At the end of it was a red cloth-covered stump that did not look hand-shaped.

Bethany remembered the explosion from Julie's pistol, the bullet striking Igraine's hand as it clutched the edge of the portal.

*Julie destroyed her entire hand!*

A bit of bile rose at the back of Bethany's throat. She breathed deeply to keep herself from retching.

"Oh, this?" Igraine said with a mask of casual indifference. "I must applaud the lovely Julie Houston Jackman for her fortitude. Or, I would if I still had two hands." She sighed dramatically.

Bethany took the opportunity to swing the slap she'd promised at Igraine's face.

But Igraine was faster than her. She caught Bethany's hand and held it fast, her fingers bony but strong. "Did you learn nothing from me, pet?"

"That was for trying to distract me from stopping the tidal wave, you self-righteous—"

Igraine twisted her hand. "Ah ah ah. None of that. I do not tolerate name-calling from my witches."

"Hag," Bethany finished with venom. She yanked herself free and took several steps back, shaking her hand. "I'm not one of your witches. You're the reason I had to help at all. Your arrival here killed Danya, who was helping Kenna stop the waves."

A flash of remorse passed over Igraine's haggard face. "An accident, I assure you," she said, her voice measured. "A most tragic accident."

Bethany glared at her, not sure what to say in response.

"Anyway, enough catching up. Would you have rather I let that vermin attack your parents?"

Bethany swallowed. This woman had tortured her for days, invaded her mind, burned her paired journal with Luke, and used her to set a trap. It wouldn't have been out of the question for Igraine to let the corgi-rat ruin her parents' lives, too. Instead of answering, Bethany reinforced her shield until it glowed bright.

"Interesting that Davan was with them," Igraine said, sounding almost bored. But her eyes gleamed with delight.

Bethany knew her tactics by now but still took the bait. Regardless of what Igraine had done in Valona, she had saved her parents from being attacked by a monster. "How do you know Ender?"

"How do *you* know Pendragon's last scout?" Igraine demanded, unable to hide her surprise.

"I asked first," Bethany shot back.

Igraine paused for a long moment, assessing Bethany with a sharp, hawk-like stare. "I've had eyes and ears inside Camelot for centuries, little dove. I knew when Davan Ender left for his secret mission, and I knew when Tomás Artair left for his. I knew when he returned and told Sargateth that his daughter was the fabled Seventh Sorceress. And I knew the moment Septim's tortured spirit seized the Prince's mind. Nothing happened within the walls of that wretched city without me knowing about it." She cocked her head like a curious dog. "Do you even know why Davan is with your parents?"

Thinking a mile a minute, Bethany shifted, pushing past the pain in her arm. "Because I told them to call him," she said, not seeing any harm in telling the truth. Igraine probably had little experience with the truth, anyway. "He taught Emma's history classes at university. He's the only one left who could get my parents to Camelot safely."

Igraine laughed. "Oh, child, Pendragon has kept so much from you. They should have stayed on Earth."

Though intrigued, Bethany didn't want to get sucked into Igraine's mind games again. She'd barely been in the King's presence, even during Septim's curse. Why would he tell her anything?

"Morgan hasn't changed at all, has she?" Igraine continued. There was an edge to her voice, but Bethany could tell it wasn't aimed at her. "Still protecting herself, her twin, and her king before showing any respect to her witches."

Bethany didn't think that was fair. She'd seen the melancholy and regret on Morgan's face when asked about the portrait of Igraine in her office.

"Didn't you ever wonder why my beautiful assassin was willing to die rather than risk exposing me when she triggered that curse I gave Septim, while he was inside Prince Argent's head?"

*Wait, what? Septim's curse was really Igraine's?*

"The loyalty my coven daughters show me is not out of fear, Bethany Celeste."

Bethany had learned about psychological manipulation tactics like this in school—had even used some against bullies—but this was another level entirely.

"What are you saying?" Bethany finally asked, both the rational and stubborn parts of her brain losing to her deep-seated curiosity. Her shield dimmed.

"I'm saying that I respect my coven daughters by telling them the truth, unlike Morgan. She hasn't told you a thing, has she? And yet you're one of her battle witches." Igraine moved closer, and a flicker of her artificial youth returned.

"Pendragon sent Davan to find his rivals—the other Earthly spawns of Arthur. And now that Davan is returning, it means his mission has concluded. You've met King Aragon. How do you think he will react to his last scout bringing usurpers into his throne room?"

"What?"

The corner of Igraine's eye twitched. "Your King will believe that your parents can dethrone him."

Bethany laughed. She couldn't help it. The idea that anyone could think her parents were long-lost royals was absurd. Jack and Audrey Hawkins were too down-to-earth. Too into internet memes and dad jokes. They had no interest in governing anything larger than the garden.

But Igraine's frown only deepened. "You haven't been around Pendragon long enough to truly know him or his propensities toward suspicion, child. Davan is taking your parents right into the lion's den."

"You don't actually think my parents—or *me*—are related to you, do you?"

Igraine scowled at the reminder that Arthur was her child. "Who can say you aren't?"

"Don't make me barf," Bethany said and mimed gagging. "If I'm related to you, I'll eat my hat. If I had a hat. Besides, my parents can handle themselves, magic or not."

Igraine looked frustrated that Bethany wouldn't budge. "They are in danger, whether you believe me or not. I can protect them. I can protect *you*."

"In case you haven't noticed, *we're* in danger." Bethany narrowed her eyes and pointed up at the black hole for good measure. "Why haven't you used that claw yet to escape this death trap? It's not like we have a lot of time."

Igraine's gaze followed Bethany's finger, but there was no recognition of danger in her eyes when she looked back at her. She adjusted her damaged arm against her chest, a tinge of pain sweeping across her ancient face. "While I don't know what that is, I do know it has made stable portals a near impossibility, even with the anchoring obelisks. The only chance I, or anyone else, has of escaping is—" she cut herself off, twirling around to block yet another corgi-rat with a flash of magic.

After it ran away squealing, Bethany couldn't ignore Igraine's labored breathing. A pit opened in her stomach at the thought that if some random monster caught Igraine by surprise, Bethany might lose her chance to get off this planet. She reached into her waist pouch and curled her hand around the hot chocolate, not sure yet what she was doing.

Igraine straightened, but her shoulders trembled against the overwhelming gravity. "I need your power, Bethany

Celeste," she admitted. Bethany stared at her. "It would take more than I have to open a portal large enough—for long enough—to Perga's Scepter. The Titan Obelisk is the oldest and most stable obelisk on Talahm. And I must find the right place to open it. That is why I'm out here. If I cannot find the right place to anchor, rescuing the village is but a fool's hope."

"You'd evacuate the Fifth Travelers?" Bethany asked, surprised. She felt like she was missing something important, just beyond the tip of her awareness. It didn't feel right that this mighty sorceress needed *her* power to yank an Olis claw through the air and slip through the gap.

Igraine cocked her head again. "I sent scouts on missions just like every other kingdom with an obelisk, Bethany. I lost many to the uncertainty of the fifth passage. If they ended up here, I cannot say, but these people are just as much my responsibility as they are yours."

"You need an army, and this one is ready-made," Bethany realized as the pieces clicked in place.

But Igraine's face showed disappointment, not agreement. "I wish you had been one of my witches from the start, not a lackey of Morgan's."

"You put that sentence back in your mouth!" Bethany demanded with disgust.

Igraine ignored her outburst. "I would have kept nothing from you, and I would have given you the gift of transparency and truth. I keep no secrets from my witches."

The dichotomy between how Igraine had treated her in the depths of Valona and how she treated her now threatened to tear Bethany's mind in half.

"Why should I trust you?" she said, trying to avoid thinking about the torture Igraine had put her through. "Aside from the fact that we're both stuck here unless we work together, give me one good reason not to kill you now and pluck the claw from your dead body."

Igraine smiled as if Bethany was a kitten masquerading as a lion. "Because I know something you don't know about Lancelot's infamous Prophecy."

Bethany narrowed her eyes. "You mean the Prophecy that says Emma and Luke are the ones who will 'seal out the forces of evil' when the world is supposed to end? Heard it. Old news."

Igraine's grin widened. "It doesn't end where Merlin said. The rest of it explains exactly what will become of the Seventh Sorceress if someone with powers like mine doesn't intervene."

Bethany stared at her.

*That's a new one,* her rational brain piped up. *Even if she's fibbing about Davan, is Emma at risk now?*

*She's eight hundred years old and knows a lot more than we do,* her stubborn side answered silently with a little more sense than Bethany realized that part of her had. *If King Aragon thinks we're rivals—if he knows something about Emma's destiny that wasn't in Lancelot's Prophecy—what would he do to keep it a secret? Or to keep them from coming for us?*

Bethany's rational side didn't answer for a long, painful moment during which Igraine raised a single, perfectly sculpted brow that looked oddly out of place on her wrinkly old face. *Whether she tells us the rest of the Prophecy or not, she's our ticket off this rock. And she needs us to do it.*

Feeling far too much like she was making a deal with the devil, she handed Igraine the sealed cup of hot chocolate. "We don't have time to waste."

# CHAPTER TEN

# THE SHADOW STAR

The voyage from Bearsmouth to Keldvaar took *The Sea Wolf* along Petra's northern coast. Julie spent hours at starboard, admiring the rugged landscape and view of Skypoint's mountain range.

What she wouldn't give to ride through Petra's countryside on horseback!

She'd had almost three months now to get used to having Tom back. And, not that she was counting, twenty-five days to reacclimate to his presence. But nothing had prepared her for the close quarters, or for the memories and feelings he dredged up.

All the reasons she'd fallen in love with him in the first place clashed with the reality that he'd left them. Left *her*.

His unwavering sense of duty. His love for knowledge and history. The way he'd danced with her in the streets of the cities they explored, singing while he spun and dipped her to the applause of strangers. Julie's heart longed for the days when she was oblivious to this secret world and their worst fights were about Tom forgetting to ask for a receipt at the store.

But the longer she was here, the more she had to face the reality that there was no going back to Earth. And when she added everything about this world together, she didn't really *want* to.

They were less than a day from Keldvaar according to the charts and figurines in the navigation room, and Julie could finally see the tapering end of the mountain range that formed Petra's spine. Somewhere beyond those peaks lay a pristine jungle seething with Nephilim.

After being captured by Igraine, Julie's surprise meter had recalibrated enough that this didn't shock her.

Magic was real. So were dragons and flying cats. Why not the Nephilim?

A chuffing sound came from behind her. She recognized it as the noise Mountains made when he wanted attention but wasn't willing to start a conversation. He reared up and rested both furry forelegs on the railing next to her, his massive paws dangling over the edge. She still had to resist the urge to pet him, because if she did, he'd bite her hand clean off.

"Have you ever been to Keldvaar before?" She had her suspicions but had no real way to get him to talk about it until now. He crossed his paws, and Julie suspected he didn't know how adorable he looked.

"My last time in the great city was in the year 2805. I'm sure much has changed since then."

Julie had no frame of reference for the dating system used here. "How long ago was that?"

Mountains glanced at her, rolling his eyes at her perceived dimwittedness. "Almost two hundred and two years ago." He sighed, resting his chin on his front legs and pointing his nose in the wind. "I doubt any of the Olii have checked on the shield in that time. While I can't be certain, there is a speck of possibility—"

Julie held her breath. That did not sound good.

"—that some Nephilim may have wormed their way into the city."

The sea roared in Julie's ears.

"What?!"

Mountains' ears twitched. "I'd wager no more than three, for sure. But it's no matter. The Elvara Bow can easily handle them, and in such a large, bustling city, it's highly unlikely we'll encounter any at all."

"You're telling me this *now*?" she said with her deadliest mom voice.

Mountains adjusted his head to look at her, his golden eyes somewhere between calculating and remorseful. "If I'd said a thing about it during Catigern, the council wouldn't have paid attention to anything else. If we'd sent a letter from the port, my precious sister wouldn't have anyone left to send to the Scepter to fulfill the Prophecy. And if I'd told Firstborn before today, he'd go rampaging off to fix it by himself. We'd be without the bow *or* the key, without the Olii, and without a plan. Tell me, how was my silence a bad idea?"

Julie's hands turned clammy. She had to tell the others—to warn them of what they were about to walk into.

And they didn't have much time.

When *The Sea Wolf* sailed into Keldvaar's port the next morning, Julie couldn't believe her eyes. The northern "hook" of Severna hadn't looked that large on the map in the ship's navigation room, but the port itself sprawled across a staggering two miles. On either end, the city itself simply stopped, lush trees and massive foliage hugging city walls taller than *The Sea Wolf*'s main mast.

Those walls stretched behind the city, and, according to Mountains, were the boundary of the shield imprisoning the Nephilim.

The deck thrived with activity as the crew prepared for arrival. Sargateth paced, his arms crossed and still clearly incensed that Mountains had kept his information quiet for so long. Morgan was calmer, standing on the forecastle deck with a bag already slung across her back, as if she were a scholar on her way to study at the library. Morgan had tried to convince them that only she and Sargateth should go retrieve the Khozek, but Tom's cool head prevailed. Emma needed more exposure to Olis magic, Luke went wherever Emma went, and if their children were going, so were he and Julie. End of story.

And, after all, Tom had been to the Shadow Star before without running into trouble with Nephilim.

Even though his admission had cut their planning time short, Mountains had challenged the outrage with questions. Had they seen an explosion of possessions in the last two centuries? Was there evidence of the Nephilim attempting to conquer the world?

The answer to both was no.

The only person Julie knew who had ever been possessed was Argent, and that spirit hadn't been a Nephilim.

They would be quick and stealthy, slipping underneath enemy noses to take the Khozek and be back on the ship before anyone knew it.

Hundreds—if not thousands—of ships crowded the docks. As they drifted closer, a dinghy with port officials approached, and William threw down the ladder.

Sargateth watched the officials like a hawk, despite the fact they were only checking the ship into the port.

Meanwhile, Julie couldn't take her eyes off the city. Keldvaar stretched high into the sky like most modern American cities—much higher than Camelot.

Standing on its own on the west side of the city, the Shadow Star was Keldvaar's pride and joy. No other buildings blocked the view of the library from the port, perhaps so everyone could see it when they arrived. Built in a starburst shape with fourteen points, the spires reached into the air like the most intricate and ostentatious Gothic cathedrals. At its center, the tallest steeple pierced the sky like a needle, a bright green pennant with gold trim flapping in the breeze.

Keldvaar had compensated for their clear reverence with towering buildings on the eastern half of the city. Sloping upward from the bay, the streets rose to the peak of a hill where a castle sat, its view of the port unimpeded.

It left the impression of a lopsided city, one hastily built, and additions justified because of a long-ago ruler's quirks.

Julie felt the itch return—the itch she hadn't scratched since she and Tom had backpacked across Europe together. Her yearning for adventure must have shown on her face, since Tom leaned against the railing next to her with a smile she knew all too well.

She kept her face stoic, unwilling to answer his warmth.

"We won't have time to explore, you know," Tom said over the rising sounds of the port. "Not even the miles of stacks in the library."

Julie sighed. "I know." She watched the variety of ships as *The Sea Wolf* glided closer to one of the docks, taking a deep breath of salty air. It reminded her of Seattle, and a flash of nostalgia swept through her.

Tom stiffened—one of his Visions. Julie lifted her hands to catch him if he fell. She knew now that her husband had never had epilepsy. Had never suffered a seizure. They had all been Visions. Prophecies. Right in their own home.

Another reminder that he'd lied.

He relaxed, and as soon as he opened his eyes, she asked, "What was it?"

Tom grumbled, his scowl clear beneath his beard. "Just flashes of the library halls. Faceless scholars. Nothing significant or useful."

Shouting from behind them made Julie twist. Airwitches hovered behind the sails, pulling up the ropes to cinch the canvas at the crossbeams. The ship slowed, and Cordelia directed *The Sea Wolf* toward a dock, making slip between two ships of equal size. The port officials clambered back into their dinghy, and the woman stuck a short piece of wood in the water behind the boat before they zipped away to meet the next incoming ship.

An almighty rattle came from aft, and a moment later the anchor splashed into the bay. *The Sea Wolf* came to a stop, its hull gently bumping against the dock. When it did, the captain took a long swig from her ever-present bottle of honeywine.

Sargateth started toward the gangplank and Julie watched as Argent approached him. The young Prince's face was drawn with concern, and Julie sensed danger. She hurried over to them, leaving Tom alone at the railing.

"Something doesn't feel right," Argent said as she got close enough to overhear. A muscle jumped in his neck. "I think I can sense them."

Sargateth froze. "The Nephilim? How many?"

"I don't know. If Mountains is right, it can't be more than two or three. But I should go with you just in case."

Sargateth looked like he wanted to object, but Argent's gaze never wavered.

"Let's get a move on, then," Julie interrupted quietly, resting her hand on Argent's shoulder blade. She felt his muscles relax, and he gave her a small, grateful smile. "No time to waste."

Though the port and lower streets of Keldvaar seethed with color and chaos, it wouldn't be hard for anyone to track their large group. But with their short window—and the possibility, however slim, that they could encounter a Nephilim—they had to take that risk.

Mountains had looked thunderous when they'd told him that the only way he could join their search for the Khozek was to take a human form. He'd refused, muttering insults and empty threats, but ultimately agreed to stay hidden in the darkest corner of the ship's hold in case Cordelia's additional bribes to skip Keldvaar's full inspection failed.

Despite Mountains' reassurances, the group couldn't even use the Elvara Bow to defend against the Nephilim if needed, as Sargateth informed them that all weapons were forbidden from the library. Even smuggling in a dagger would result in arrest, and the Keldvaar courts weren't friendly to anyone who threatened violence in the Shadow Star.

Sargateth and Argent led the group into the city, followed closely by Morgan and Luke. Emma hurried down the gangplank next, waiting for her parents at the bottom.

Tom crossed first, offering his hand for Julie at the end. She took it as she jumped onto the damp but sturdy wood of the pier, ignoring his expression of delight and the way her body electrified at his touch. She'd avoided physical contact with him as much as possible, afraid that she'd do something she'd regret. Julie tugged her hand free as they started down the pier to the road leading into the city.

Tom could walk much easier in his braces after Luke and Sargateth had made some adjustments to them during the voyage. Covered by his robes, only the shimmering runes near his ankles were visible. And if Julie listened closely enough, she could hear the soft clink of metal.

As they walked, Julie longed to disappear among the people of Keldvaar—to explore the side streets and soak up the culture.

Even in the clothes procured for her in Camelot—thankfully not a dress—Julie felt like she stood out. Spring was turning into early summer, and though they were right on the water, the heat of the city still seeped through everything. She felt like she was in her twenties again, traveling across Europe with nothing but her backpack and a visa stuffed into her back pocket. Her blood sang out for adventure unlike the way it had on the ship. Being at sea had its novelties, but what she really wanted was culture.

She kept one eye on Argent at all times, her heart pounding whenever he stared too long in one direction or abruptly stopped walking, even if it was just for a second.

Julie wondered if his tension wasn't just from watching out for Nephilim.

She'd noticed changes over the last few days in how Argent and Emma interacted, and she could tell something had happened between them. There was a distance she'd not seen before, even now as Emma guarded their rear.

It reminded her of Tom in the months before he'd faked his death.

Despite Tom's pace and the distractions that Julie slowed to admire, they made good time through the city. Soon, the giant central spire of the fourteen-pointed library loomed overhead.

Intricate carvings of dragons, snakes, and constellations covered the library's exterior, only visible up close. She couldn't even count the flying buttresses that held up each of the library's arms, and could only imagine the view from the top of the center steeple.

Massive double doors made from solid steel stood between Julie and perhaps the greatest library she would ever see in her lifetime.

"Center spire elevator," Sargateth softly reminded everyone as they entered a smaller, human-sized door cut into the two-story metal barrier.

She ducked after Tom into the huge entry hall, breathing a sigh of relief when nothing happened. She'd taken the gamble that whatever magic identified weapons at the door didn't know what a firearm was.

Emma closed the door behind them. The elevator would only go down so far, and the rest of the trek would be on foot.

His gait awkward, Tom walked past the sweeping library counter that followed the curve of the tower itself. Multiple patrons milled around the lobby, several of them at the counters. More people could be heard in the stacks that encircled the entire bottom floor.

"There's close to a hundred and fifty librarians here," Tom said with unmasked excitement despite their urgent mission. "At least ten of them man the counters day and night."

"Not important right now," Julie hissed, trying to break Tom's schoolboy attitude. But a hundred and fifty librarians? *There must be thousands of patrons at all hours, and any one of them could be a threat.*

Argent stopped walking. Hanging back, he invaded Julie's personal space and whispered directly in her ear. "I think there's one in here."

Julie forced herself to act normal, following Tom and the rest of their party past the circulation and reference desks. Argent hurried ahead until he caught up with Sargateth.

One of the librarians, a tall, wiry, shrewd-looking man with narrow shoulders and a thin waist, peered at them with sharp, eagle eyes as they walked past. A bright red starburst pin was stuck lopsided on his lapel.

"Can I help you find anything?" he asked, his calm, warm voice a stark contrast to his appearance.

"No, thank you," Tom answered, a brief smile lifting the corners of his lips.

"Very well," the librarian demurred. "May your time in the Shadow Star be fruitful."

Tom led them into a long, wide hallway with open archways on either side which led to different sections of the library. The walkway ended in a large, circular room with more halls branching off in all directions. In the center of the room was a shiny metal cylinder fifteen feet wide that extended all the way up into the spire. As she looked closer, Julie spotted intricate designs etched into the metal, many of them thin runes with just a hint of magical light pulsing in them.

"This is the elevator," Tom said, hobbling around to the doors. "The others have already gone down." He pressed a larger rune on one side, and after a minute, the doors slid open, revealing a cylindrical carriage.

Julie scoured the walls for a number pad but came up empty.

A smug grin on his face, Tom pressed a thicker rune on the inner wall, and it lit up, white magic shining through the strokes. "Kato. Beneath." The elevator started its descent, much smoother than any elevator on Earth.

Julie had to force herself to take a deep breath, and she ignored the long look Tom gave her. Now was not the time to tell him about the tiny cages she and Bethany had endured in Igraine's fortress.

"I came here with Renault long before the war, when King Hadrian ruled and Renova had peace for a few years," Tom revealed with a tight smile. "My father wanted me to broaden my horizons before I took his mantle. The Shadow Star is the largest library in the world. I was in heaven."

Julie could almost picture him thirty years younger, his eyes bright with wonder at such a vast archive of knowledge. She imagined him begging to stay for lifetimes, even as duty called him home. The parallels to their life together on Earth made her heart twist. As a cop on Earth, he'd spent hours in the library on the weekends, usually taking Luke with him. It was no wonder her older child lived and breathed books.

When the elevator slowed and the door opened without a sound, Julie sighed. She brushed her hand against the handle of her gun hidden at the small of her back, ready to draw it if they were ambushed.

They left the carriage without incident, watching the door slide shut. She heard the soft whirring as whatever magical mechanisms worked to lift it back to the ground floor.

"This is the lowest public level," Tom said, hobbling down a corridor that mirrored the hallway above. "There are the others."

Julie peered past Tom into the shadows cast by the shelves stuffed with books. Morgan was pacing back and forth while Sargateth leaned with one shoulder against the end of the furthest stack. Behind him, she caught Argent's profile as he talked with Luke.

"Argent, did any follow us down?" Sargateth asked, fear tinging his voice. His kind green eyes were sharp, fixed behind them on the distant shape of the elevator.

The Prince walked back toward the lift, his hand fidgeting where his quiver usually hung at his belt. Julie kept her eyes glued on him until he shook his head. "No. I think it was only the one spirit in the vestibule, but I couldn't tell if he was embodied."

"Nevertheless, we must remain on guard," Morgan said.

"Come close and pay attention," Sargateth said, the tension clear in his shoulders. His eyes darted around, as if searching for enemies hiding in the shadowy stacks. He'd said very little about the Khozek's hiding place—only that it would take a great deal of magic to undo the protections he'd woven around it. "Before we descend further, you must know what to expect."

"More than what we went over on the ship?" Julie asked, not bothering to mask her irritation. After Catigern, she'd wondered why the eldest of the Olii insisted on keeping things close to his chest when he saw how badly it affected those around him. "More than what Mountains already told us?"

"Mountains has centuries of bitterness in him," Sargateth replied without a trace of compassion. "The Khozek is locked behind wards with enough magic to erase your very sense of self if you do not follow my every instruction. Emma may accompany Morgan and me to each checkpoint to observe, but everyone else must remain behind until we undo each layer and call you forward one at a time. Do you understand?"

When he had extracted everyone's agreement, Sargateth turned to the wall behind them, where a ripple of magic revealed a door with seven concentric circles of runes at its center. He pressed both hands into the design, the symbols lighting up where he touched them. Then he twisted the circles, and the deep echo of a lock sounded from within the door.

"Welcome to the heart of Atlantis."

# CHAPTER ELEVEN
# THE ATLAS

"Atlantis?" Emma exclaimed, her mind kicking into overdrive as her heart started galloping. Looking sideways, she searched Argent's face for any hint of surprise but found none. He'd been harder to read since they'd eavesdropped on the conversation about the letter from Renault, and the work on the ship had kept them from spending much time talking.

Luke looked as though the gears in his brain had jammed. "As in, the lost and destroyed island metropolis city of Atlantis? The one Plato said sank beneath the waves 'in a single day and night of misfortune'? *That* Atlantis?"

"Yes," Sargateth answered. "But I don't know who Plato is."

Luke made a keening noise. "What does Atlantis have to do with the Nephilim?"

Sargateth paused, looking perplexed. He got distracted when Morgan slipped past him, hurrying down the passage. She stopped abruptly about fifteen feet in, and a light blue ward rippled into view, blocking the way forward. She and Sargateth both relaxed. "Everything. Atlantis was a Nephilim city judged in the great flood like the rest of Earth. Its wreckage here spans the entirety of Severna."

Luke turned white, and Emma grasped his shoulder. "Atlantis was the size of an entire *country*?"

Sargateth shrugged, beckoning them to follow him down the hall. The mission here was simple. Get into the room where Sargateth had hidden the Khozek, swap it with the hastily made replacement, and get out.

But Emma knew from years of experience that simple did not mean easy. Despite being allowed to observe, she wanted to learn something from these masters. Except for raising the platform to Skypoint, she hadn't felt useful since breaking out of Valona. Her power itched for an outlet.

"I want to help undo the wards. Let me learn Olis magic," she said, feeling hopeful.

Sargateth halted, turning around with a hard expression. "Olis magic is not like human magic—including yours," he said. "One wrong move, one accidental touch.... There are few things that could take *you* down, Emma, but these wards are one of them. We do not have time to waste."

Emma tried to suppress the stubborn, angry part of her personality that her schoolteachers had tried to squash.

It didn't work.

"I walked through the curse that knocked you and your sister out, in case you forgot."

"A human creation—"

"Sargateth," Argent cut him off from the open room behind them, "should we encounter a Nephilim, wouldn't it work in our favor for Emma to know Olis magic?"

The Archmage's face spasmed. "Prince—"

"Let her help, please," Argent finished quietly.

Sargateth gave him a funny look. "All right, then." He led her down the rest of the corridor to where Morgan had just deconstructed the first ward. Luke trailed behind them. "Hold out your hands."

Emma did, mimicking the gesture Sargateth had used to open the door.

"What do you feel?"

Emma closed her eyes, casting out her awareness. In the background, she sensed all the warm bodies nearby—the

Ancients, her family, her Prince—but saw the lingering evidence of what had once been a ward. It dissipated like a fine mist until nothing was left, but further down the corridor another ward appeared, almost like in the video games Bethany had loved playing on Earth.

"Powerful magic," Emma answered, not opening her eyes as she began walking toward the next ward. Sargateth beckoned the rest of the group through the first checkpoint. "It's a warning."

"What does it say?" prompted Morgan from ahead.

Emma listened, each step taking her nearer to the magic.

*Unwelcome.*

*Cursed.*

*Outcast.*

*Flee, flee, flee.*

"The warning isn't meant for me," Emma realized out loud. In the magic of her mind's eye, she watched the shapes of her mentors look at one another in surprise, as if they hadn't expected her to discern that. Luke hovered behind them, close enough to protect them if needed, but far enough that he wouldn't get caught in any backlash.

A final step brought her close enough to the next ward to touch it, but Sargateth's warning rang clear in her mind.

"How do I undo it?"

Sargateth and Morgan sandwiched her in the narrow corridor, their instructions complex. Emma committed the motions and unfamiliar words to memory, even if she didn't know what they meant.

Magic was about intent, after all, and she intended to get through these wards as fast as she could.

The Khozek awaited them.

Every ward brought them deeper underground, and the more Emma worked to undo them, the harder and more complex they became. By the time they came to the last barrier, her entire back was drenched with sweat, her legs shaky.

She'd wanted an outlet, but perhaps she'd gotten more than she'd bargained for.

Releasing the last ward, she let out a sigh of relief and sucked down the rest of the water in her waterskin.

The corridor opened before them. They gathered on the edge of a cliff, looking over a cavern with large swaths of wreckage as far as the eye could see. Broken pillars and huge megalithic cut stones toppled on their sides, covered in carved images. While it may have once been a city, now it was just one part of the miles of broken dwellings, most of it swallowed by the vast jungle beyond the walls of Keldvaar.

Sargateth hadn't been lying when he called it the Heart of Atlantis. It looked like the remains of a temple.

"Over here," the Archmage said, leading them around a curve in the rock to another door. "The last checkpoint."

A prickle crept over Emma's scalp and down her neck.

Sargateth and Morgan stood together, pressing their palms on the concentric circles of runes.

The runes turned red, and the door disappeared, revealing a tiny chamber with a wooden chest resting on a pedestal. The wood was old and worn, glowing with hundreds of tiny runes.

The Khozek.

Argent let out a choked shout, yanking Emma's attention back to their surroundings. "It's here!"

But then *five* hulking figures melted out of the shadows, dressed in what looked like the armor of a royal guard.

"No," Argent whispered, the terror in his voice filling Emma's entire being with sheer panic.

"Hello, Raphael," a male voice said from the darkness behind them.

Sargateth spun, his eyes wide and wild.

"Six. There's six. *How can there be six*?" Argent muttered frantically as Emma looked to the Ancients for direction, but all of Sargateth's attention was on the sixth Nephilim. Morgan planted herself in front of the guards, looking like she would like nothing more than to whack them all across their helmets with her staff... which was back on the ship.

"My, my, it has been a few centuries, hasn't it?" the voice continued.

*Centuries? Raphael? What is going on?*

"What? Don't tell me your years serving humans have addled your memory, old chap."

"That is not a name I've worn for three hundred and fifty years," Sargateth said sharply, though his voice wavered with six Nephilim around them. "Who are you, and how do you know that name?"

The owner of the voice came into the light. He towered over Luke and Tomás by at least a foot, the wide sweep of his red cloak making him look larger. The too-wide grin, the dark eyes, the broad shoulders, and impossible height made him seem not quite human. Even Renault's ever-changing eye color didn't make Emma feel as uncomfortable as this newcomer did.

From behind him, the librarian with the crooked pin on his lapel appeared.

"Lord have mercy, it's *seven*!"

"May I present," the librarian said in that smooth voice of his, "King Cleopas Rhakmar of Keldvaar."

"Thank you, Ebe," Rhakmar said with a grin that showed far too many teeth. Some of them looked sharper than normal.

"Cleopas? You cannot be the same Cleopas I treated with in 2366," Sargateth breathed, the fear and confusion painted on his face like badly done makeup. He shoved to the front of their tiny party to face the king and his steward. "How are you alive?"

"He's possessed by a Nephilim," Argent spat, his features twisted with revulsion and fear.

Emma forced her face into a neutral expression, slowly breathing to control her racing pulse. Besides her mother's firearm, their only weapon down here was magic. But in such close quarters, she couldn't risk using it against an enemy even the Olii feared.

"Oh, well spotted," Rhakmar applauded. "But who are you? A timid sapling with all the hallmarks of a royal?" His eyes widened, and his grin stretched impossibly large. "Color me shocked that a Pendragon has stepped outside of his fiefdom. Tell me, who is left to war with Ralador?"

No one answered him. Tomás shifted, placing himself in front of Julie, and Emma saw her mother's hand rest on the grip of the gun hidden beneath her shirt. Luke looked ready to raise a shield at any moment.

"Remarkable control you have, Raphael, even if this one holds your bridle," King Rhakmar scoffed, pointing a long, pale finger at Prince Argent. No one bothered to correct him. "I know your history, Pendragon. Seven hundred years of nothing but wars with your southern neighbor. I should be relieved you haven't the resources to expand your bloody empire here.... Unless you're sniffing around for weaknesses." A wild smile stretched across Rhakmar's face. It seemed too wide now that they could make out his other features. "You'll find none. Come closer."

When no one moved, the shadowy guards closed in behind them, forcing them away from the open door to the Khozek.

"What could be so urgent to persuade the ruler of Renova to abandon his home? Could it have something to do with all the interesting creatures that show up whenever we feel the ground shake?" Rhakmar made eye contact with them all, lingering on Argent for a beat longer than Emma would like. Emma's fingers finally found Argent's, and the direct skin contact helped them mentally connect with less effort.

*He thinks you're the King.*

*Let him,* Argent answered without hesitation, though his presence felt walled off from her. *We gain nothing by telling him otherwise.*

"I've heard rumors, you know," Rhakmar continued, unblinking as he stared at them. "Rumors that the Seventh Sorceress was born... on Earth. And other rumors that she's here now, to fulfill a silly Prophecy made by a crackpot."

Emma didn't react, but her father tensed, his exoskeleton creaking in response.

"Touched a nerve, have I? Seems the rumors are true, then." He took another look at Emma. "I must admit, of all the traps I've set, none of them have captured nearly as many fine specimens as this one."

"What do you want, Cleo?" Sargateth pressed. "Making it through the shield is one thing, but not leaving the city or releasing the rest of the Nephilim? What are you playing at?"

Rhakmar cocked his head. If he'd been wearing a crown, it would have slipped off with the angle. "Sadly, I can't overpower the Khozek. The vast majority of my brethren, the rest of the Nephilim, are still trapped in the jungle by your shield. I know their hearts, and their hearts delight in the deepest evils. But evil alone does not make one strong enough to break through Olis magic." He leaned forward so far that Emma thought he'd tip over, but instead it increased the intimidation factor. "Are you *sure* you don't remember me, Raphael?"

The confusion on Sargateth's face made Rhakmar burst into great peals of laughter that echoed through the vast ruins. "King Atlas of Atlantis, at your service," he said with a smirk and a mocking bow.

Emma's heart dropped to her feet.

"But you're supposed to be dead!" Sargateth breathed, and Emma had never imagined that the great Merlin could be filled with so much fear. "When we put the shield around Severna's borders, I shot and *killed* you with the Elvara Bow! Why aren't you dead?"

Atlas's grin somehow got wider. "Ah yes, the famed bow of God's Wrath. You cannot kill a Nephilim, Raphael. Even the Lord knows this. You can only kill his host." He seemed to like having a captive audience. "Cleo has served me well, though I'll never find a host who could rival my first bodily form—the body you did, in fact, kill."

Emma couldn't help but notice that Rhakmar, or Atlas, hadn't actually answered Sargateth's first question. Why hadn't Atlas gone off to take over the world?

"I must thank you, though, for moving the Khozek inland—*and* for changing the borders of the shield to accommodate all the greedy folk who live here under my rule. Without the Khozek unfettered by the ocean, neither I nor my strongest brethren could have escaped your prison."

"It's *Sargateth's* fault?" Emma blurted in astonishment, and the anger she'd been fighting for weeks bubbled up again.

Sargateth not doing more to search for Magdalin before she surfaced in the Trident.

Sargateth not fighting against the King's decree to keep her, Luke, and Argent from rescuing Bethany.

Sargateth forgetting to tell them where the Skypoint entrance was.

Sargateth constantly keeping secrets until it was too late. *Sargateth, Sargateth, Sargateth.*

Atlas let out a delighted cackle, and Sargateth grasped Emma's shoulder. She shook him off, rage filling her chest and bursting out in a wave of magic focused directly at him.

He stumbled. "Emma, it's not—"

"Stop holding things back from us!" she continued, momentarily forgetting the audience. "We all have things at stake in this!"

"Ooh, I like you," Atlas crooned with a smile. His skin seemed too tight over his face, as if worn out, even though he appeared to be in his mid-sixties. "The power of a chosen child bottled up to fix the messes of others. Here's what I'll do," he said, adjusting his cloak as if it had been crooked. "I'll talk to you because you don't appear afraid of me. The rest of your silly band either don't want to open their miserable mouths or don't want you to, which means I will answer your questions. Send Raphael and his twin to wait in the tunnel, and I'll tell you everything you want to know."

"Not a chance," Sargateth growled. He and Morgan moved as one, placing themselves in front of Emma, her family, and Argent.

This seemed to please Atlas. "How precious," he said with a twisted grin. "You still think you have the upper hand." He addressed Argent now. "Instruct your pet kittens to leave."

Dread bubbled in Emma's chest. She didn't want to face Nephilim without the Ancients.

Argent radiated indecision. Amazingly, Sargateth and Morgan both looked to him, playing along with Atlas's assumption that Argent was, in fact, the King.

Argent spoke slowly and carefully. "I will not force them into ill-advised obedience."

The expectant smile slipped off Atlas's face.

"I didn't agree to this," Emma said, regretting that she spoke when Atlas's returned his full attention her way.

"The conditions under which you find yourselves are not optional. You cannot afford a fight. You will lose." He sighed, inspecting his fingers as if one of them had a hangnail. "Besides, I have tantalizing information that will help you on your little quest."

"You're going to let us go?" Emma questioned sharply, wondering what the catch was.

"That sounds awfully like a question I will only answer once those two depart," Atlas said in a quiet, dangerous voice.

Slowly, Sargateth turned face Emma. He placed one hand on her shoulder and pressed the replacement power source into her hands. She glanced down in astonishment, then shoved it into her pocket. "It's already active. All we must do is leave it in that room," Sargateth whispered so softly she almost missed it. A burst of warmth spread from her shoulder across her chest, and the tendrils of her birthmark writhed on her skin in response. "Do what you can, but do not underestimate his ability to deceive you. You have fifteen minutes until I come back for you with every ounce of my power."

Emma had never felt such a dire weight of expectation before, not even when this very same man had told her the Prophecy she'd been born to fulfill. She swallowed past the lump in her throat and dropped her chin in acknowledgment.

Sargateth faced Atlas, walking past him without a word or backward glance. Morgan followed him.

Emma's stomach tied up in knots.

Two of the five guards trailed after the Ancients, and Atlas watched until they disappeared around the curved overhang. Then he turned his attention back to Emma, Luke, their parents... and Argent.

The last three remaining guards promptly restrained Luke, Tomás, and Julie. The fake librarian, Ebe, slinked forward at lightning speed and seized Emma's upper arm in an unshakable grip.

"What are you doing? Let us go!"

Ebe's strength was far beyond any human. But unless they had gone through the Blacksoul rituals, there was no way these men could do magic.

Atlas took a menacing step toward Argent, who held his ground despite his obvious fear. "Now that we won't be interrupted by frivolous Olis platitudes, we can get down to business."

In the blink of an eye, he seized Argent by the throat, and Emma screamed.

"Quiet yourself. I have no murderous designs today," Atlas admonished, the boom of his voice threatening to rattle the stone ceiling. "Don't you wish to know how *I* came to expect you?"

Emma's heart skipped against her ribcage. Argent desperately tried to pry his way out of the Nephilim king's grasp, but these beings were supernaturally strong.

Instead of choking him, Atlas forced Argent to walk backwards into the chamber with the Khozek. Ebe followed, dragging Emma with him. Her skin already felt bruised from his crushing grip over her bicep. As they crossed the threshold, Ebe pressed a tiny rune on the door's edge.

Now closer, she could see more than just the pedestal and the chest.

The room was hewn from solid gray stone. The only light came from the runes pulsing on the chest containing the Khozek. Atlas entered and sidestepped the pedestal to the rear, where a familiar obelisk had been hidden from view. He kept Argent in his clutches, but at least the Prince could breathe. Emma could still feel his fear and resurgent trauma—it hadn't been that long ago that Igraine had tried to kill him by strangulation.

"Tell me, Seventh Sorceress Artair, do you know what this is?"

Emma breathed hard through her nose. In the back of her mind, she wondered how he knew so much about her. "Yes."

"Does it surprise you to learn that the magnificent shield protecting the rest of the world from the debauched evils of Severna's Nephilim also prevents the wild, rogue portals from opening inside our borders, including within the city proper?"

It did, in fact, surprise her, but then—

"So why is an obelisk here?" Atlas asked the question for her. "I'll let you in on a little secret, Emma."

*Seriously, how does he know my name?*

"The device you seek amplifies more than just magic. It turns out that Raphael's lovely creation doesn't care what it amplifies, as long as it's powerful enough. Such as intent. Desire. Will."

Panic raised its snout within Emma's stomach and sniffed around.

"This is why I have an obelisk. This is the only place in all of Severna where you would ever see a portal spring to life."

Something didn't add up. "If you have access to a portal, what's stopping you from using it? Why haven't you left Keldvaar to conquer the worlds?"

A spasm of annoyance flitted across the King's taut face. "Portals are one-way from the source."

Emma already knew that. "So, the ones that open here.... You don't have anything you can open a portal *with*. No captive Olii. No gauntlets. Someone else is opening them *to* here. But who? Why?"

Atlas cocked his head at her again. Still trapped, Argent shifted, trying again to pull the Nephilim's hands away from his throat.

"The Khozek is also why I've held onto this body for as long as I have, but sheer desire cannot outlast the ravages of time. I have an... *associate*, if you will. I believe you know her as the Vorcana of Grimhold, and she opens them because we have a deal."

Emma's entire world screeched to a halt. That was Igraine's title from centuries ago—what she'd first called herself as the Grand Mage of Ralador.

"And what deal was that?" Emma asked breathlessly, almost on autopilot as she tried to wrap her mind around the fact that Igraine was the informant. Her family mirrored her restlessness just outside the door.

The Nephilim King turned his head, his gaze sharpening once more on Argent trapped in his firm grip.

"She promised me a male host that can do magic."

And Argent's terror flooded Emma as though it was her own.

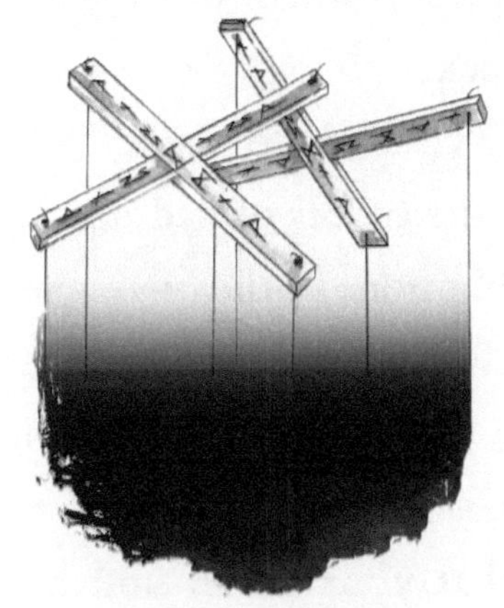

# CHAPTER TWELVE

# STRINGS

From outside the chamber, Emma could hear the muffled sounds of her parents and Luke struggling with the Nephilim guard. Her mental timer for Sargateth's promised return had ticked down to ten minutes. She didn't know whether to stall or to try getting them out of this mess herself.

She wasn't as good at negotiating as her mother, and Sargateth's promise to come back in all his power could lead to catastrophic destruction.

She frantically searched for a way to free Argent without endangering the rest of them or blowing their mission to retrieve the Khozek.

Argent... who couldn't do magic.

"I hate to be the bearer of bad news," Emma said, not hating it at all, "but none of the men here can—"

"Oh, hush, child," Atlas interrupted, his long, spindly fingers caressing Argent's throat. Argent had both hands tight around Atlas's wrists, but it did no good. "I know perfectly well that your father and brother can wield. But I'm not interested in them. Their magic is imperfect. Restricted. The Vorcana promised me her power inside a man who could handle it—a man who could handle *me*."

"You're out of luck," Emma said firmly, wincing when Ebe squeezed her arm and yanked her back a little. "She did that ritual on Septim, not Argent. You'll have to lodge a complaint with her the next time she opens a portal for you."

"Oh-ho!" Atlas's eyes widened. "You're the Princeling, not the King! I should have known. My eyesight is getting so bad, you know, with dear old Cleo's body being over six hundred." He bared his teeth in a wicked grin. "But I knew there was something special about you. Once a soul has been touched by the rituals, nothing can erase it."

"It wasn't done to his soul!" Emma insisted with a raised voice. Ebe's fingers dug into her skin. His hot breath on the top of her head made her want to vomit. "Whatever Igraine promised you, you can't get it from us!"

Atlas's face twisted in anger. "You are in my domain, stealing from me, walking into *my* trap—and you think you can tell me what I can't take for myself? I am King here, Emma Artair. The only King with power." He drew in a deep breath as if preparing to take his last. "It matters not if he didn't personally endure the rituals. Septim's soul imprinted on this sapling for six years, no? The abilities of a mighty spirit such as myself far surpass that of the strongest human man. I tasted all of your souls the moment I encountered you today, and out of all of them, his is the best suited to my needs. It will be *much* easier to perform the Blacksoul Rituals on him."

Argent's eyes fixed on Emma, filled with a swirl of determination and fear.

"I won't let you take him," Emma said, ignoring the pain of the steward's grip. She couldn't process the fact that the vendetta against the Pendragons went even deeper than Igraine.

Atlas chuckled. "I have wanted nothing more since the Olii trapped me and my brethren here," he said, his voice a soft but poisonous caress. He forced Argent closer, his eyes fluttering shut as he drew in another deep breath.

As if he could smell Argent's soul.

"No!" Emma cried out.

Argent's hands pulled at Atlas's wrists, but it was like trying to move a mountain.

Emma tried to distract him instead. "You said you had information that would help us on our quest. Did you lie?"

"I lie quite often," Atlas admitted with a pleased smirk. "But not about that."

"Then what is it?" she prompted, barely able to hear herself over the pounding of her heart and the dulled shouts of her family struggling against the guards outside.

Atlas's black eyes zeroed in on hers. "Simply that you have no time to lose if you want to beat the Vorcana to the Scepter. She's coming with an army."

Emma's attention split between Argent and this new revelation, and her jaw dropped. "How do you know that?"

Atlas gestured carelessly at the obelisk. "She called on me just a few days ago from that pesky world she got herself trapped on. If you thought she didn't know you'd be coming for this," he pointed at the chest containing the Khozek, "then you are sorely mistaken. But enough chatter. I have a new host to get used to."

Atlas took another long, sickening sniff, this time with his nose pressed against Argent's scalp. Argent's eyes were squeezed shut, his features twisted with resigned determination instead of terror.

"Wait!" Emma cried out, desperate. "Isn't there anything else you want?"

Argent's eyes popped open, and Atlas met her gaze with a calculating expression. The Nephilim King stared at her for a solid thirty seconds, and each tick of Emma's mental clock made her want to die.

"There is one thing," Atlas finally said, as though savoring the fear choking the room. "I will give you a choice. Either way, you'll all walk out of here. I'll even let you take the Khozek."

Heart thundering, Emma's eyes darted between Argent and Atlas. She couldn't see a way out of this awful position.

"What is it?" she asked, her throat dry.

"Raphael gave you a little trinket before he left. If I'm right, and I'm rarely wrong, he wanted you to leave it in place of the Khozek, no?"

Emma nodded before she could stop herself.

"Very good. Your choice is this. Either I take dear, sweet Argent as my next host right here, right now, and you can waltz out with the Khozek and leave that little trinket behind to power the shield. Or, I will let your Princeling go, unharmed, if you take that trinket with you and let Raphael's shield fall."

"Emma, no!" Argent yelled, struggling for breath when Atlas's hand tightened around his throat.

Argent's voice exploded in her head. *I'm not worth the lives of everyone they'll kill if you let the rest of the Nephilim out!*

"Make your choice, Emma dear," Atlas crooned.

Breathing hard, Emma squared her shoulders as much as she could with Ebe hovering behind her. There was no way to get out of this without sacrificing something, and she was not about to give up Argent.

*Emma, no! Don't do it! I'm not worth it!*

*Yes, you are! I'm not going to lose you!* she projected back to him. *I won't let him possess you.*

Emma's insides twisted at Argent's obvious shock and disappointment—in her. "I'll take the ward stone with me," she said quietly, barely able to hear herself over her pounding heart and terror. "Let him go."

Atlas immediately released Argent's throat. Argent seized the Khozek's chest with both hands and scrambled away, past Emma and out of the room. Atlas steepled his fingers. "Ebe, if you would."

A sharp crack split the air, and Emma screamed in blinding pain.

The steward had shattered the bone in her arm.

She fell to her knees, barely aware of anything except the white-hot fire in her arm. She heard the sounds of a scuffle outside, the sharp report of two gunshots, and then a cool, numbing sensation eased down her arm until the spots in her vision cleared.

Luke dragged Emma to her feet and shoved her through the door. Their mother had shot two of the guards in the kneecaps, and the third kneeled with his head in his hands. Tomás had a large shield up and was covering Argent as he retreated toward the tunnels, and Julie kept her gun trained on the Nephilim behind her children.

Atlas advanced toward them, Ebe at his flank. They appeared in no hurry, nor did they show any concern for the injured guards.

As soon as Emma and Luke made it past Tomás's shield, Julie squeezed off another round that buried itself in Atlas's right shoulder. He stumbled against Ebe.

"I would take you as a host, Julie Artair, if the Blacksoul Rituals worked on women," Atlas wheezed with a deranged grin. While the shot hadn't been near any vital organs, he didn't seem surprised or angered by it. "I like your spirit!"

They hurried back down the path to the tunnel, where Sargateth positively glowed with pent-up power, looking ready to charge into battle at any second. Morgan had a tight grip on his shoulder, and their two Nephilim guards melted away into the darkness.

"What happened?" he asked, voice strangled. "They cut off the sound somehow; I was just about to come for you—"

Argent sprinted up the corridor without acknowledging anyone, the Khozek's container still clutched to his chest. Emma and Luke ran after him, but as they did, dread pounded in her heart.

A stitch formed in Emma's side as she struggled to keep up with Argent's pace back to the ship.

Her mind swirled with fear that she'd just made the worst mistake of her life, but also, if she hadn't, Argent would be living out his worst nightmare. How could he have been serious? Did he really expect her to let Atlas possess him right in front of her just so they could leave the shield intact? How did they know Atlas hadn't been lying that the other Nephilim were still trapped behind it? Or that Atlas would have kept his word after gaining a new body?

There was no pretense of stealth now. They had to get back to the ship, and fast, if what Atlas said was true.

If Igraine really was coming with an army.

Their pace drew curious gazes, but nobody tried to stop them. There were no shouts from behind as if the Nephilim guard was on their tail, and she didn't know if that scared her more. In her frantic glances backward, she only saw Luke, and she hoped that the Ancients had done something to speed up her father's pace. They must still be way behind them.

Far ahead of her now, Argent sped up the gangplank and disappeared among the throng aboard the ship. She barely caught sight of his head ascending the stairs to the navigation room, and he had ducked inside as she made it to the pier.

Weaving through the people milling about the docks, her arm throbbed under Luke's numbing charm, her lungs burning.

Emma hurried up the gangplank to the main deck, intent on talking to Argent. She couldn't think straight, and the shattered bone in her arm worked quickly through Luke's magic.

"Weigh anchor," Luke barked from down on the pier. He sounded like he was underwater, but so did the rest of the port.

She spun around, the heaviness of her decision clawing at her insides. Luke and William spoke furiously to each other, but Emma couldn't hear them over the pounding in her ears. Dazed, she stumbled to the stairs, her fingers white every time she gripped the railing. Her legs wobbled. She hadn't recovered from undoing the wards into the Heart of Atlantis before the mad sprint back to the ship.

Finally, she reached the door to the navigation room and fumbled with the handle. When she opened the door, the chest was on the table, and Argent paced a hole into the rug, one hand fisted in his hair and the other pressed hard against his side where the Direwolf had raked him. He looked up at her when she entered, and the despondent expression on his face sapped the rest of her strength. She crumpled to her knees.

Argent didn't move. "Why didn't you just let him take me?" he asked in an anguished whisper.

She couldn't feel him in her mind. He'd cut her off from his thoughts—his emotions.

"Emma!" came Luke's powerful voice as he pounded up the stairs and burst in behind her. Renault's hawk, snoozing on its perch in the corner, squawked and ruffled its feathers, startled awake. Luke helped her to her feet and forced her into a chair. "Let me see what he did to you."

The anchor outside lifted with a great rattle.

Argent came around to the front of the chair and cupped her chin with his palm. "Why did you do it?"

"Do what?" Luke asked, now zooming in on the projection of her broken arm. The bone looked like it had exploded.

"I told you, I couldn't let him take you," Emma whispered, tears collecting at the corners of her eyes.

"Emma, you put the entire world into the hands of an enemy that the Olii imprisoned for a reason. If I'm taken out, whether by death or possession, there is another who can inherit the throne."

"What are you guys talking about?" Luke interrupted, still working on Emma's arm.

Argent touched her cheek, letting his hand fall away before she could lean into it. "I love you, but I should never have left that place if it meant the safety of Talahm and of Earth. Avoiding my greatest fear is not worth more than the lives the Nephilim will slaughter."

"Wouldn't you have done the same for me?" Emma asked, the tightness in her throat making it hard to get the words out.

Argent opened his mouth as if to answer her but closed it again, his jaw tight. "I don't know," he finally said, twisting Emma's heart in a vise.

The ship picked up speed, and Emma quickly glanced at the porthole. There weren't as many ships around them now, and she blinked away the tears as she watched the lone, tall tree on the distant cliffs that marked the halfway point out of the bay.

Drained and scared, she looked back up at Argent. "I thought you knew by now that the very last thing I'd ever do is let you die or be possessed. No matter the cost."

Luke paused his healing. "What happened? In case you forgot, I was stuck outside with Mom and Dad, and we couldn't hear anything. I thought you put up a silencing spell."

*The rune Ebe pressed must have cut off the sound.*

Emma's stomach twisted into even tighter knots, and her anxiety ratcheted through the roof when the door to the navigation room burst open. Sargateth entered, followed by her parents, the King, and Morgan. But before Morgan could close the door, Mountains slunk inside.

A sonic boom echoed across the bay, and a subsequent pressure wave pushed the ship forward. Emma gripped the chair to avoid being thrown from it. The others stumbled, but her mother caught her father and kept him from falling.

"What was that?" Julie asked, her hands lingering on Tom's arm.

Emma swallowed, unable to dislodge the lump in her throat. They were far enough away from the city that there was no going back, especially if that explosion was what she thought it was.

She dug her free hand into her pocket and withdrew the replacement stone. She couldn't bring herself to look Sargateth in the eye.

"Atlas made me choose. Let the shield fall, or watch him possess Argent." She watched as Sargateth's slim fingers plucked the ward from her lap.

The Archmage's hand curled into a fist over the stone. "Then that was the shield collapsing. The Nephilim are free."

# CHAPTER THIRTEEN
# THE WAY FORWARD

"Do you have any idea what you've done?" Sargateth asked in a low, dangerous voice.

Luke methodically put the shards of Emma's shattered bone back in place, not quite sure how to feel about his sister's decision-making paradigm. She'd been distracted and off her game since Valona.

Since they lost Bethany.

"Ouch," Emma winced, trying to pull her arm out of his grip.

"Sorry," Luke whispered.

"Emma Artair, I am speaking to you!" Sargateth said, loud and angry.

"Hey, don't talk to my kid like that," Julie snapped, coming over to Emma's other side. She offered her hand to Emma, who squeezed it until it turned white.

Luke glanced at his sister, not surprised to see tear tracks marking her cheeks.

"I saved your next King from being a Nephilim host," Emma answered between short, choppy breaths.

Luke met his mother's wide gaze with a small, confused shrug. He didn't fully understand what had happened between Emma and Argent.

Sargateth's face turned reddened. "That shield was the only thing keeping the Nephilim from turning Talahm into a field of blood."

Emma swallowed hard and forced herself to look at him. With a halting voice, she told them what had happened in the chamber.

Sargateth towered over her. "I have to agree with the Prince. Now there's nothing stopping them from spreading across this world like locusts." Shoulders trembling with rage, he spun away and rummaged through the drawers built into the far wall, pulling out a parchment, inkwell, and quill.

Luke only had five bone shards to put back.

"Sargateth?" the King asked, but watched Emma, a curious look in his eye.

"Renault must be warned to prepare for Nephilim invaders," the Archmage answered tersely, "both embodied and not. Camelot has no defenses against demons."

Sargateth ruined the first sheet of parchment with blots of ink, and Luke reached into his bag for the ballpoint pen he kept with him at all times. He tossed it to Sargateth, who snatched it from the air without looking and scribbled a note. Once he folded the parchment and tucked into the hawk's harness, Sargateth opened the back window and sent the bird on its mission.

He turned back to Emma, but she cut him off. "We can't go back and undo what I did. It's done. Can you stop pretending that any of you wouldn't have risked the exact same thing if it was *your* loved one in his place?"

Luke's heart raced as he tried not to picture Atlas threatening to possess Bethany.

Sargateth took another step forward, but Argent blocked him. "We have more productive things to attend to," he said with authority. "Septim's mark on me means I can sense the spirits. If, in fact, we are pursued, I will know."

With only one bone fragment left, Luke was almost done healing Emma's arm. He watched from the corner of his eye as Argent moved to the table and inspected the locking mechanism with the King. Sargateth retreated to the far wall, his arms crossed.

Mountains, who had flopped down on the middle of the carpet and was doing his best to be in everyone's way, gave a small, unexpected chuckle.

"What are you laughing about?" Morgan asked coldly, standing next to her brother.

"Just the mess you've landed yourselves in," he answered with a drawl. "You all emerged unscathed, no?"

Emma's eyes snapped open as Luke finished putting the last shard back. "One of them broke my arm without even trying!"

Mountains eyed her as Luke wrapped both hands around her bicep and squeezed, the final bit of healing magic making her skin glow. "You look just fine to me. Perhaps someone should break your bones more often."

The door swung open with a crash, and Cordelia entered, looking vexed. The feather in her hat drooped over the brim. "If anyone cares, we're now heading straight for the Glass Channel." She took a swig from her ever-present bottle of honeywine and made a beeline for the chest on the table. "Is this it? This is what we stopped in Keldstink to get?"

Emma got to her feet and swung her arm, recovering her range of motion. She looked ready to slug Mountains in the face. "We would have been better prepared if we'd known that more than one or two Nephilim had gotten through. There were *seven* of them in the library!"

"I was merely guessing," Mountains replied with disdain. He ruffled his wings, wincing when the bad one jostled. "You should be thankful I warned you at all."

"Enough!" King Aragon interrupted, banging his fist on the table. "The fact remains that we have it now, and we are one step closer to locking Igraine out of this world forever."

Emma sat back down and leaned forward, resting her elbows on the edge of the table. Their prize covered a quarter of the map. "Are we, though? Igraine has been opening portals to Atlas in the very room where that was stored." She pointed at the chest. "Besides Bethany, what's stopping her from waltzing right back?"

"We'll just need to cut off Langoth entirely when we reach Perga's Scepter," Aragon said tightly.

"After we rescue Bethany," Emma said, and Luke felt a sense of déjà vu.

When King Aragon didn't answer, Luke glanced at Argent, who stayed silent. Both royals wore impassive expressions, and neither met his eyes.

"Oh, come on," Emma pleaded, planting both of her hands flat on the table as she stood. The chair caught on the carpet behind her and toppled over. "You can't really think she's some long-lost descendant from Earth come to take your throne!"

"That was a private conversation. I wasn't aware my son had told you about it," the King said, furious.

"We overheard together," Argent corrected, looking appropriately guilty.

Emma had told Luke about the letter that same night, but he hadn't truly believed it until now. "Emma," he warned, but she didn't listen.

"The last thing Bethany would want is to lord power over anyone," Emma continued angrily.

Luke yanked her backward, clasping his hands firmly around her now fully healed arms. "Shut up and look!" He pointed at the chest, now rattling on the table. The runes turned red at the hinges.

Everyone in the room froze, staring at the box.

"What is it doing?" Julie asked, more curious than afraid.

"Amplifying, in this case, your puny human emotions," Mountains answered from the floor in the most bored voice imaginable. "You know, its entire purpose for existing."

"And why we have it," Sargateth said, letting out a huge breath.

Emma pulled out of Luke's grip. "There's one more thing. Atlas said Igraine has an army. And that if we want to make it to the Scepter before she does, we need to hurry."

King Aragon gazed at the chest with clear interest. "Can this increase our speed? Get us to Perga's Scepter faster?"

Luke's heart filled with hope as the ship surged forward.

"Magic can't solve that, *your Majesty*," Cordelia Roque grunted from a dark corner of the room, and the ship slowed again. She sounded halfway tipsy from the honeywine. "And as captain, I won't allow it. Rogue portals are popping up everywhere. The last thing we need is extra speed if a portal opens right in our path."

Furious, Luke kicked the leg of the table before he could stop himself. "Then why are you in here getting drunk instead of up there at the wheel?" The chest rattled again, red creeping over the runes on the lid down to the sides of the box.

"Enough," Sargateth said with unnatural calm, his eyes tracking Cordelia as she picked herself up with a huff and left, bottle still in hand. "We cannot risk the mission with our anger."

Mountains picked at his teeth with an intact claw. "Speak for yourself. I'm not the one getting ruffled by simple logic."

Julie faced Mountains, her hands on her hips. "Could I have a word with you? Outside?"

The Olis must have seen through her blatant attempt to remove him from the situation, but he obliged without a word. Julie opened the door and slipped out after him, easing it shut with a soft click.

"She's good," Morgan said with a long sigh. She leaned her forehead against the smooth wood of her staff. "I wish I had ten of her in the Coven."

"Even if she could do magic, you couldn't have her." Tomás crossed both arms over his chest.

Something else had been bothering Luke since the revelation that Igraine was in contact with Atlas. "If part of her plan was for Atlas to trap us, then the next time she calls on him, she'll know he failed. Why would he have let us leave at all, especially with the Khozek?"

Argent padded around the table, standing next to Emma, though not close enough to touch. "You think she was hoping to get the upper hand at the Scepter by having Atlas take us out of the equation entirely?"

"Isn't that what he tried to do?" Luke asked quietly in response, shrugging one shoulder. "It's what I would have done if I was her."

The room fell silent. Luke watched the King and Prince share a glance that spoke volumes.

Emma fixed both of her sharp, cobalt eyes on Sargateth. "Without the Khozek, would Keldvaar's obelisk even be able to handle a portal opening?"

"Probably not, but we must reach the Scepter as soon as possible. If she uses Mountains' claw to reach the Titan Obelisk at the Scepter before we can block her, then we really will be at risk of living out one of the Prophets' Visions."

Tomás rubbed the corded scar on his neck. "But if Atlas was truthful.... If Igraine is coming with an army, that requires a very different battle plan than facing her alone. We know there are unknown combatants on the field—both Visions showed as much. They could be the army Atlas spoke of."

Sargateth drummed his fingers over the chest, and the runes dimmed. "Agreed," he said.

King Aragon made a noise of dissent. "There won't be an army to contend with if we push hard to reach the Scepter. We must seal the Titan Obelisk from *all* portals."

The part of Luke that wanted to yell at the King about rescuing Bethany warred with the part of him that didn't want to experience the consequences.

"We must weigh all the options," Tomás said before Luke could decide where to land. "If we fail to seal her out, we must do all we can to tip the scales in favor of Luke's Vision. Otherwise, we risk trapping ourselves in the failure of mine."

Hours after dinner, Luke sat in an uncomfortable chair alone in the navigation room, his eyes fixed on the darkened chest holding the Khozek.

*This is the answer to our problems? A magic stone carved from the Sal Dorhana's ceiling a millennia ago?*

A single lit candle flickered from the center of the table, casting long shadows. The rear window, though small, showed an abundance of stars.

Luke wanted nothing more than to have Bethany back unharmed.

He sat up straight in the chair.

*Amplified will and desire.... Can I just wish her back? Right here? Right now?*

The chest hummed, the vibration making the candle sputter. One by one, the runes came to life, soft gold like Bethany's hair.

Luke's heart hammered against his ribcage as he thought about Bethie. Their stolen kisses in Camelot's hallways the night before he'd gone with Emma to the Trident. The fierce love in her eyes when he'd found her beneath Valona. The promises they'd made to each other in the hundreds of shared journal pages.... His hands curled over the armrests, his fingertips numb with the pressure.

*I want her back right now. Screw fate—give me Bethie!*

The runes flared so bright Luke had to cover his eyes.

A hand came down on his shoulder, and Luke nearly jumped out of his skin. He breathed hard through his nose, trying to see past the bright spots in his vision. "Bethie?"

"Unfortunately not," King Aragon replied.

"I didn't hear the door," Luke said, feeling dumb. He'd been so lost in his desire to rescue Bethie that he hadn't heard the door. "Sorry. I was just…. Never mind. What can I do for you?"

The King didn't answer, instead walking past Luke to right the chair Emma had toppled over in her anger. He then went to the small window, undoing the latch and pulling the glass in on its hinge.

A rush of sea air filled the cabin, and Luke took a deep breath.

"I grew up with your father," King Aragon said, his eyes fixed on the night sky. "We became like brothers. Though we always knew he would be my Prophet and I his King, it never stopped us from seeing each other like family."

Curious, and now coming down from the adrenaline spike, Luke joined the King by the small window. Aragon's tan face and dark curls were bright in the light from the stars.

"One of the Prophet of Camlaan's many duties is to help protect the throne from threats, Seen and unseen. Tomás has never failed me."

Guilt gnawed at Luke's stomach.

King Aragon's put his hand on Luke's shoulder, tightening his grip before Luke could shrug it off. "I lost one son to war, and you served my only remaining heir on a silver platter to the witch pledged against us."

Luke tried to twist away, his heart galloping. "Sire—"

"I wonder how it feels," Aragon seethed through clenched teeth, both hands now wrapped around Luke's neck, "to gasp for air the way my son did that day?"

Luke choked as Aragon's fingers dug into his airway, cutting off his breath. *This can't be happening!* He scrabbled at the King's wrists, desperate. Was this what it felt like when Igraine held Argent with magic against the wall? Choking the air—the life—out of him as he dangled there?

And then, King Aragon's face transformed. Old and stretched, his smile became wider than it should be, his black curls melting into a wavy gray topped by an audacious crown. Stormy eyes turned as black as the void between the worlds.

Not Aragon.

*Atlas.*

Luke struggled, twisting like a fish, but Atlas was stronger. Darkness tinged the edges of his vision, bright stars popping off one by one as the blood vessels burst in his eyes.

"My will be done," Atlas whispered.

Luke's chest burned for air. He kicked and thrashed until his limbs felt too heavy.

He sagged, and just as his eyelids drooped shut, Luke jerked awake. He scrambled out of the chair and pressed himself against the far wall. Each breath felt like a full-body cleanse, his heart beating with renewed energy. The navigation room was empty. The rear window was closed, and the candle on the table had burned itself out. Emma's chair was still askew on the floor. And the chest with the Khozek sat in darkness, not a single rune lit.

The similarities with his dream in Camelot's tower made him sick. Luke watched the door for any chance that the King would enter, staring at the handle for what felt like hours.

Finally, footsteps approached, and Luke tensed. He crept across the carpeted floor as quietly as he could, all the while trying to get his breathing under control. He would ambush anyone who—

"Sire." Sargateth's soft voice carried through the door. "If we push at full speed, we could reach the Scepter within three weeks. Four if the north seas are rough."

"Is that with or without the Khozek's help?" King Aragon said, just as quietly.

Luke could see their shadows through the pane of stained glass embedded in the door.

"Without. Cordelia is right. The seas are too treacherous to risk amplifying our will for speed."

"We don't have time to waste," Aragon disagreed with a hint of a growl.

There was a long pause, as if the Archmage was thinking. He started walking again, his voice growing fainter. "We could perform a test. Let me confer with Morgan on the best course of action to see if we can't use it to...."

Luke strained to hear the rest of that sentence, but it was lost to the wind and the creaking of the ship. He stayed as still as a statue for several more minutes, mind racing, and wondered if he should ask Argent if he sensed any Nephilim on board. What if Atlas had snuck past them all? But the Prince had acted normal throughout dinner, and there was no sign that any spirits had infiltrated the crew.

No... something else was going on.

He had to find Emma.

Luke couldn't make himself truly invisible like Emma could. But his privacy ward worked just as well on people as it did on places. After applying it to himself, he snuck out, sticking to the shadows just in case.

Emma was on duty as an airwitch tonight, but when he scanned the rigging for her, all he could make out was a vague figure hovering behind the main sail with both hands stretched out, driving the ship forward.

Luke had hated heights ever since he'd watched Daniel fall to his death, overly aware of every wrong move that could send him tumbling. So, when he started up the rigging, the hole in his stomach from his waking nightmare yawned to accommodate the extra anxiety.

When he got close enough to make out the airwitch's features, he was startled to find Coven Mage Evie Watson, not Emma.

He must have been so surprised that he let his privacy ward drop, because Evie made eye contact and waved.

And then she morphed into Emma.

Luke lost his grip on the rigging and started to fall backward, but magic caught him and carried him all the way up to the crow's nest.

He struggled in the air, frantic to get away from yet another person changing in front of him.

"Hey, Luke, it's just me—"

"Prove you aren't going to kill me!" Luke yelled, not caring if anyone heard him.

"I—what?"

"Prove it!"

Emma—or the person who looked like Emma—let him go when his feet touched the wood planks of the crow's nest, and he pressed himself against the edge, raising a shield between them.

Still hovering in the air with a confused expression, Emma stared at him. *Is this good enough?* She asked, projecting her voice into his head. *I would never hurt you—you're my brother! What's gotten into you?*

Luke finally relaxed and dropped the shield, sagging. Emma landed next to him and touched his shoulder.

He flinched, and she took a step back, her hands up.

"How did you do that?" he asked, his heart pounding.

Emma shrugged. "I was just blowing off steam by practicing some harder magic. It's a body swap thing I first tested out in college when I was trying to get away from some creeper following me through campus."

Luke relaxed a little. "And where's the real Evie? Does she look like you, if you were swapping bodies?"

Emma glanced down at the deck. "I think so. She's asleep in the crew's quarters."

Luke took a few deep breaths and, without preamble, asked, "Remember what I told you about Amity stabbing me and then turning into Igraine?"

Emma frowned. "You mean your nightmare?"

Luke shook his head. "I don't think it was a nightmare. I don't even think it was a Vision in the usual sense. But something isn't right." He told her about what he'd just experienced, glad that she'd taken him somewhat seriously the first time—and that their relationship had improved enough that they could trust each other with things like this. It made him feel more like her Sentinel. "It doesn't help that all the Nephilim are out now," he continued, trying to couch it without appearing to blame her. "If one of them does manage to take the King as a host, nothing would stop him from trying to kill us."

Emma sucked in a deep breath. "Argent would warn us before it came to that," she said quietly. "You know, I used to think the King wouldn't abandon any of his subjects, but you've heard how he's been talking. He's shut down any mention of saving Bethany before we deal with Igraine."

"You believe me?" Luke asked, relief flooding through him.

Emma made a 'so-so' motion with her hand. "I don't *disbelieve* you. But I won't risk losing Bethany forever just because Aragon thinks she's not worth the risk." She closed her eyes, her brows furrowing. "I can still feel the connection to Bethany that I made when we were in Valona. It's really thin, though. She's alive, at least."

Luke let the tension bleed from his shoulders. He envied Emma's ability to connect with people like that. He desperately missed what it felt like to be connected to Bethie, even if it was through Emma's doing.

After a few moments of silence, Emma continued, sounding strained. "Argent figured out how to stop projecting his thoughts to me all the time, which is great for his privacy. But now I think he's hiding something. He hasn't let me in since Atlas made me choose between him and the shield."

Luke let out a breath. "Do you think—"

Emma shook her head. "I still refuse to believe he'll betray me, but you've said it yourself. Visions always come to pass, even if the interpretations are weird. The fact that you and Dad had competing ones gives me hope that the Khozek will do exactly what Mountains thinks it will to rescue Bethany. Neither of you Saw Bethany on the battlefield. As far as I'm concerned, if you didn't See it, it won't happen. We're trying to create an ending neither of you Saw, which means we can't take the risk that Bethany somehow gets left behind or trapped on Langoth. How do we know if she survives unless we get her ourselves?" She took a breath. "And if Aragon has a problem with that...."

Rebellion stirred as Luke stared out across the silent ocean, little blips of light appearing and disappearing with astonishing regularity—a minefield of portals, all across the water.

He formed the words in his head, rolling them around before making them real. But it was the most real he'd felt since the last time he'd kissed Bethie.

"I would steal the Khozek or fight Igraine myself—even if I die—before I let him abandon her there."

# CHAPTER FOURTEEN

# AS THE WORLD TURNS

It was a few nights later that purple flashed through Argent's nightmare. A ritual chamber, deep underground, was lit by a hundred candles and the glow of Igraine's demonic eyes. Shadows danced across King Aragon's body where it lay splayed across the flagstones.

He lay still in death, but he spoke nonetheless.

*It doesn't matter which Pendragon, as long as one reigns in Camelot. Join me, my son. If both of us die, she will live forever.*

Argent startled awake, his heart pounding, cold sweat coating his skin. Of all the traps they'd encountered beneath Valona, the one that had messed with him the most had been the memory trap. While he didn't remember the memory he'd experienced—it must have been Septim's—his unconscious mind unhelpfully filled the gaps with his worst fears, now worsened by the Nephilim.

Atlas wanted *him* as a host.

Even though the Nephilim King let them go, the fact remained that his soul had been touched by the rituals.

One of the airwitches yesterday had spotted a ship trailing leagues behind them, not yet close enough to identify its colors. William dismissed it as a merchant ship passing through the normal Helcari shipping lanes, but Argent remained on high alert. So did his father and the Ancients.

*What if Atlas is coming after us?*

Slipping out of his hammock, he sat on the edge, curling his toes into the hard planks. He focused on the rough grain and the pitch of the ship as it sailed northeast. Blinking through the darkness, he froze when he saw Emma peering at him from the folds of her own hammock, her eyes wide with questions.

He hadn't talked much to Emma since the disaster in Keldvaar. He still couldn't quite wrap his mind around her willingness to offer up the world to the Nephilim in exchange for one man's soul. But every time he pictured her panic and desperation in that chamber....

Everything had happened so fast.

They had not discussed such matters like his father and mother had. The more he thought about it, the more he wished he'd prepared her for a situation like the one they'd found themselves in. Despite the visceral relief that he was sound of mind and in full control of his soul, his stomach twisted with the reminder that the rest of the world now faced his worst nightmare.

Emma rolled and landing on all fours like a cat, warily approaching.

"Nightmare?" she asked, crouching in front of him.

Argent could only nod. They stared at each other for a long moment before he finally touched her cheek. Her eyes fluttered shut as she leaned into his hand. "It wasn't the worst one I've had," he whispered, so as not to wake the rest of the snoozing crew.

She grabbed his hand, using him as leverage to stand. Then she pulled him to his feet. "It might still be clear enough to watch the stars," she said, her tone hushed as she wrapped them both in the spell that hid them from everyone else. Her voice turned hesitant. "Did you still want to do that with me?"

An idea sparked. "Yes, with a detour first."

He led her through the center aisle of the crew's quarters, silently pushing open the door to the stairway leading above the decks. At the top of the stairs, the cold night air swept through him, and he realized they were both still in their bedclothes.

Emma's warming magic caressed him, and he relaxed into the touch of her hand on his shoulder. Despite their different opinions on sacrifice, he could not imagine spending the rest of his life with anyone else. They could work past this.

Lanterns lit the darkened ship, and an airwitch stood at the helm. A few others were stationed around the deck and the rigging like well-dressed gargoyles. Emma's magic hid them completely, so when one of the witches passed within a few feet of them, she never glanced their way.

"What's the detour?"

Argent didn't answer, instead tiptoeing across the deck to the captain's quarters. Hidden in the shadows, he pulled Emma close to his chest, unable to stop himself from nuzzling her hair with his nose. "Have you ever tried honeywine?"

"No—" her face broke into a grin.

Argent couldn't help but match her smile. "Captain Roque has too many bottles, don't you think?"

"You haven't stolen a thing in your life, have you?" Emma asked, giggling into his chest. Her relief over his willingness to engage with her again was palpable.

The words were on his tongue before she even finished her sentence. "Besides your heart? Not a one."

Emma stilled, looking up at him with those striking eyes. "I would love to raid my great-aunt's stash with you."

Argent couldn't help himself—not even with the threat of the Nephilim on their tail. He kissed her, both hands cupping her face, searing her into his subconscious. If Atlas *did* catch up to them and overtake Argent's body, no spirit could take away his memories of Emma Artair. When he pulled away, she followed for more, and his heart felt like bursting. "Honeywine," he said to center himself.

"Honeywine," she breathed with a smile.

Argent carefully tried the handle to Cordelia's quarters, but it wouldn't turn.

Emma laid her palm on the door frame. A second later, the lock disengaged.

When Emma pushed the door open a crack, Argent realized he had no idea where Cordelia stored her alcohol. But as his eyes adjusted to the darkness of the captain's quarters, he almost laughed in disbelief.

Bottles occupied nearly every flat surface except the floor. There wasn't a sliver of space on the small table in the corner, and the books on the shelves built into the walls wore bottles for hats. Even the squat purple love seat beneath the porthole had bottles stuffed into the cracks between the cushions.

Emma picked up a bottle from the table, shaking it before she set it back down. Empty. "Where did she get all of these?" she asked softly, even though her magic cloaked all sound. "Why is she even still the captain?"

"Drunkenness has never dulled her instinct on the seas," Argent whispered back. While Cordelia had often imbibed on the voyage to Helcari, the number of bottles was entirely unexpected. Perhaps her fall from grace after Valona had impacted her more than she let on.

Emma crouched in front of a cabinet when a snore pierced the still room.

They both froze.

Argent's breath quickened when a shadow on Cordelia's gigantic bed rolled over.

"Not Elaine," Cordelia muttered in her sleep. "It should have been me...."

Knowing the complicated relationship Cordelia had had with her sister, Argent crept closer, hoping she would say more. Emma wrapped both arms around his waist, one hand clenched around the neck of an unopened bottle of honeywine.

"I believe we have a date to get to," she whispered.

Her breath against the shell of his ear sent a pleasant shiver down his back.

They slipped outside, and Emma paused just long enough to re-engage Cordelia's lock. "How do you feel about the crow's nest?"

Argent craned his neck. The top of the main mast stretched high above them. He'd often gone up to the roof of the citadel with Adam, dangling their legs over the edge in their careless youth. Other than riding Emma's platform up to Skypoint, the last time he'd been that high up had been when Septim used him to shoot Tomás Artair with a poisoned arrow. "I'm not opposed," he said, but it sounded off. Insincere.

Emma's face softened in the lantern light. "We can go to the bowsprit instead."

Argent shook his head. "Crow's nest. I know you won't let me fall."

Emma's face lit up. She took his hand and led him to the base of the mast, still invisible to the witches on duty. She hugged him close, the bottle pressing into the small of his back. Then, she kissed him, and it startled him enough that he almost missed when their feet left the deck.

The wind tugged at their nightclothes as she lifted them up to the crow's nest, but he couldn't take his eyes off her. His heart, full of love for her, warred against the intrusive thoughts that her decision to sacrifice the shield had exposed her indifference toward the greater good.

When they landed inside the narrow perch, Emma gave him the bottle and laid both of her hands on the planks, closing her eyes.

The crow's nest morphed, becoming wide enough for them to lay down fully stretched out. Argent didn't think he'd ever get used to her power—her casual use of magic to do things he'd never considered. He peered over the edge, the moving lanterns marking the watch.

"They won't be able to tell," Emma said.

He turned his gaze upward. The sky blazed with a hundred thousand pinpricks of light, the stars casting their shine from billions of miles away. Emma had once explained to him what light years were, but the science didn't compare to simply basking in the Lord's creation. Across the dark waters, portals opened and closed, forcing the ship to take a tortuously slow pace north through the Glass Channel.

"Come here," Emma said.

When he glanced back down, he did a double take. She'd conjured pillows and a thick blanket that looked like it belonged on his bed during winter.

She'd also made the boards as soft as a mattress beneath them. As he leaned back against the pillows, she took the bottle and pulled out the cork.

The smell of sweet honey filled his nostrils. "After you," he said. It would take all his concentration to behave appropriately tonight.

Emma took a swig. "I can see why Cordelia's addicted to this stuff." She held the bottle up as if trying to see through the dark glass and took another drink.

Argent had not touched alcohol since Septim had been in his head. Pushing those memories aside, he drank deeply from the bottle. Despite the sweet taste, his throat burned a little.

"Do you want to talk about it?"

"The nightmare?" he clarified, replacing the cork and setting the wine to the side. The alcohol warmed his stomach. "No. Those are not images I want to replicate in your mind."

When she didn't reply, he turned fully toward her and watched her face. She looked like she was struggling to vocalize what she wanted to say, but when she met his gaze, she quickly looked away.

"I do want to talk about what happened in the library," he said, knowing it would kill the mood. But they had to. It would eat away at him until they did. "I should have taken the initiative to discuss with you ahead of time how we'd handle such a situation."

She looked at him in bewilderment. "Why on earth would we have to plan for something like that? Never in a million years would I even *consider* letting you get possessed!"

"We were all fools to step foot in that city without weighing the risk."

"Mountains thought there were three, max!"

"Then we were fools to trust him!" He reached for her right hand, holding it firmly so she couldn't pull it away. He kissed it and then planted her palm against his heart. The tesseract burned on his skin. "I will not deny that I'm here with you right now because of what you did. But it came at the cost of this world now being exposed to the one thing I longed to escape for six years. You know this, Emma! If I could have, I would have killed myself to end Septim's possession."

Emma's face crumpled, and she tried to reclaim her hand.

"I believe we can fix it; I just don't know how. But many will lose their lives in the process."

She didn't say anything for a while. Then, her arm relaxed, and he lifted her hand to his mouth, kissing the white ridges on her palm.

"I'm sorry," she admitted. "But I don't know what else I could have done. I know *you*, Argent. *You're* important to me. It's hard to value the unknown multitude over the known few."

He let out a sigh of relief. It was progress. But the conversation led them back to the topic he'd put off since he confronted his father about Renault's letter. "About Bethany—"

She yanked her hand away.

"I don't have a simple answer for you, but I would like to explain if you'll listen."

Emma's eyes were blue fire in the night, burning brighter than any of the stars above. "If the explanation is anything but 'We're saving her,' then we have a problem."

Argent licked his lips. "I doubt that she's a distant relative, but that's beside the point. What's important is that Mountains' plan to extract Bethany with the Khozek opens up the opportunity for Igraine to force her way through."

"Don't turn this into another 'sacrifice one for the many' scenario!" Emma said, raising her voice. "You're talking as if you don't even *know* Bethany!"

He took hold of her chin, forcing her to look him in the eye. "I don't. Not really. I didn't spend years studying her soul like I did yours through our journals. I know her far less than I know you—"

Emma grabbed the bottle of honeywine again and wrenched the cork out.

Argent snatched it away before she could take a drink. "Considering the possibilities does not mean I've already decided what to do."

"You and your father both want to sentence her to death," she accused, getting to her feet. Clenching her fists, she turned her back to him.

"Neither of us want that," Argent disagreed sharply. "This is not about Bethany Hawkins *or* her parents. I don't care if they're related to us. I *do* care if facing Igraine outside of prophecy will put us in an even worse position than if we didn't have the Khozek or the Elvara Bow at all."

Emma's voice was quiet but harsh. "I won't let you kill my best friend."

Argent sighed. He should have known she wouldn't budge on this. "I'm not *trying* to kill her. I don't know how likely it is that the Khozek can tip us toward an outcome not prophesied. But please understand that my father's first priority, and mine, is protecting the worlds from Igraine's promised tyranny. Talahm is already facing unprecedented danger from the Nephilim."

Emma was quiet for so long that Argent almost continued, but his patience was rewarded by her slight intake of breath.

"When you were so eloquently explaining why you thought I should have let you become a Nephilim host, you said something about there being someone else who could carry on your dynasty. You didn't mean Bethany, did you? Is your mom having another kid?"

Argent sighed, getting to his feet to stand next to her. "It was at the bottom of Renault's letter. My father didn't know. So yes, it's not just the world population or Renova's people Father and I have to think about. It's this new sibling, too."

She crossed her arms, tilting her weight to one hip. "I'm glad for your parents, really, but Bethany isn't the only one trapped there. What about the Fifth Travelers? The people we rescued in Valona weren't there on vacation. Igraine took them from Langoth. What if there are more still trapped who belong to your kingdom?"

He'd identified a dreadful prospect while brooding over the conversation with his father, and he'd agonized about how to broach it with Emma. "Bethany has been at Igraine's mercy not once, but twice. We have no way of knowing that Bethany is even fully herself. I have to allow for the possibility that Igraine may have affected her the same way she affected my father."

Emma's face showed her struggle between loyalty and logic. Finally, she looked at him, her eyes wary. "I don't want you to be right. The last thing I want is for Bethany to be compromised. But even if she is, I'll still do everything possible to rescue her from dying in a black hole. No one deserves that, except Igraine." She paused. "And the Nephilim."

"Emma," he whispered, threading his fingers through hers. He tugged her palm to get her to face him. "I will do whatever is in my power to get her back, but I must be prepared for the possibility that we cannot rescue Bethany before we're able to lock Igraine on Langoth." He brushed a strand of jet-black hair away from her cheek, his heart warming when she leaned into his hand with a sigh.

"I don't want to think about what will happen if I'm forced to choose."

Foreboding stirred deep within Argent. "It's my duty as heir to entertain all options."

"Tell me this," Emma said, grasping the front of his sleeping shirt with both hands. "If you were King, what would you do?"

His heart sped up. "I'm *not* the King—"

"But you will be," Emma pressed.

Argent wrapped his hands around her wrists. "I've never wanted to rule—"

"—and that's what will make you a great King," she interjected. "All else equal, if you were in charge, what would you do?"

He tightened his grip. "I would do what I'm doing right now. Weighing the possibilities. I don't know how the tides of fate will treat us at the Scepter, but I must be prepared for every option." He kissed her forehead, then gently pulled her down to the soft blankets. "Whatever happens, we face it as we are strongest. Together."

Lying next to him, she stretched out and snuggled into his side. "I don't want to go back down to my hammock." Emma hesitated for the briefest moment, but Argent heard the catch in her breath. "Will you stay with me until sunrise? If it doesn't bother you?"

Argent propped himself up on one elbow and traced the curve of her jaw with the tips of his fingers. "Why would it bother me that the most beautiful, powerful witch in the world not only loves me but would break into the captain's cabin with me for a nightcap?"

Emma blushed, but she didn't look away.

"You are not afraid to fight for what you want, and I will take your fierceness a hundred times over, even if it means the crew gossips about us in the morning. Let them."

This time, she reached up to kiss him, and it took everything in him not to reel back in shock when he felt her hand slip under his tunic and press against his scars from the Direwolf.

Tendrils of magic spread across his skin, finally finishing healing his side. Her tesseract pulsed against him.

He wrapped his arms around her back, crushing her against his chest, hands splayed across her shoulder blades. She was his air. The promise of a life beyond the Scepter. The only reason he was still alive. He'd never been touched like this before—never thought anyone, including Emma, would even want to. Septim had kept him completely isolated. Every caress of his mother's hand across his cheek lost between his skin and his soul. Six years without human touch that he could truly call his own, and now, safe in Emma's embrace, he could feel everything.

Several bliss-filled minutes later, Argent drew back, resting his forehead against Emma's. Her desire for him filled her eyes, and his breath caught.

He pressed a gentle kiss to her lips, savoring her with every piece of his soul.

If they made it past whatever awaited them at the Scepter, he would have her beside him until the end of all things.

Argent woke the next morning in a warm cocoon of blankets with Emma's hair tickling his nose. Amazingly,

Emma's magic had hid them overnight. When Argent rubbed the sleep from his eyes, he froze at the sight of an airwitch hovering just behind the mast, her eyes sliding right past the crow's nest as if it didn't exist.

The ship had picked up speed, too.

Argent gently shook Emma awake, breaking into a grin when she smiled at him like the cat that caught the sparrow.

The airwitch called down to the decks. "Ship sighted! Colors of Keldvaar!"

Argent's stomach dropped. He got to his feet, pulling Emma up after him. The vessel was still far behind *The Sea Wolf*, but it was now close enough to see the green flag on her mast. How was Atlas chasing them so quickly?

More shouts and clamoring came from the main deck, and when Argent peered over the edge, he watched as his father and Sargateth hefted the Khozek's chest to the base of the mast behind the wheel. Cordelia must still be dead asleep in her quarters.

"Oh no, they're going to try teleporting the ship," he whispered anxiously. His father had told him a few days ago of his plans with the Ancients to use the Khozek to get them to the Scepter faster through a series of jumps north.

"*Teleporting?*" Emma asked. "Since when can they do that kind of magic?"

Sargateth produced the key and opened the box. Even from up in the crow's nest, Argent could see the vibrant cobalt blue threads covering the dark object. Sargateth laid both hands over the Khozek, and Aragon gripped Sargateth's shoulder.

Two seconds later, the ship vibrated. The ocean and the distant pursuing ship shifted back and forth, fast enough that Argent wondered if his vision had malfunctioned. With a great heave forward, *The Sea Wolf* shuddered, and the ship flying Keldvaar's colors disappeared.

A sharp cry came from the bow, and the ship turned hard to port. A moment later, a gaping portal flew past them, barely missing the ship's side.

"Whoa, that was close!" Emma yelled, grabbing Argent's waist and pulling him down low so he could better stabilize. "What just happened?"

"I think we just moved a few leagues north," Argent answered, peering through the slats in the railing. Nothing about the surrounding ocean had changed other than the fact that the pursuing vessel had dropped from sight.

Down on the deck, Sargateth had fallen to his knees. Aragon crouched in front of him, his hands supporting the Archmage's face.

"Sargateth doesn't look so good."

Emma tugged on his arm. "Argent? What is *that*?"

Her finger shook as it pointed across the bow.

A single large tentacle poked above the waves, sending a shockwave down Argent's spine.

"KRAKEN!" he bellowed.

No one moved.

Emma cursed, remembering the cloak of privacy she had produced, and Argent felt her magic lift off them.

"KRAKEN!" Argent screamed again, and it jolted the crew below into a frenzy. "TELEPORT!"

Morgan hurried over to her brother and the King, placing her palms on the Khozek.

The ship vibrated again, this time more violently, and their surroundings changed once more.

Shouting erupted on the deck below, and the ship slowed with enough force to press Argent against the railing before he could even open his eyes.

"Is it gone?" Emma asked, breathing hard.

Argent blinked until he could see again. The shadow of an island loomed in front of them.

"We have a bigger problem," he said, transfixed by the minefield of portals between them and the Glass Isle.

He struggled to his feet, clinging to the edge of the crow's nest as he got a better view of the sterncastle. Cordelia spun the wheel, wearing a furious expression as she slowly navigated them past the portals. William ran in the direction of the crew's quarters.

"You both should get down," the airwitch on duty said stiffly from where she floated behind the mast, her muscles straining as she controlled the wind in the sails.

The ship tilted hard, sending Argent tumbling back to the planks.

Emma managed to stay upright, watching the horizon behind them. "We need eyes up here," she answered, and with a wave of her hand she reverted the crow's nest back to its original form.

"I'll watch for the Kraken and the Keldvaar ship. You two make sure we don't hit a portal," Argent said, sounding more authoritative than he felt. He wished he was on the sturdy deck below, but if he insisted on Emma taking him down, the distraction might cost them everything. What use would he be on deck?

They'd assumed the Kraken was still in The Sleeping Sea, where it had nearly destroyed *The Sea Wolf*. A worse thought arose... what if there was more than one?

The next thirty minutes passed tortuously slowly. Emma joined the airwitch on duty, hovering around the fore topmast and shouting back and forth with William.

The ship had slowed to a snail's pace, weaving between open portals. Packed together, they were sometimes close enough that there was barely a foot of tolerance on either side of the vessel.

*Could using the Khozek be making the portals worse?*

Between watching for their pursuers and the Kraken, he only caught snippets of what was happening on the deck. The last jump had the same effect on Morgan as the first one had on Sargateth, and Luke tended to the Ancients.

It made him think back to when he'd watched Luke's futile efforts to break Septim's curse over Sargateth. His stomach twisted with the reminder of his role in all that.

Something caught his eye on the horizon—the faint outline of a ship. His heart thundered against his ribcage.

"They caught up!" he yelled, waving his arms overhead until Cordelia looked up at him. "Keldvaar!"

Luke helped Sargateth and Morgan to their feet. Both Ancients pressed their hands on the Khozek, their shoulders hunched.

Wide-eyed, Emma landed back in the crow's nest and flung her arms around him, pinning Argent to the mast just as the ship began vibrating at high speed again.

In the blink of an eye, the sky went dark, and rain poured in droves from the black clouds overhead. Choppy waves pounded against the hull, and in the distance, Argent could make out a coastline that did not match what he knew of the Glass Isle.

They were now *much* further north.

The airwitch behind the mast screamed.

In front of the ship, a purple light cut through the waves. It sped into the air like lightning, its center splitting open into the largest portal Argent had ever seen.

The airwitch yanked her hands back in a fruitless effort to backfill the sails and slow them down.

A half-second later, the ship tilted starboard, sending Argent and Emma tumbling to the edge of the crow's nest. The portal's gigantic gaping maw stretched across *The Sea Wolf*'s path.

But it was too late.

The bowsprit dipped into the black void, and as the ship turned, the hole swallowed the front of the ship and sheared off the figurehead with an almighty crack.

Argent's heart almost stopped when the blackness flickered to life, and he saw a familiar face with a long blonde braid over her shoulder, their enemy beside her.

The portal closed on its own. The mast beneath them cracked, and with a great lurch, the ship listed sideways, sending Argent and Emma into a freefall toward the waters below.

# CHAPTER FIFTEEN
# ILLUMINATED

"I hope you convinced her not to murder us all," Hela said stiffly when Bethany and Igraine walked into the settlement's commissary tent.

Bethany didn't feel great about it, but they didn't have much choice. She filled a plate with roasted fish and a thin slice of bread made from hardy wheat grown in the camp's makeshift greenhouse. "She's got the Olis claw, knows how to use it, and wants off this rock as much as we do." Even if she'd somehow managed to overpower Igraine, she wouldn't have the faintest clue where or how to look for the place Igraine said would connect to the Titan Obelisk at

Perga's Scepter. "Without combining our power, she can't open a portal large or stable enough to save everyone in this village."

Hela narrowed her eyes, glancing between them as Igraine levitated food onto a rough wooden plate. "And what's her price?"

"Why don't you ask her?" Bethany sniped, tired of playing ping-pong with strong personalities. The first bite of her meal tasted like every luxury dish she'd ever longed for on Earth.

"Make one wrong move," Hela whispered to Igraine, "and I'll—"

"—thank me for saving your sorry hide," Igraine answered cheerfully.

Bethany left the tent, shivering when she passed through the thin warmth charm. Misha stood outside, leaning against his staff with both hands wrapped around it.

"I thought you said she was dangerous," he said without looking at her.

Bethany swallowed her mouthful of bread and fish. "She is. But she promised us a way home. And I believe her."

Misha snorted. "There's no way home. Not from here. Don't get our hopes up."

"You're not exactly in a place where your hopes could sink any lower. Don't you know what that is up there?"

Misha barely glanced at the black hole, indifference written on his wrinkled face. "The end, I assume, with how you're talking about it. But the tides will kill us before that happens."

Three screams from the infirmary tent tore through the camp.

Struggling through the gravity, Bethany dropped her plate and ran across the courtyard, her hand alight with fire. The cries pierced the dead silence of the settlement so sharply they hurt Bethany's eardrums. She burst into the tent, ready with a ball of fire primed to throw at—

She skidded to a halt, unable to make sense of what she saw.

And smelled.

The light from Bethany's fire cast long, spindly shadows against the tent wall, illuminating a creature of impossible proportions. It crouched over Lincoln, who curled protectively over his sister. Kenna tried to get up from her bed, but she was still too weak to move. Bethany coughed, choking on the stench of rotting flesh that had consumed the entire tent. The creature swung around, its red eyes gleaming from the sockets of its bone-white, skinless skull. Massive elk-like antlers sprouted from its head, one end catching on the lantern that hung in the middle of the tent. The lantern crashed to the ground, its light flaring before it died among the broken shards of glass.

Bethany gagged, throwing her fireball at it, dodging to the side when the wendigo lunged. She'd seen sketches of this thing before in Emma's mythology books, but never thought she'd fight one.

The fire hit the white, patchy fur covering the wendigo's barreled chest and sizzled. The creature opened its jaw impossibly wide, letting out a shriek that almost paralyzed Bethany. It leaped across the tiny room, a long, unnatural tongue sliding over needle-sharp teeth as if tasting the air. Bethany tucked and rolled, gritting her teeth against the pain of re-injuring her arm. On her knees, she launched a torrent of blistering flames at the wendigo, fighting the sheer terror that seeped into her bones from having met its gaze.

"Get out, get out, get OUT!" she screamed, the temperature in the tent skyrocketing with the intensity of Bethany's fear. The wendigo raised its spindly arms to protect its face, its taut, ashen skin blistering. Slowly, the creature slid away from them until it reached the far side of the tent and melted into a shadow that slipped under the fabric's edge.

A heartbeat later, Bethany looked at Lincoln and Penny. They didn't move, both curled so tightly they resembled pill bugs. But she caught the slight rise of Lincoln's shoulders. *Good. They're still breathing.* Kenna had sunk back into her thin mattress, eyes closed as if her adrenaline had fled.

Bethany's coven tattoo pulsed, warning her a split second before a firm hand clamped over her shoulder.

"It's gone," Hela said in a shaky voice.

"What was it?" Misha asked as he entered the tent, far less startled than the rest of them. When Bethany met his gaze, his concern was clear in his beady eyes.

"Wendigo." If she hadn't seen it, she wouldn't have believed it. "Do all the things that go bump in the night come from this planet?" she asked, only half joking. Her adrenaline had peaked, and she was not looking forward to the upcoming crash.

"*Pizdah!*" Misha cursed and spun on his heel, ducking back into the courtyard. "Lock down the camp! A wendigo got past the perimeter."

Bethany cautiously approached the Emrys. She hesitated for only a moment before touching Lincoln's shoulder. He started to unfurl himself. "Are you guys okay? You don't have a hankering for human flesh, do you?"

Lincoln jolted, staring at Bethany with wide, confused eyes. "What?"

"No madness with a side of cannibalism?"

Next to him, Penny recoiled.

"Good. That's how they reproduce, you know. I don't need more wendigos standing in front of our way out."

Lincoln dry heaved.

Bethany patted his back awkwardly before getting to her feet. "Yeah, that was my reaction too when I first read about them."

She looked around the tent, relieved to see Rissy tending to Kenna. The old woman looked like she'd lost consciousness again, her half-moon tattoo dormant and stark against her pale skin. Living in perpetual darkness seemed to have sucked the color right out of her.

Bethany pressed her lips together. "I'll go after the wendigo."

Hela grabbed her good arm. "Take Harlow with you."

"No need for that," Igraine said casually, entering the tent with her usual flair. "I love a good hunting party."

Bethany rolled her eyes, but she couldn't deny that she'd appreciate the help.

"Oh, don't worry pet. I won't bother you with vapid talk. I know the concentration it takes to stalk prey."

With that creepy sentiment hanging over her, Bethany shoved past Igraine and slipped under the tent's edge where the wendigo had escaped.

She watched with amusement as Igraine copied her, straightening her hair and smoothing down the front of her dress after she stood.

Bethany and Igraine tracked the wendigo's prints, veering around the edge of the camp toward the cliffs.

Almost as if it expected to return.

Shoving down her fear, she cast the invisibility spell she'd learned from Emma and kept moving. She ignored the look of delight on the old hag's face.

It wasn't long before the monster's stench filled her nostrils again. Out of the red darkness, its glowing eyes moved eerily, like a dog licking its wounds while keeping guard.

Bethany stopped, shivering. Igraine patted her once on the arm and pointed off to one side before disappearing. She could only hope that meant Igraine planned to approach from the opposite direction so they could trap the creature in a pincer move.

Bethany's brain screamed at her to turn around, to flee this unholy creature, but the entire camp could succumb to its power if left alive. They fed on strength, which explained why it had gone to the infirmary first.

Kenna was still a powerful witch.

*"I can smell the frantic beat of your frail heart, fiery one."* The wendigo's hissing whisper sent spiders skittering down

Bethany's back. She hadn't known they could talk. "*Magic cannot mask the scent of fear.*"

Speaking would do her no good. She built up the fire in her hand until it felt too hot to hold. All she had to do was burn out its heart, and the settlement would be safe.

The familiar tear of an opening portal behind the wendigo caused a different kind of horror to well in her. It turned, its massive antlers bobbing with far more grace than the creature should have.

Like the other portals here, the hole shimmered to life. The image made Bethany sick to her stomach.

The portal looked up at her alma mater's communications building from the base of the wide, sloping hill students called Thompson Flats. Chad Halliwell walked down the cement path, his hands shoved into deep pockets.

Emma's bully.

The wendigo swung its head back toward the heat surging in Bethany's hand, as if assessing its chances.

While Bethany still held a stadium-sized grudge against him, Chad didn't deserve to face down a wendigo. She dropped her invisibility spell and threw the fireball, letting out a wild shout.

"Bethany Hawkins?" Chad blurted from the other side of the portal. He looked stunned and terrified at the same time. She didn't blame him. The portals were *weird*. And seeing a wendigo would top any crazy college experience.

Igraine materialized near the side of the portal and shanked the wendigo right through the heart with a red-hot peg—the peg attached earlier to the prisoner chain in the infirmary. She didn't have time to dwell on how or when Igraine had gotten that.

Igraine held the creature halfway through the portal, and the wendigo thrashed, shrieking.

"What day is it?" Bethany screamed at Chad. It was their only chance to actually figure out the effects of the time dilation.

To his credit, Chad didn't hesitate. "July 18th," he answered.

The tear started to zip itself back up. With it, the last of her vindictiveness toward him dried up. "You see something like this again, you run away faster than you ever did in football," she shouted, "or you'll die!"

The last thing she saw of Chad Halliwell was his wide, fearful eyes.

With a keening scream, the wendigo fell apart at the seams, its bones and sinew no longer held together by whatever dark magic had created it. Its entire back half was gone, probably steaming on the grass in front of Chad back on Earth.

Igraine staggered backward, and Bethany sent another burst of flames at the wendigo's remains, burning them to a crisp.

*If we make it back to Talahm, I hope we can stop these stupid portals opening wherever they want.*

"Friend of yours?" Igraine asked, bent over with her hand pressed against one knee. Only the front half of the wendigo's skull and antlers remained, still smoldering.

Bethany stared at the place Chad's face had disappeared behind the curtain of the universe. "He could have been, once. If he hadn't been a tool."

Igraine straightened, nudging the wendigo's skull with one toe. "I do not know that insult."

Bethany turned back to the camp, trudging slower than she'd like. "It means he treated people like objects and didn't care who he hurt." She glanced over her shoulder at Igraine, unable to resist the dig. "Kind of like you."

"I told you, my dear, that I am transparent with and compassionate to my witches."

The infirmary tent came into view. "I'm not your witch."

Igraine paused, the silence between them heavy. "I have high hopes for you, Bethany Celeste."

Ignoring that lest she barf, Bethany brought up the other thing that had been bugging her. "How come all the portals here are see-through? That's never happened before."

"Oh, didn't I tell you?" Igraine said, delighted. "I make it a practice to illuminate them. You never know what might be lurking on the other end."

Bethany couldn't deny that logic. "But aren't you worried about someone seeing something they aren't supposed to? Chad will have nightmares for the rest of his life. Not that he doesn't deserve it, but—" she cut herself off. Why would Igraine care about that? "Never mind." She entered the infirmary.

Kenna had woken up. She sat on the edge of the bed, and Rissy Clement helped her sip a small cup of hot chocolate. Harlow talked in low tones with Penny while Lincoln listened, his eyes fixed on the tent flap like it might let another beast inside.

"Where's Igraine?" Rissy asked. Beside her, Kenna tensed.

"Right here," Igraine answered, walking in. "The wendigo is dead."

Kenna glared at her. "Just like Danya, no?"

Igraine stared at the leader of the Fifth Travelers, raising an eyebrow. "Danya was an accident. I killed the wendigo on purpose."

Kenna's face reddened, and her eyes flashed. "And I suppose you expect us to be at your mercy because of it? I've heard all about your supposed promise," she spat, gesturing to Bethany's coven sisters, who must have told her about the deal. "These people are *mine*. They've trusted *me* to keep them safe all these years. I will not have you pretending to be a queen even if you *can* provide a way back to Talahm."

Bethany kept her eyes on Igraine, who had an abysmal track record with handling insults.

She didn't disappoint.

"And how long, exactly, is it until the next wave hits? How long until you spend yourself so thoroughly that you expire and sentence *your people* to drowning, just because you couldn't take the word of the only witch—and actual queen, by the way—offering you a way out? How long have you wished for your homeland, only to taste bitterness when you lay your head to sleep?"

Kenna struggled to her feet, and Rissy belatedly stood to help her. "I see no markings of royalty on you," she said, scathing. She pointed to the elaborate tattoos on her face. "My mother was the last princess of the Helcari Empire before it crumbled. I have weathered this wasteland for thirty years."

"Darling, you're delusional. Helcari collapsed *four hundred* years ago. I should know. I watched it happen."

Bethany inserted herself between Igraine and Kenna before they could go for each other's throats. "She's not delusional. The black hole slows down time." She'd figured out the math after getting the date from Chad. "Time on Earth is twice as fast as on Talahm. A hundred days have already passed on Earth since I left, like, two weeks ago."

Igraine stared at her, unblinking. Bethany almost expected a cricket to chirp and break the silence.

"Don't you get it?" she pressed. "Pendragon is a whole month ahead of us. We're way more behind than you think. Every second counts."

*That* made Igraine's eyes widen.

Wordlessly, the old hag abruptly left the tent. Bethany exchanged a tense glance with Hela before following Igraine out.

In the sky, the accretion disk loomed. Its red smear across the sky defied comprehension. As far as she knew, no one on Earth had ever seen a black hole, not even in photographs of deep space. At its center, spaghettified matter spiraled around the blackest spot Bethany had ever seen, so dark and deep it caused her eyes to itch. What Emma wouldn't give to see this! If Langoth weren't doomed to join the rest of the red matter falling into the event horizon, it might have been worth trying to return and study its physics.

Still trailing Igraine, her breath caught. *I've used all four of my trips—everyone here has. What happens now if we try to use a fifth?* An even worse thought intruded. *Will I ever see Luke again?*

High above them, another portal opened. Bethany backed away in horror, yelling for Igraine. The tear grew twice as long as the tents were tall and split wide open. A cascade of freezing water dumped into the center of the camp. Bethany shouted, trying to gather the water in a huge ball before it could flood the space—again. Hela sprinted from the tent, and she worked with Igraine to strengthen Bethany's magic. But the water wouldn't stop, as if it were emptying Talahm's seas.

Igraine grunted, and the dark portal revealed the soft pinks and oranges of dawn on one side and the ever-flowing deep blue of the ocean on the other.

A long wooden pole pierced the tear, followed by the snarling face of a wolf. Bethany watched in slow motion as Luke flew across the portal, over and beyond.

She screamed his name, but the tear snapped shut, shearing the massive figurehead from its home and sending it crashing into the center of the camp. Bethany, Igraine, and Hela lifted the massive ball of water high above the camp and exploded it, turning it into mist and a light rain.

Brushing the stringy hair from her face, Bethany turned back to the wreckage, her heart pounding and thoughts racing.

"Cleo must have scared them into making a mistake," Igraine said to herself, a sharp edge to her ancient, crackly voice. "But this will not slow them for long." She grabbed Bethany's arm, forcing their eyes to meet. "King Aragon will do whatever it takes to secure his dynasty, including locking us here forever." She pointed at the sky with her chin. "I'm close to finding the anchor. But we must hurry. Otherwise, we will all die."

# CHAPTER SIXTEEN

# THE PRICE OF FORGIVENESS

Julie turned a page in Renault's massive book, trying to ignore Tom as he struggled to fasten his exoskeleton. As time wore on, she found it harder and harder to keep the stone wall between them intact.

She could almost admit to herself that she missed him. That she might even forgive him.

She just wanted her family back.

William had come down earlier to tell them the plan with the Khozek, insisting that they stay below decks until it was over. It had been almost half an hour since the last shuddering made the planks along the walls and floor glitch back and forth through reality, and she felt antsy stuck down here with her—did she want to call him her husband again?

Tom finished snapping his exoskeleton together and creaked to his feet.

Shouting erupted above decks as the ship heaved again, the vessel making another jump forward. Julie dropped the book and tightened her hands around the fabric of her hammock until it stopped.

The ship lurched sideways, and a great cracking thundered through the crew's quarters from the front of the ship. The force threw her several feet through the air, knocking all the breath out of her when she landed, skidding across the floor.

A heartbeat later, more wood broke above them, and she heard the ominous whoosh of something falling.

*Did we just lose a mast?*

The impact against the water caused a frightening splintering sound to her right.

Water swirled into the room from a gash in the ship's hull. Julie scrambled to her feet, frantically searching the room for her husband. He must have been thrown in the confusion. The lanterns hanging from the ceiling were all either out or low, and the light from the hole in the ship's side diminished as water flowed in.

"Tom!" she screamed, the water rapidly coming up to her waist as the ship sank.

"Julie!" he responded from the floor ten feet from his hammock. He tried to get to his feet, but the exoskeleton wasn't designed for recovering from a fall.

Julie waded toward him, the water rising so rapidly that she barely made it halfway before his black hair slipped beneath the waves.

"Tom!" She struggled through the water but got caught on the now-submerged hammocks and the other waterlogged items floating around.

Julie started treading water. Her heart beat frantically against her chest. Tom's exoskeleton was dead weight, and she was sure he couldn't stay afloat using his arms.

Julie's eyes burned in the saltwater, but she forced herself to keep them open as she swam toward her husband. His eyes were tightly closed, his cheeks bulbous with his last breath. She grasped him under his arms and heaved, trying to lift him.

With a gasp, Julie's head broke the surface. Tom was too heavy, and she couldn't touch the floor anymore.

She coughed and sucked in a breath, but another surge of water sent her back under. Tom hadn't gotten any more air.

Panic overwhelmed her. This couldn't be the end—couldn't be how her family died—and this wasn't how she'd ever imagined her last moments.

A dark, glittering figure swam through the hole in the ship and zoomed up to her. Emma's nightclothes billowed around her in the water like a ghost, her birthmark shining against the darkness.

Straining to hold her breath, she made eye contact with her daughter and let her take over the rescue. Julie kicked off from one of the support pillars, swimming toward the ocean. The only thing she could do now was trust that Emma would save Tom.

The ascent consisted of the longest ear-popping seconds of her life, and by the time she broke the surface, her lungs were a microsecond from bursting. She gasped for air, flailing as rainwater plastered her hair to her face.

A great splash a few feet away sent her back under the waves, but swimming had returned to Julie just like riding a bike. She kicked both feet and resurfaced, watching Emma fly through the stormy skies with her arms wrapped around her father's chest. She landed on the listing deck of *The Sea Wolf*.

Julie swam to the edge of the ship. The vessel had sunk enough that she could climb up to the railing without needing the rope ladder.

"Mom!" a voice yelled from the water, and Julie looked over her shoulder to see Luke swimming toward her. He must have been thrown forward when the impact happened.

But there was nothing in the water that they could have hit.

She clambered over the railing and leaned down to help Luke, pulling him onto the deck with all her strength.

With Luke safe, she frantically looked around. Destruction reigned. The central mast holding the crow's nest had cracked near the base, and most of it hung over the side of the ship. Barrels and boxes were broken to smithereens, their contents spilling across the deck. Glancing around for Emma and Tom, she registered the missing figurehead.

Sargateth limped down the stairs into the flooded quarters, and Morgan jumped into the air to hover in front of the ship.

"Luke!" Emma screamed, and Julie's heart seized.

Emma had laid her father on the deck next to the collapsed mast. Luke rushed over and fell to his knees, conjuring a hazy medical projection over Tom's limp body.

His eyes were closed, hair plastered against his face and neck.

Paralyzed with disbelief, Julie couldn't move.

Luke did something else, and a stream of seawater poured out of Tom's mouth. But his chest remained still.

Emma rushed away, diving back into the water to find others who had been below deck.

Like Mountains.

Julie's heart felt like it had stopped in her chest. "Tom!" she screamed. Tearing across the remaining distance, she knocked Luke out of the way. She climbed on top of her husband, threading her hands together to start chest compressions. Never had she ever imagined that she'd need to give her husband CPR, never thought that the next time she'd touch his lips would be to breathe life back into him, never thought—

"I'm not losing you," Julie said ferociously, pressing rhythmically into Tom's ribcage. "You're not allowed to die again!"

Two breaths. Thirty more compressions.

Screams echoed around her. Luke continued to work his healing magic.

Julie had never been more grateful for magic than in this moment, but ultimately, nothing else mattered.

Only Tom.

"Come back to me!" She screamed, hating how stupid she'd been this whole time, making him pay penance for his sins rather than recognizing the gift of him *being alive*.

Finally, he coughed and started breathing on his own, his eyes fluttering open.

Sobbing in relief, Julie fisted his robes and yanked him up. She savored the weight of his body against hers, his arms coming together behind her back, *him*.

Luke sat backward and wiped his stringy hair from his face before getting to his feet. There were others who needed his healing.

"Jewel," Tom breathed, his voice ragged. His arms tightened, and he crushed her against him.

The decades-old endearment shattered the rest of her. "I love you, you idiot! You stupid, beautiful man, I love you! I can't lose you again, do you hear me? I cannot lose you!"

"I love you," Tom whispered repeatedly, pressing his nose to her neck so that his beard tickled her collarbone. He kissed the hollow where her neck met her shoulder, the touch like fire on her skin.

She clung to him until she couldn't restrain herself any longer. Heart pounding so loud that she couldn't hear the shouts across the ship anymore, she grabbed the sopping wet hair at the back of his head and forced him to look at her. His captivating green and gold eyes were red from the saltwater.

Julie kissed him, hard.

It was everything she remembered and so much more. He was fire and ice rolled into one. Her hands pushed further into his hair and pulled him closer, and his hands slid up to cup her cheeks, his thumbs caressing her soft skin. She could feel a buzz like a soft electric current, and she realized it was the charge of his magic.

And then she remembered every time she'd felt that magic during their marriage on Earth. Every time he'd touch her, it felt like sparks lit the pressure between their skin. He'd always been like this, but she'd never known it for what it truly was—a man gifted with magic meant to protect the ones he loved. And he *had* protected his family, even if he'd done it in a way she wished he hadn't. She realized all this during their kiss, and when he pulled away, she gripped his shoulders even harder, following him for another.

When her eyes opened, she saw his shining back at her.

He stroked her hair again, a soft laugh accompanying the smile that spread across his face. "I've missed you," he breathed. "I missed *that*."

Julie rested her forehead against his, their breath mingling. "Twenty years, Tom. I went to bed every night wishing you were there. Knowing you couldn't be because you were dead."

Tom's hands stilled.

"I prayed countless times that you could come back for just one night, for just one kiss—" She shuddered, sucking in a deep breath. Her fingers brushed against the rough, corded scar on his neck. "You've always been the only man for me. To have you back, to have all my family together again—this is the greatest gift God has ever given me."

A choked sob escaped Tom, and he tightened his arms around her. "I love you, Jewel. I wish I had not kept so much from you, and I'm sorry I did."

"Don't you ever leave me again." She couldn't keep her voice from wavering.

"I promise," Tom said, pressing another electrifying kiss to her lips. Suddenly, he pulled away, looking around with fear in his eyes, as if he only now remembered how he'd ended up in this position. "Jewel... where are the kids?"

"They both rescued you," Julie said, her breath catching again. "They're helping with the ship now. I don't know how far we are from land." Tom coughed again, and Julie held him steady, rubbing her hands across his back. She brushed his floppy hair away from his face and tucked the streak of white behind his ear.

She peered through the rain and wreckage. A bright light like that of a shield shone from the entrance to the crew's quarters. Whatever magic Sargateth used had stopped the ship from sinking, but there was too much damage. The groans and cries of the injured crew filled the air, and Julie could only hope that Luke could heal them all.

Glancing around their immediate surroundings, her gaze fell on Prince Argent in soaking wet bedclothes. He crouched over the still body of one of the ship's airwitches, his head bowed.

Julie's heart sank. She still didn't know what had happened, but at least one person was dead.

Loath to leave Tom, she worried about what they were going to do next. Reluctantly, she got to her feet and carefully approached the railing.

Julie swallowed the lump in her throat.

A dark coastline loomed in the distance.

It was far enough away that without magic, they'd *all* be dead.

Together, it took Morgan Le Fay and Emma nearly two hours to shepherd the broken ship to shore.

Sargateth stayed below deck, expending the rest of his massive power. With his shield, he forced all the water from the interior of the ship and was now holding the ocean back from the gaping wounds in the hull.

Two Royal Coven witches had died. Julie only felt a little guilty for her disappointment that Cordelia was not one of them.

She got their names from Argent and vowed to remember them.

Meg Wycliffe. Skilled in fire and energy manipulation but unable to swim. Drowned before Emma could pull her from the belly of the ship.

Charlotte Peck. An airwitch who'd never even seen the ocean until the supplemental crew had reached Bearsmouth. The mast had hit her when the ship surged sideways, and she'd fallen to the deck, dying on impact. Charlotte was the one Julie had seen Argent kneeling over.

Numb, she wondered how many more would lose their lives before they made it home to Camelot. If they even got that far.

If they managed to defeat Igraine.

Standing at the railing with Tom, Julie shivered violently, wondering if this was payback for the times she'd chastised her kids for not wearing jackets in cold weather. Her husband tightened his hold around her, and she pressed her cheek against his chest, hardly able to process that she'd almost lost her chance at forgiving him.

Just before they ran the ship aground, the rain petered out, revealing a thin, sandy shore with craggy rocks and a sheer cliff beyond. A group of six people stood on the beach, waiting.

Julie instantly tensed.

Morgan and Emma touched down onto the deck, and Sargateth struggled up the stairs, collapsing at the top with a heavy sigh. Morgan found a box and immediately sat on it.

The ship sagged in the sand, tilting far enough to one side that Julie had to dramatically shift her weight.

"Did you see—"

"Natives," Morgan answered, sounding just as tired as her brother. "Though I cannot say which tribe, as I'm not sure how far north we are."

"We were aiming for Port Benga," Sargateth wheezed, still flat on his back.

"This does not look like Port Benga," William said, stomping across the deck. Water dripped from his bushy salt-and-pepper beard. "This looks like Sapphire Falls."

"What do they want?" Julie asked, looking back at the group. One of them had started walking toward the beached ship. "What if they're possessed?"

There was a beat of silence.

"Only one way to find out," Argent said, approaching with his father. "I go down and talk to them."

If someone had told Julie when she worked as a CEO that she'd negotiate alongside a magical flying cat and two royal descendants of King Arthur, she would have laughed for a year straight.

But now, with the threat of these natives possibly hosting Nephilim, even if unaware, Julie didn't feel like laughing.

They trudged through the wet sand with difficulty.

When they were within thirty yards of the strangers, Argent whispered, "I can't sense anything. I don't think the Nephilim have made it this far."

"We still cannot take any chances," King Aragon replied.

"We need supplies," Julie reminded them. "And help rebuilding the ship."

Morgan stopped walking and dug her staff into the sand. She still looked drained from the effort she'd spent saving the ship. "Yes, food and wood. If they are not overtaken by the Nephilim."

Their stopping point chosen, Julie watched with cautious curiosity as the natives approached.

An older woman with light gray hair and dark eyes led them, a staff with no gem in her hand. Dark brown furs were draped over her shoulders, and a gold necklace glinted at her throat. "I am Sami," she said, clearly assessing if they were a threat.

"I am Morgan." Julie didn't blame her for not sharing her true nature as an Olis.

"We are the Children of Sapphire Falls," Sami continued, gesturing behind her toward the rest of their small group. One was an old man, but the rest were young warriors—both men and women. The old man slowly trudged forward, standing next to Sami. For nomadic natives, they were well-dressed in leathers and furs that belied great wealth.

A hundred yards down the beach, another portal opened. Everyone turned toward it, clearly worried about what might come out.

But the tear only yawned open and then shut, leaving a thin amber line in the air.

Sami relaxed. "You need help, yes?" She gestured at the shipwreck.

Julie glanced at Argent out of the corner of her eye. He appeared relaxed, and she surmised he still didn't sense any nefarious spirits among them.

"Clearly," Julie said, taking over. "Food, clothing, supplies. And timber for repairs. Can you help?"

Sami and the old man glanced at each other with calculating gleams in their eyes. "Help, we can. But everything comes with a price, yes?"

"I'm sure we can work something out," Julie answered, secretly delighted to get her hands dirty negotiating again.

King Aragon cleared his throat, but Julie shot him a look that would have made her children wither in place. Thankfully, he refrained from interrupting.

Behind them, the rest of the crew made their way to shore, salvaging whatever they could from the hold.

"Excellent," Sami said, clapping her hands together. Chunky gold bangles rattled on her wrists, and the corner of her mouth lifted in a smirk. "You have some work to do before we can help, yes? You may find us on the ridge when you're ready to do business. Let it not be said that the Children of Sapphire Falls do not help strangers in need."

Before Julie could reply to that odd statement, Sami and the others abruptly turned and filed away without a backward glance.

When the natives were out of earshot, King Aragon cleared his throat again. "Lady Artair—"

"My husband may serve you, but I don't. You and the bonehead twins—" she pointedly glanced at Morgan, "—put all our lives at risk with your stupid scheme. And for what? To outrun a ship that we have no proof Atlas is on? Look at the cost! Now we're stuck here for who knows how long, spending resources we can't afford to fix a mistake that *you three* should have had the foresight to avoid." She glanced at Argent. "Not you, honey. I meant Sargateth."

"I know," Argent replied, looking like he carried the weight of the world on his shoulders.

Julie resisted the urge to rest her hand on the Prince's shoulder, instead zeroing in on the King. "Well? What are you waiting for? We have to see what we can salvage to afford help."

She stalked away, not feeling an ounce of fear about how the King might respond.

They had more important things to do.

Like rebuilding the ship before Igraine beat them to the Scepter.

# CHAPTER SEVENTEEN
# SAPPHIRE FALLS

"You oafs wrecked my ship!" Cordelia screamed at King Aragon and the Ancients shortly after they made it back on board. Her captain's hat was crushed in one hand, the feather broken. She'd smashed a bottle of honeywine on the deck, adding to the debris, and the odor of alcohol wafted freely.

Argent expected his father to dress Cordelia down for her disrespect, but was surprised when he calmly let it wash over him. Sargateth and Morgan, on the other hand, looked caught between guilt and anger.

"The greatest sailing vessel in the history of the world, and you brought it to utter destruction because of your stupid, wretched impatience! But no! Don't listen to the veteran of the seas. Surely you must know more than my decades of experience—"

"Cordelia," King Aragon finally interrupted, now starting to look irritated. "Shut up."

Cordelia snapped her mouth closed, but her eyes burned with malice.

"I realize you've been kept in the dark about certain aspects of this voyage, but I am the King of Renova, and you are my subject. You are in my employ, and I will not have your foul mouth polluting the ears of the rest of my people."

Argent felt a keen sense of satisfaction at the growing horror on Cordelia's face. The last time he'd felt like this was when he put her in the brig on the way back from Valona.

"Yes, the ship is wrecked, we lost supplies, and, worst of all, it cost the lives of two of my Royal Coven's witches. I do not make light of that, nor am I going to pretend that we did not make a grave mistake."

Cordelia opened her mouth again, but King Aragon held up his right hand, gesturing for her to stop.

"But *nothing* gives you the right to speak to your King like this. And nothing prevents me from taking away your rank as Captain if you do not mind your tongue. I've had enough of your petty attitude."

And with that, King Aragon turned on his heel and returned to shore to help set up camp with what little they had left.

Argent went into the ruined crew's quarters to pick through waterlogged remnants. He couldn't get the sight of Bethany standing with Igraine out of his mind.

The most he'd interacted with Emma since being thrown from the crow's nest had been a brief embrace before they headed ashore. There hadn't been time to tell her what he'd seen before being pitched into the water, and now he worried that he shouldn't.

If Bethany was working with Igraine, what did that mean for their mission? Could his eyes have been playing tricks on him? Since when did the portals show what was on the other side, anyway? And if Bethany was being controlled by Igraine, what would stop Bethany from helping Igraine through if they used the Khozek to rescue her?

He was sure Emma hadn't seen her best friend through the portal. Otherwise, she wouldn't be talking about anything else.

Argent fell into a rhythm moving between the ship and shore. He helped set up makeshift tents using canvas and backup sails and dug bonfire pits in the sand. All the while, he thought about the dilemma of what to say about it, if anything at all.

It was late afternoon before they were ready to confer again with the Children of Sapphire Falls on top of the cliff. Thankfully, he'd found the Elvara Bow and his quiver among the rescued, if damp, supplies. He strapped it across his back and climbed up a well-worn trail with his father, Julie, and both of the Ancients.

At the top of the cliff, land spread out as far as the eye could see. Plains and shallow hills were covered in grass and shrubs. When he looked north, the land looked colder where it transitioned into the Northern Reaches. But nestled between the beach and the distant craggy mountains was a dense, sprawling forest that had to be hours away on foot.

Timber for their ship.

Sami and the old man sat by a small fire, roasting rabbit on a spit. A tent with purple trim and silver braids embroidered along the edges stood behind them. The warriors were nowhere to be seen, but Argent suspected they weren't far off.

"The Children of Sapphire Falls seek trouble with no one," Sami said as a way of greeting, poking at the fire with a long iron stake with filigree that looked out of place. "But

I sense in your spirits that you are wary of trouble coming to you."

Argent exchanged a loaded glance with his father.

"I am Oren. Your ship is badly damaged, yes?" the old man said, though he ended the statement like a question.

"Yes," Julie said, bewildered. "In addition to what we've already mentioned, and if your people are willing, we need extra hands to speed up repairs."

Argent scanned the area for the warriors, finally spotting one camouflaged amongst the rocks about thirty feet away. He tensed, hand twitching toward his bow, even though he still could not sense any demons among them.

"You would do well to keep your weapons to yourselves," Oren said, but there was no threat in his voice. "Let us discuss prices while Runi and Nico show you the safest path into the Sapphire Forest." He pointed at Argent, Sargateth, and the King, leaving Morgan and Julie to hammer out the details.

The camouflaged warrior got to his feet and came over, followed by another one who had been better hidden.

Argent strained to sense anything different about them, but the feeling he'd gotten in Keldvaar didn't make itself known.

They were clean.

Nico and Runi led the men inland along a rocky path toward the trees. The longer they walked, the more Argent's heart sank.

Even with help, they were going to be stuck here a long time.

Despite the fact that the Sapphire Forest lay across distant, difficult ground, they found plenty of trees to turn into planks for repairing the ship.

Though the Children of Sapphire Falls had agreed to help them repair the ship, Sargateth and Morgan harvested as much wood as possible in the waning hours of sunlight, flying it to and from the forest until there was enough material to get started.

At dawn the next day, witches from the tribe showed up to shape and levitate planks into place, taking direction from William and a disgruntled Cordelia—both of whom knew the ship inside out.

Emma, who had immediately jumped in to mold and reshape the raw wood, worked nonstop, only taking an interlude for the brief but somber funeral for Meg and Charlotte.

The sun had started to set when Argent collapsed on the sand at the base of the cliff, his back pressed against the smooth sheer stone and sleeves rolled past his forearms. The ship had been dragged fully ashore onto a makeshift dry dock, exposing the massive hole that stretched from the crew's quarters all the way down to the hold. That explained why the ship had started sinking so fast. Not only had they lost the mizzen mast, the figurehead, and a good portion of the bow, but also most of the supplies they'd picked up in Keldvaar were now lost to the bottom of the Glass Channel.

But the tears in the ship weren't the worst of the damage.

Luke had worked with William to do a full magical diagnostic of the ship. It had revealed a catastrophic break between the wheel and the rudder, likely from the final, frantic jump. They'd need a complete reconstruction if they had any chance of navigating to Perga's Scepter.

Shading his eyes against the setting sun, Argent watched as magical lights blossomed to life above the ship, letting a second shift take over. Emma was among the last to leave, but she found him within minutes.

When she leaned her head against his shoulder, he threaded his fingers through hers.

"How long do you think it will take?"

Emma took a long, dragging breath. Her thumb rubbed circles against his hand. "Weeks," she whispered, sounding more upset than she had when Mountains refused to open a portal in Camelot. "You heard Luke and William talking. It's bad."

Argent felt a twist of anxiety in his stomach. Even with the food supplied by the Children of Sapphire Falls, he would need to hunt for fresh game. "Is there anything we can do to fix the ship faster?"

Emma shook her head, blowing a strand of hair away from her face. "The Khozek got us into this mess, so while I think it could really speed things up, I'm hesitant to touch it. Luke and William also don't want to mess up the steering on accident. We're better off paying these people to help us, even if it takes longer."

"I wonder if the Khozek draws the Nephilim to it," he thought out loud. "If moving it from beneath the bay into the bowels of the Shadow Star allowed Atlas to use its amplification, who's to say he isn't attuned enough now to follow its trail like a hunting dog?"

Emma stilled next to him. "I'd bet anything Atlas manned the ship chasing us."

"Me too." Even if his suspicion about the Khozek was incorrect, Argent considered the sheer number of people working on the ship. If Sargateth's artifact chose to amplify the wrong person's will, he shuddered to think what further delays might happen. While he thought they all wanted to get to the Scepter as fast as possible, it was impossible to truly know a person's heart.

And if using the Khozek created a beacon, they shouldn't use it until it was absolutely needed.

Emma tugged her hand from his and shoved it through her hair, her shoulders rounding as she hunched forward.

Argent shifted so that she was in front of him. Without asking, he dug his fingers into her shoulders, working his thumbs into the knots in her muscles.

She relaxed, her shoulders drooping. "You have no idea how good that feels."

By the time his hands tired, Emma's breathing had deepened. He rubbed his palms down the sides of her arms, and when she leaned back into his chest, his heart leaped.

Across the water, the sun touched the horizon. The clouds slowly cycled through different shades of orange and red, then purple.

"I'm sorry I let you fall," Emma whispered into the first chill of approaching night.

"What?"

"From the crow's nest. When the portal took off the figurehead. Before we went up there, you said you trusted me not to let you fall, but I did."

Argent tightened his arms around her and kissed the top of her head. He wrestled with what to tell her. "It caught us all by surprise."

He felt her tense.

"What's wrong?"

Emma blew out a big breath.

Argent frowned. Witnessing Julie finally break down to let Tomás fully back into her life showed him how much a person could lock away. He'd done his share of keeping secrets and holding grudges, and he didn't want to do it anymore. "Don't say 'nothing.' You wouldn't let me get away with that answer when we spoke through our journals."

"I can tell now when you're shutting me out." She tapped her temple. "And while I don't want to be in your head all the time, I can't help but think that you're hiding something."

This was going to be harder than he thought. He knew the danger of poor communication—he'd watched as much between Emma and Luke during their quest to Valona. He just hadn't expected the same thing to happen between them.

And he didn't want to lie. That would instantly destroy the trust that already seemed to be weakening.

He described what he'd seen through the portal quietly and slowly. Bethany, still dressed in the half-destroyed coven armor she'd been wearing in Valona, had stood next to Igraine Pendragon.

As if allied.

"Portals aren't see-through," Emma said when he'd finished.

"I agree that I've never seen one like this before, but how else do you explain—"

"I don't know. Maybe it was a side effect of your dad and the Ancients using the Khozek. And besides, I was up in the crow's nest too. Why didn't I see them through the portal?"

"Were you even looking at it?" he asked, shoving down his rising irritation. "It happened a split second before the portal closed. We've all seen how fast the rogue ones disappear."

Emma scooted away from him and stood up, brushing the sand from her legs. Her face showed her skepticism.

"You don't believe me," Argent said softly, his heart sinking.

"You said yourself that you've never seen a see-through portal before. How convenient that the first one you see just happens to show Bethany working with the enemy." She said, voice scathing.

Argent's ire rose. "Yes, convenient that I saw something that now forces me to seriously consider implications that I did not want to!"

"And what's that?" Emma asked, putting her hands on her hips.

His mouth felt too dry, and he leaned his head back against the rock. "The same thing I brought up before the ship wrecked. If Bethany is being controlled by Igraine, we need a better plan than 'pluck her from Langoth with the Khozek and hope Igraine doesn't take the chance to escape.'"

Emma's hands curled into fists. "She would never—" She cut herself off, shocked. "Oh no!"

Argent scrambled to his feet and took her by the shoulders. "What? What's wrong?"

She grasped his wrists, terror clear on her face. "I can't feel my tie to Bethany anymore! She was there just a few days ago, but now I can't tell if she's dead or if the connection has just failed!"

Argent cupped her chin, forcing her to look up at him. Her bright cobalt eyes were wild with fear. "If I really did see her through the portal just yesterday, then assume she's alive."

She took several deep breaths, then pressed her forehead against his. "What if we don't get there in time?"

Argent was torn. For Emma's sake, he didn't want to purposely lock Bethany out of their world. But he also didn't want to face Igraine in combat. Every hour they spent rebuilding the ship was another moment for Igraine to claw her way back through. "Then our only choice is to let Luke's victorious Prophecy unfold. Even if it costs us."

"A Prophecy that didn't show Bethany anywhere on the battlefield," Emma said. "We have to get there before Igraine does."

Three days later, Argent asked his father to go hunting with him. He'd brooded over the growing rift between him and Emma about Bethany, Luke wanting to use the Khozek to fix the broken steering, and his own fear of the object drawing in the Nephilim like moths to a flame.

It also didn't help that if they used the Khozek, and finished the repairs in time, Argent would have to make a choice he really did not want to make.

Now, more than ever, he needed his father's advice.

They scouted a mile past the constant stream of men and witches cutting timber to levitate back to the dry dock. They mostly travelled in silence, quietly passing through the trees. The farther they got from the ocean, the more

Argent felt his mood improve. Even the occasional empty portal opening and closing didn't bother him.

"Do you hear that?" his father asked, finally breaking the comfortable silence between them.

Argent cocked his head and focused. He could just barely make out the sound of a waterfall. "Is that Sapphire Falls?"

"Let's find out." Aragon took the lead, weaving through the trees until they came to the edge of a deep canyon.

To their right, crystal blue water thundered five hundred feet to the bottom of the cleft, churning up clouds of mist. Hardy shrubs clung to the sides of the waterfall, and bright green moss crept over the wet rocks.

A gentle breeze wafted mist from the falls across their faces, and Argent closed his eyes, enjoying it.

"You have never asked me to do this with you before, so I suspect you had an ulterior motive," the King said. "What is bothering you, my son?"

A surge of unexpected gratitude welled up in Argent's chest. "I don't remember much from before the war... but I don't remember you ever asking me that."

The King opened his mouth as if to reply that *of course* he'd asked that question before, but he closed it again, saying nothing. He gestured for Argent to continue, both eyes fixed on his son rather than on the beauty of the waterfall.

Argent breathed deeply, savoring the clean, fresh scent of the forest mixed with the water pounding against the rocks below. He shared that he'd seen Bethany standing with Igraine in the moments before the portal closed, as well as the fact that Emma was set on enacting Mountains' plan unaltered.

"I agree that Bethany being the end of the Earthly Pendragon line is a moot point," he said, leaning against the trunk of a nearby tree. The edge of the unstrung Elvara Bow dug into his shoulder blade. "But I can't get Emma to see that Igraine is a far greater danger."

"You may never get her to see it your way," Aragon said with a sigh. "There are things on which you will never see eye-to-eye. Such things are both the curse and delight of being in a relationship with the woman you love."

"But this is about the fate of the world!" Argent's frustration spilled over.

"Against the fate of her best friend," Aragon reminded him. "And even so, I cannot change my position."

Argent deflated. It was the same argument Emma had used after saving him from the Nephilim. "Bethany's absence in the Prophets' Visions has convinced her that the only way to save Bethany's life is to use the Khozek as Mountains intends."

"From what I understand of Tomás's past prophecies, someone's absence in a Vision is not a guarantee that they are not present in how it unfolds," Aragon said softly.

"Then why did we leave Renault behind?" Argent asked, confused.

King Aragon gave him a half-smile and faced the waterfall. The sun neared noon, and the cloud cover had parted enough for the rays of light to create rainbows through the mist.

"Because someone must protect Camelot. Your mother is a formidable witch, yes, but Renault is half Olis. His power and affinity for the dragons is the city's first and last defense. I was relieved that Luke did not See him in his Vision. And I am even more thankful now that he is able to protect your mother and the new child."

Argent pushed away from the tree and walked past his father, unable to keep still. They should circle back soon if they wanted to find game and carry it back before nightfall. "Then the solution is to face Luke's Prophecy, not attempt to thwart fate," he said, stepping carefully away from the drop-off and back into the trees.

"We should still try to make it there as quickly as possible," Aragon disagreed, following him. "I know you don't want us to use the Khozek, even if it's just for the steering issue—"

"Ignoring prophecy leads to disaster," Argent interrupted. "And as Luke will tell you, trying to change it makes it worse. What if Atlas *had* taken me back in Keldvaar?" He unsheathed the bow, holding it up for his father to see the intricate carvings along its entire length. They glowed a pale blue, their ancient enchantments still as strong as the day Sargateth shot Atlas with it. "He would know we had this and do everything in his power to obtain it. And that means that I would have been pitted against you on the battlefield."

His father was quiet as they walked through the forest. The sun slipped back behind the clouds, and their surroundings darkened.

But Argent's mind kept turning. He thought back to his suspicion that the Khozek was now like a homing beacon. "If we use it and it draws the Nephilim to us, what is our defense? I can sense them, yes, but I would be powerless against Atlas taking me as his next host."

Aragon grabbed his arm and made him turn around. His face was sharp and fierce, his gray eyes flashing. "I'd become Atlas's host before I'd let him take you."

"Don't say that! You don't know what that means," Argent retorted, seizing his father's forearms. The edges of

Aragon's bracers dug into his hands. "You do not want to know that pain."

"It was my fault Septim took you," his father said with fervor. "My fault that I did not see the change he wrought in you. *My fault* that you lost six years of your childhood—and I lost my chance to truly know you as my son."

A lump rose in Argent's throat. "What about the Ancients? Atlas would control them."

"I would pass their oaths to you first," his father insisted.

Stunned, Argent's mouth fell open.

"Facing Igraine in open combat, even if it tips toward Luke's version of the Prophecy, is still a far worse outcome than if we can make it to the Scepter before she arrives. If using the Khozek draws Atlas to us, I say let him come. I would give you the crown and offer myself in your place."

"He wants a man who can do magic," Argent said, his throat dry. "He would force you through the Blacksoul Rituals."

Aragon took Argent's face in both hands. "You are not listening to me, my son. I do not care what pain I may endure if it means ultimate victory over Igraine and Atlas. I failed in my duty as your father to protect you from Septim. I will not fail you again."

Now that Argent had agreed to use the Khozek on the steering mechanism, the ship's rebuilding leaped forward. With that out of the way, they were freed up to tackle the major damage, including patching the hull and crafting a new main mast.

The first tense moment came when one of the lookouts spotted a ship in the distance, but it continued north without incident. Afterward, Luke raised a massive illusion in front of the beach, hiding them from sight.

When the second ship sailed past, William reminded them that the Helcari shipping channels continued this far north. Still they kept watch, even though none of the vessels got close enough for them to identify their colors.

Despite the precautions, Argent couldn't shake the feeling that the Nephilim would show up at any moment.

The Children of Sapphire Falls proved eager to help them with every additional need—for a price. Argent wondered just how much they were spending, but it wasn't as though they had a choice.

A fortnight after the wreck, everyone gathered around the two deer roasting over a large bonfire, and William wheedled Cordelia into sharing a single bottle of her precious honeywine. She claimed a whole one for herself while the other made the rounds.

The ship was almost finished. Emma and Luke told Argent that they could probably set sail in the next couple of days, and he itched to feel the sway of the deck beneath his feet again.

Argent had just taken a swig and handed the bottle to Emma when Sami and Oren approached from the cliffs. The warriors Runi and Nico hovered behind them.

"Forgive our intrusion," Sami said with a bow. "The last half-cycle of the moons has passed quickly, and you will be ready to depart soon."

Sargateth and Morgan got to their feet, casting a glance at Mountains, who eyed the remainder of the second deer's carcass. He'd largely stayed out of the way during this unexpected interlude, but he never passed up an opportunity to insult someone.

"Great power is gathered here," Sami continued, her voice barely audible over the crackle of the fire. The crew fell silent. "The Olii have not graced these shores for many years, and now three gather on a mysterious journey north. You did not expect to stop here, let alone like this, yes?"

A strangled laugh escaped the eldest Olis.

"Your destination is past the Northern Reaches; else you could have journeyed on foot."

Argent's heart rate picked up. He strained to sense any Nephilim, but they were still free of the demons.

"Perga's Scepter," Sargateth answered, catching everyone off guard. Argent hadn't expected the Archmage to be truthful.

Surprise passed through the two leaders. They each made strange gestures with their right hands as if to ward off danger.

"What is it?" King Aragon asked, getting to his feet.

"You do not know? You set your faces toward the Scepter but—"

"But the Scepter is far, and the stories travel by mouth, not bird," Oren interrupted. "You speak like you are from the west. Far you have traveled thus, and you have leagues yet to go. But the Scepter is a place of death and despair."

"Have you a guide?" Sami asked, waving at her partner to be quiet.

Cordelia's maps were old, but they had nothing else. Sargateth shook his head.

Sami tsked. "If you want to survive the Dragontooth Caverns, you need living memory."

Argent recalled seeing the caverns marked at the northern tip of the Scepter on Cordelia's navigational maps, but he hadn't realized they'd need to go *through* them.

"What are those?" Luke asked.

"The only entry point to the top of Perga's Scepter from the north," Sami explained, one hand curled around her staff. The other was hooked through the crook of Oren's arm. "If your destination is the Titan's Obelisk and the ruins of the Jade Temple, the caverns are your only option."

Cordelia got to her feet. The conversation seemed to have revived her snark. "And how do you know any of this? No one has set foot on Perga's Scepter for a thousand years."

Sami cocked her head at Cordelia. "Tales told to keep the captains away."

"People still live there?"

"Live there? Never. One need not put roots into the land in order to cross it, or hunt. Or pay homage to the dead."

Sargateth frowned. "Does anyone from your tribe have experience of the Scepter?"

At this, Sami hesitated, her eyes darting to Oren. She tipped her head. "One does."

"And what is your price for such a guide?" The bluntness of King Aragon's question startled them all.

Sami and Oren glanced at each other, silently deliberating. Then, Sami said, "An exchange. For Oren to lead you through the caverns, Julie Artair must stay behind."

"Absolutely not," Tomás immediately answered, struggling to his feet on the shifting sand.

Julie stood with him, resting a hand on his shoulder. "Tom, if that's the price—"

"I don't care," he said, seizing her hand and threading their fingers together. "I won't be parted from you again."

The King cleared his throat. "Is there another option?"

"No," Sami said. "That is our price. Bring my husband home safely, and we will return Julie to you in equal manner."

Argent's heart sank. Next to him, Emma dug her fingers into the top of his thigh.

"Jewel, no," Tom whispered, this time more quietly.

"There's no use fighting it," Julie answered. She leaned in and kissed his cheek before moving around the log to present herself to Sami.

"Mom?" Luke and Emma said together, both of them taking steps toward her.

Tomás finally caught up to his wife, struggling with the sand, his stiff legs, and the exoskeleton. "Jewel, you don't have to do this."

Argent wanted to look away but couldn't.

Julie grasped her husband's hand so tightly their fingers turned white. She looked around at Sargateth, her children, the King, and even at Argent. "I know why it has to be me. There's not a soul from *The Sea Wolf* besides me who won't play some key part up there or on the ship."

Argent couldn't help but admire her fortitude against such authority.

"I don't want to lose you," Tomás said.

"On that, we agree. But if the way there isn't as easy as you think, you'll never make it."

Argent looked away when Julie leaned in to kiss her husband, who looked at a loss for words.

"Take a journal," Tomás croaked. "Write to me every day."

Argent could sense the unspoken *to let me know you're still alive.*

"Of course."

Sami cleared her throat. The fire crackled—the only other sound in the night. The crew of *The Sea Wolf* looked somber in light of what amounted to a hostage exchange.

Julie faced the elders of the Children of Sapphire Falls. "I will remain with your tribe in exchange for Oren's guidance to the Scepter until they return."

CHAPTER EIGHTEEN

# THE DRAGONTOOTH CAVERNS

Light snow fell as the last slip of Ekranom faded from view, the northern chill deepening with each passing league. Emma wrapped herself and Argent in warming charms, but even with the thick winter furs they wore to abate the wind, it didn't seem strong enough. Ice had begun coating the railings, and the airwitches had to constantly shake out the sails.

Here, Emma felt magic in the air itself. It raised her hackles, especially after the close call in Keldvaar.

They'd lost so much time to that rogue portal. She hated almost every minute spent on the beach, not just because she didn't like sand in every crevice, but because she couldn't stop worrying that a ship would appear on the horizon with pursuers from Keldvaar. The implications of what it might mean for their return if none came worried her even more. On top of that, she worried that another portal would appear without warning, ruin all their hard work, and make them miss their window to save Bethany.

The decision to not continue teleporting jumps and instead rely on a constant rotation of airwitches pushing them at top speed compounded her fears further.

They'd sacrificed speed for guaranteeing the ship would make it intact, and now Emma wondered if that had been the right choice.

The one bright spot was that her parents finally made up and behaved like normal married humans again... even though they'd been separated once more.

While the Khozek had certainly helped repair the ship's steering, Emma had watched Argent's nerves fray every time a ship came within sight of the beach.

If Atlas really had been in that first ship following them, why let Argent go at all?

The airwitches pushed *The Sea Wolf* through increasingly choppy waters, now laced with chunks of ice.

At last, the Scepter's coast unfurled along the starboard side of the ship. Cordelia's cracked and yellowing charts would have had them navigate to the cave opening yawning in the distance, but Oren had crossed out that location on the map with messy ink strokes.

Emma kept her eyes on the cliffs looming in the distance. Her mind flashed back to the sight of her mother and Bethany kneeling beside Igraine with ropes around their necks deep beneath Valona.

Part of her was thankful that her mom had stayed behind in Sapphire Falls.

A headwind had exhausted the airwitches, and Emma and Cordelia helped when the gusts became too strong.

Emma's gloved hand found Argent's as they stood on the new wood of the repaired prow. He gave her palm a squeeze, but she felt wary rather than comforted.

He'd blocked her out of his head again.

They stood together in silence for a moment, and Argent planted a kiss on her head and then left. She watched him navigate the rolling deck with ease to go talk to his father. While she was glad that the relationship between the King and Prince was miles better than it had been mere months ago, she had a bad feeling—one that had nothing to do with the possible Nephilim on their tail.

"You ready?" Luke asked, coming up next to her. He must have waited for Argent to leave.

It made her wonder if he sensed it, too.

Emma studied her brother. The months without Bethany had weighed on him, and he had new worry lines across his forehead, his beard grown out to the point he looked like their father. But his eyes were bright with anticipation.

"No," she answered honestly but quietly. She wondered if her voice had gotten lost in the wind when he didn't reassure her. "What if we're too late?"

Luke draped his arm over her shoulders, and she leaned into him, reminded of when he'd protected her as a child. "I think we'd know if we were too late. Besides, Bethie is a witch of Renova. A fighter with your blood running through her veins. If anyone has to be worried, it's Igraine."

He sounded so sure of himself, but when Emma turned her head to look up at him, she saw his tight jaw and the furrow of his brow.

"There's no other option."

Emma breathed deep, the frigid air almost numbing her throat. She let it out slowly through her nostrils. The closer they drew to Perga's Scepter, and the farther they sailed from Sapphire Falls, the worse Emma's anxieties became.

And now, if they wanted to reach the Jade Temple ruins where the Titan Obelisk was, they had to trust an old man who had not seen this side of the world for decades. Only Oren could lead them through the treacherous Dragontooth Caverns.

But first they had to find the correct entrance.

Emma's adrenaline rose the moment Oren pointed out the craggy outcrop hiding the caverns. The crew worked in a frenzy to prepare for the landing party. The high winds and the wild waters meant they couldn't get as close to the entrance as they would have liked. Nor could they spare as many of *The Sea Wolf*'s witches as originally planned.

Cordelia shepherded them into a longboat, insisting on going with them to the battlefield.

When William let the longboat down, he saluted. "Give 'em peril!"

Emma couldn't believe that ten humans and three Olii had fit, especially since Mountains was in his true form, still refusing to "debase" himself. The presence of the witches on board helped steady the passage across the rough waters and toward the hidden entrance that Emma was surprised Oren could even see.

But even as the prow of the longboat bumped against the high ledge that formed the mouth of the secret entrance, Emma couldn't relax. In silence, she scrambled onto the rock, peering around sharp edges that reminded her of the lava tunnels beneath Renova and Ralador. She hoped there weren't any magical traps in these dark caves.

"How far to the top?" Luke asked Oren, pointing into the darkness as the rest of the crew scrambled out of the boat. Cordelia lashed a rope around a rock, knotting it so they wouldn't become stranded.

Oren raised two gnarled hands, holding them about three inches apart. "We have come this far, yes?" He looked around, nodding at the boat and then the ship riding the waves. It had been at least a quarter of a mile to the cave, if not more. Oren stretched his arms out as wide as he could. "The broken temple is far enough away that we'll spend a night inside the darkness, yes. Oh, to be one who can fly."

Argent took a few steps into the blackness and stopped, his face paling.

"We're not alone," he said, his voice echoing. "Nephilim are here."

Argent told Emma that he could sense the Nephilim at the very edge of his awareness, but never close enough to see—if indeed they were embodied.

None of them knew what to do if confronted with a disembodied spirit, and when Emma asked the obvious question out loud, it was Oren who answered.

"In my distress, I call upon the Lord without ceasing. He delivers me from all troubles, yes?"

Emma didn't find that practical, but it made her think more when Luke started muttering memorized Bible verses under his breath.

After Valona, Emma could do without sleeping in enclosed spaces. They had reached the cavern's mouth at midday, despite the sun hiding behind the clouds, and had spent hours making slow progress through the pitch-black caverns. They navigated winding ledges cut by stalactites and stalagmites, and the slimy, slippery ground that offered an easy fall to certain death.

Leading the group, Oren guided them while Argent looked out for demons, the Elvara Bow strung and ready to go.

The twists and turns took them higher and deeper into the caverns. Emma and a few of the other witches cast balls of light to lead them, but Oren set their pace. No one spoke for fear of losing their concentration, and the only sounds were their breaths, the measured footsteps, and the creak of Tomás's exoskeleton.

At least Mountains could walk on his own, though he kept to the rear of their single-file line. Luke had told her that he wouldn't risk sapping his magic to carry the obstinate Olis, not that Mountains even tolerate such humiliation.

Everyone stopped moving, and Emma tensed carefully behind Oren and Argent to avoid slipping over the edge.

"What's wrong?" Luke's voice rang out from the middle of the line.

"Nephilim," Argent whispered, but Emma was sure everyone heard him. "Blocking the way ahead. They're not moving like they have been."

In the eerie silence that followed, Emma's heart rate ratcheted up, and dread passed through them all.

"Oren, do you know a different way to the top?"

Oren wrung his hands together. He could have been mistaken for a frightened rabbit. "Perhaps, perhaps," he said, his voice trembling. "It was many sets of tens ago, yes? I was a much younger man then, with brighter eyes. Double back, double back. Another path through the dragon's gullet, yes?"

Everyone plastered themselves against the jagged wall as the elderly but spritely tribesman shuffled past. Emma and Argent both followed, needing to stay near the front to create light and danger-sense.

"We cannot waste much more time," Sargateth muttered softly, but the sound traveled in the tunnel. He carried the Khozek's chest, while Morgan guarded the key.

"What is waste?" Oren replied. "Time is never wasted; it only passes, yes?"

The old man's constant questions at the end of his statements grated on Emma's nerves, even though it seemed a hallmark of his tribe—or perhaps of the Ekranom peoples.

"The sooner we can reach the temple, the better chance we have," Morgan said stiffly from the rear.

*A better chance for what?* Emma wanted to ask, but she dared not. She slowed down, focusing on the ground. Each step felt more treacherous than the last, since going downhill on slippery limescale was a lot harder than going up.

More than once, she almost went over the edge, finding her balance at the last second.

Oren led them back the way they'd come for at least an hour. Then, on a thin ledge with a bulge in the middle, the elderly guide slipped into a hidden offshoot that none of them had noticed on the way up.

"Ah, here is the wily throat!" Oren shouted from inside. His voice echoed loudly, and Emma slapped both hands over her ears. She could've sworn the cavern shook a bit.

"Quiet!" Mountains hissed. "Or you'll bring the whole wretched island down on us!"

Oren ignored him. "Not far now, not far now at all until we can rest our heads, yes?"

Despite her dislike for the old man, Emma looked forward to a good night's sleep. Though she suspected it wouldn't be as good as she hoped, considering what they'd face come morning.

And what could sneak up on them in the night.

"Are we being followed?" she muttered to Argent as they followed Oren up the narrow shaft. "Or hemmed in?"

"Hard to say," Argent whispered back. "It's like they've been leading us further up and further in but didn't want us to go the way Oren took us. If Oren didn't know a second path through, we'd be stuck. Or worse, have to face them." He was silent for a few seconds. "There's nothing in front of us now, but this whole cavern could be seething with them."

The first hint of Perga's Scepter's topside was the gust of freezing air that whistled through the tunnel.

"Close, yes, quite close," Oren muttered from the front, his words carrying back on the wind.

Emma adjusted her cloak, wrapping it tighter around her shoulders. She risked using a tiny bit of warming magic to keep the bite out. Her adrenaline hadn't let her get much sleep, and she kept conjuring images of what awaited them at the Jade Temple. Underneath her anxiety was a stark sense of dread that no matter what happened, not all of them would come back alive.

Hewn stone steps led them out of the Dragontooth Caverns and into a white wasteland. Emma had to shield her eyes for several moments while she adjusted to the brightness. A wide trail cut through tall, snow-dusted pines, and the only sounds were the ones made by their group. If any wildlife lived here, they knew when to disappear.

Sargateth, Morgan, and Cordelia staked a perimeter, however short-lived it might be, while the rest of them took a moment to rest and regroup. Oren laid down his pack on the steps leading down to the cavern's entrance. He would stay there and wait, since he couldn't help and might hurt their efforts against Igraine.

Emma hoped the Nephilim wouldn't bother him.

An ugly thought presented itself. *If Oren dies, what happens to Mom?*

Mountains sat on his haunches down the trail, his ears twitching every time a snowflake landed on his head. His great, long tail swept back and forth across the ground, brushing away snow until gray-brown permafrost appeared.

Emma watched the cranky Olis. She wondered what he must be thinking about the possibly of facing down the woman who had held him captive for a century.

*If I were him, I'd be plotting how to tear out her throat.*

Sargateth and Luke rounded everyone up before Emma could say anything to Mountains, and after Argent strung his bow, they were off again. Evie, Cara, and Dakota scouted ahead.

Walking through the thick snow was almost as difficult as navigating the slippery slopes of the caverns, and it made their progress slow. No one spoke as they walked, not wanting to be the one to give away their position.

Nearly an hour after they emerged from the caverns, Dakota returned alone, breathing hard, her face red from the cold. "We heard voices," she gasped, doubling over.

Morgan hovered, fussing over her witch.

"Evie and Cara stayed to get a better look."

Emma's heart thundered as she fought the urge to run past them to see for herself if they were too late—if Bethany was still alive. Argent's gloved hand found her shoulder, and she forced herself to breathe. She already knew what they had to do. Oren had sketched out a rough diagram of the temple ruins, including which sides sat closest to the cavern entrance and where the Titan Obelisk stood. They'd have plenty of cover from the broken stones and the overgrowth that had reclaimed the grounds in the last millennia.

Everyone slowed down, crouching to follow Dakota the further she led them. Emma wrapped them all in her invisibility spell, silencing their footsteps at the same time. It wouldn't do to give themselves away now, not when they were so close.

Around the next curve of the trail, Evie and Cara squatted like cats behind a massive stone block that had been blasted off its foundation. Emma covered them with her invisibility spell, and they relaxed, finally getting a look at the playing field.

An obelisk twice as large as any of the ones she'd seen sat in the center of an open space. Only three weathered gray pillars still stood, marking the corners of the original temple design. Cracked slabs that had once served as the ceiling littered the temple grounds, providing far too much cover for their enemies.

Voices drifted from across the littered courtyard where ten agitated Olii sat on their haunches.

The Night's Empress was nowhere in sight.

# CHAPTER NINETEEN
# THE KHOZEK

Luke and Emma had discussed this moment for months. What would happen when they finally reached the Scepter? When they either found Igraine waiting for them or seized the opportunity to lock her out of this world forever?

What they *hadn't* considered was Igraine's absence in the presence of the Olii. Luke, like his father, had assumed that they'd show up together, and it added another worry to Luke's already overburdened psyche.

Mountains maintained that they could extract Bethany first, but Luke did not trust King Aragon or the Archmage any longer. He had his suspicions about the Prince as well, even though Emma seemed to trust him. Everything pointed to them choosing to condemn Bethie to Langoth so they'd never have to face Igraine.

Luke wished he'd been the one carrying the Khozek, but King Aragon had taken it from Sargateth before Luke had the chance. The King held one end of the Khozek's chest, and Prince Argent supported the other.

Luke knew what that meant.

Relieved not to see Igraine, but now doubly worried about what it would take to rescue Bethany, Luke edged toward his ruler. The continually falling snow had created a pristine blanket over the entire courtyard, but as Luke moved closer, his feet slid on ice hidden underneath.

"They're here," Argent muttered under his breath to the King. "I don't know where, but multiple Nephilim are definitely here."

Luke filed that information away, more concerned now about how to get his hands on the Khozek. Every delay ratcheted up his anxiety, the gnawing in his gut, and the feeling that his heart had been permanently torn from his chest.

Preparing to meet the ten Olii, Emma dropped her invisibility spell.

"Brothers and sisters, we meet at the pinnacle of prophecy," Sargateth said, his voice loud across the still ruins.

The Olii turned their attention to the tree line, their ears twitching. Sargateth strode into view, only slipping a little in his human form. Slowly, the rest of their delegation followed, each person on guard.

"Where is your so-called empress, Firstborn?" Eternal Winds snapped. He shifted on his haunches, and Luke hoped his butt had frozen. "We've been here for days now with nary a portal."

*What about the Nephilim? Haven't they—OH. Sargateth didn't tell them. He sent the hawk to Renault! The Olii don't know the Nephilim are out! Why haven't they revealed themselves?*

Mountains dragged himself forward. The brief respite in Skypoint had done wonders for the Olis, as had the unexpected stop at Sapphire Falls, but the rest of the journey had undone it all. He sat right in front of the Titan Obelisk that jutted conspicuously from the ruins, his thick tail wrapping around the base.

"You're all such fools," he said, sounding far more pleased than he had since they'd left Julie on the shores of Sapphire Falls. He met Luke's eyes and then Emma's, as if sensing their anticipation to execute his plan. "This is our best and only chance to secure Talahm from becoming a dominion of ash."

Eternal Winds rose to all four paws and stretched out his wings before folding them back against his body. Three others did the same before they all padded across the snowy grounds.

"The humans have already made this a wasteland," *Forever in a Day's First Hour* muttered, flicking her tail in agitation. "A kingdom of ash would at least clean it up."

Luke watched King Aragon tense.

Argent's eyes darted between the obelisk and Emma, and his free hand kept flexing open and closed.

Luke narrowed his eyes.

*What if Argent lied about the Nephilim? What if he and his father got possessed at Sapphire Falls during one of their hunts?*

"No portals?" Sargateth repeated, his uncertainty audible. "Not even rogue ones?"

"Not here, of course," *Sharpest Edge of Diamond Skies* answered, licking one paw to wash his fluffy ear. "Or did you forget that this place is where the first gates were established?"

Sargateth ran a hand through his hair, a nervous habit Luke had picked up on over the years. The Archmage glanced toward King Aragon.

"Let's not waste time, then," the King called out, walking forward with the chest still hanging between him and Argent. Sargateth followed. "With the Khozek, we can prevent bloodshed."

Luke's stomach dropped, his heart galloping, and he stepped into the King's path. "Sire," he said in the sharpest voice he'd ever used, "we have to save Bethany first."

King Aragon didn't look at him, stepping around Luke like he wasn't even there. The ice beneath the snow did nothing to impede him.

"Argent?" Emma called out uncertainly, and the Prince's shoulders tensed.

But Luke had had enough. He chased the King, Prince, and Archmage, running fast enough to place himself in their way. He generated a thick golden shield, planting his back heel so it packed the snow against the ice. "I will not let you sentence Bethany to death." Luke kept his voice firm, unyielding. He tried not to let his desperation for Bethie bleed through.

"Luke," the King started, taking a long breath. "Move out of the way. I cannot risk the rest of this world for Bethany. Yes, she will be a casualty, and I'm sorry about it—"

"I don't answer to tyrants." Luke didn't move. He didn't take his eyes off the King. Not even when Emma crept into his peripheral vision, her hands out and ready to call on her magic.

"Tyrant?" King Aragon repeated slowly, staring Luke straight in the eye. "For wanting to protect the entirety of Talahm *and* Earth, your homeland, from Igraine's ruinous plans?"

"Prove you're not controlled by Atlas, then," Luke snapped, not caring if he was wrong.

King Aragon stared at him and then glanced briefly at Argent.

"I'd know if he was near enough to take anyone," Argent answered, sounding like he fully believed it.

Luke felt Emma's mind touch his, and he immediately welcomed her in.

*He wouldn't lie about the Nephilim*, she insisted, but Luke wasn't so sure.

"I can't let you do this either," Emma said from behind the King.

Aragon whirled around, dropping his handle of the chest to grasp the hilt of his sword. Argent let go as well but stayed next to his father, his left hand tightening over the yoke of the Elvara Bow.

Emma's disbelief washed over Luke like a flood. "Argent, what are you doing? I thought we were in this together! To save Bethany!"

"I didn't want it to come to this, but I have to protect the many." The pain in Argent's voice sounded real, but Luke didn't believe him.

Emma's cheeks flushed, her anger hot in Luke's head. She walked past Argent and the King with her fists clenched, standing next to Luke behind his shield. Argent kept his bow held low.

The phantom pain of Amity's dagger stung in Luke's chest, as well as the crushing in his throat as the King strangled him.... His breath picked up. "This isn't a dream," he said to himself. "I knew they all meant something," he said louder, drawing attention. Behind the royals, Tomás inched toward the chest containing the Khozek. "I should have known you'd betray us," Luke accused Argent. His shield flared bright gold with the upsurge of his emotions. "This isn't about stopping Igraine at all—you just want to keep your throne safe!"

Tomás's exoskeleton creaked a little too loudly, and Aragon whirled around, fully drawing Excalibur before he registered who he was drawing upon. "You too, Tomás?" he said, sounding betrayed himself.

Tomás held both hands up in a placating gesture and retreated through Luke's magic. "Bethany shares my daughter's blood, and as far as I'm concerned, that makes her one of my children. I'm done putting my family second."

The harrowing realization that the Khozek was vulnerable to those who meant to leave Bethany for dead chased away Luke's internal fist pump.

*Connect Dad, pronto,* Luke told Emma.

*Already here, son,* Tomás answered.

His father's calm mental voice smoothed the edges of Luke's fear. *We have to get the Khozek.*

As if sensing his desperation, the chest rattled.

Behind the King and Prince, Sargateth looked like he would rather be anywhere else, but the chest rattling on the ground caught his attention. He frowned at it, glancing up at King Aragon and then at Luke. Without warning, he turned to his sister, who tossed him the key. He snatched it effortlessly from the air.

"I cannot waste any more time arguing why this must happen," King Aragon said with a tinge of disappointment. He put his sword back in its sheath and started to pick up the chest.

Beside him, Luke felt Emma's magic spark. He extended his shield on both sides, catching sight of Cordelia walking toward the rest of the Olii, who watched the events unfold like a grand show.

"Sargateth, seal the obelisk," King Aragon commanded, his eyes wide with fear in the face of Emma's magic.

Emma jumped back across the shield and clapped her hands together. A crackling ball of magic burst to life between them.

King Aragon and Argent both dropped the chest again. The King moved like lightning, drawing Excalibur and opening the mechanical shield built into his bracer. Argent nocked a regular arrow, leaving the Elvara arrows in the quiver, but he looked very much like he did not want to point it at anyone.

Before Sargateth could snatch the chest, Emma showered him with direct hits that he either absorbed or deflected with his own hastily erected shield. Emma drove him back, away from the Khozek.

"Don't think you can stay neutral, Morgan!" King Aragon said, glancing over his shoulder. "You have just as much duty to keep your former apprentice from these lands!"

Luke winced at the low blow. He considered dropping the shield for a chance to cross swords with the King himself.

"Your Majesty—"

"Do not let your next words be an excuse, Morgan," the King interrupted in a soft, dangerous voice. "Break this shield into oblivion."

Behind the Grand Mage, Evie, Cara, and Dakota all looked like they didn't know what to do. Their loyalty was to the King and the Coven, like all Royal Covens, but Luke had heard their conversations on the ship about how much they wanted Bethany back.

Morgan reluctantly approached, one hand filling with bright purple magic and the amethyst of her staff starting to glow like Emma's had once before it exploded. Luke's heart rate ramped up.

Right before the magic hit, Luke sensed his father's magic joining his, and the shield flared but didn't break. His heel pressed deep into the snow, sliding a little on a layer of ice beneath.

"Again!"

*If you're going to help against Morgan too, now would be a great time,* Luke frantically sent to his sister.

*He told her to break the shield, not to hurt us! Do you want that order to change?*

Morgan lifted her staff and swung it against the shield a second time. The force sent Luke to one knee, cracks spidering through his magic even with his father's support. This wasn't the training grounds of Camelot anymore, and Morgan's strength was at least twice Renault's.

"Why are none of you helping?" Emma yelled at the Olii, four of them protected by Luke's dying shield. She continued attacking Sargateth, but Luke knew if the King ordered him to fight back, Emma would not have it so easy.

"The petty squabbles of humans are beneath us," Eternal Winds replied, sounding bored. At the edge of the temple ruins, the remaining six Olii had settled into more comfortable positions, one of them climbing onto the nearest broken pillar and stretching out both wings to drape over the sides.

Cordelia sat in front of the columns, using one as a backrest as she wrestled the cork out of her honeywine.

Mountains snarled. "This isn't a petty squabble, you buffoon. If they fight amongst themselves long enough, it will give Igraine the chance to subjugate us all."

Luke heard yawns and gritted his teeth. One more blow would break him.

Argent's eyes stayed on Emma, but his bow and arrow remained pointed at the ground. The fact that he hadn't taken the chance to claim the Khozek for himself confused Luke, but he didn't have time to dwell on it.

"Morgan, finish it!" King Aragon commanded, his gray eyes flashing.

*Fight when it falls,* Luke blasted in his mind.

*I'll take the King,* his father thought firmly. *You get the Khozek.*

Luke abruptly released his magic, and the incoming swing of Morgan's staff whistled through empty air. She overcompensated, spinning all the way around, her arms pinwheeling for a moment as she lost balance. She slipped on the ice beneath the snow and fell hard to the ground.

Tomás crossed blades with the King, pushing him away from the chest. He moved slowly, stiffly, but his skill with the sword was enough to match the King's hesitance to truly fight a man he claimed to call a brother.

Luke rushed forward, tackling Argent. The Elvara Bow skittered across the ground, and all of the arrows fell out of Argent's quiver.

Sargateth blasted Emma backward, leaping into the air and fluidly transforming into his Olis form. He soared over the skirmishes and pounced on the chest. Then he lifted off again, the Khozek's container dangling from his front paws. He landed in a roll just feet from the Titan Obelisk, scattering the Olii lounging around it.

Luke scrambled to his feet and abandoned the fight with Argent, trying to chase after the Archmage. His feet skated unexpectedly across more ice.

Emma fought Morgan, who blocked her path across the field. "Aren't you going to help us?" Emma yelled at the three coven witches, but none of them moved.

The expression on Evie's face could only be described as sorrowful.

Luke lifted both of his hands as he approached Sargateth, but he had no idea what to do. The sounds of magic clashing made it hard for him to hear anything else.

The Archmage changed back into his human form, his hands shaking as he unlocked the chest. He lifted the lid and took hold of the Khozek. It had the same coloring and undulating patterns as the ceiling of the Impossible Room—the Sal Dorhana, where both Sargateth and Morgan had been created at the dawn of time.

"This was not the deal," Mountains protested, his tail tightening around the bottom of the obelisk. "I promised to bring Bethany through before attempting to close off Langoth!"

"I made no such agreement," King Aragon said from across the stones, his voice like flint as he defended against Tomás's blows. "I am here for one purpose only—to see that Igraine Pendragon can nevermore set foot on Talahmi soil, regardless of the cost. Sargateth... do it now."

"Don't!" Luke screamed, but he had no authority over the Ancients. "Stop! I can see you don't want to do this!"

The eldest Olii's shoulders shook, his face shining with sweat and a measure of regret in his eyes. "Move," he commanded the Olii, and they all scattered.

Luke abandoned all pretense, sprinting toward Sargateth. He tackled the Archmage, both of them rolling across the unforgiving flagstones. The Khozek clattered away from them.

Luke scrambled toward it, but he suddenly found himself immobilized. Sargateth walked past him, reaching down to collect the ancient amplifier.

Luke shouted until his throat felt raw.

Sargateth knelt before the obelisk, planting the Khozek at the base. In low tones, he chanted in his native tongue until black and blue lines sped from the Khozek to the obelisk, crawling up it until all the runes were encased. A single dark thread shot straight up from the tip of the Titan Obelisk, climbing twenty feet in the air. It stitched itself around the faint, remnant scars of past portals and hung there like an ugly suture.

Sargateth's shoulders drooped, and he rocked back on his heels, hanging his head. After a beat, he got to his feet and let out a furious cry, throwing a massive ball of plasma into the forest beyond the ruins. It hit multiple trees, sending up clouds of steam filled with the splintering echoes of broken timber.

Silence swept across the temple ruins, and Luke trembled in fury.

All this way, only to lose Bethany again....

Forever.

He let out a long, agonized wail. "What have you done?"

## CHAPTER TWENTY

# TICK TOCK, TICK TOCK

Two days after *The Sea Wolf*'s figurehead arrived unexpectedly in the Fifth Travelers' settlement, Igraine finally found the anchor point.

And not a moment too soon.

Bethany finished packing up another tent when a watcher ran into the courtyard and collapsed to his knees. "Wave—incoming—less than an hour—"

Ice poured through her nerves. *It's now or never.*

Kenna, now recovered after two full days of rest, hurried the stragglers from what remained of the camp. The wave's crest inched closer to the cliffs, this one several feet higher than the last. No one would be able to break its crash against the settlement.

Igraine led them inland to the place where the portal could connect to the only stable location on Talahm—the Titan Obelisk at Perga's Scepter.

They had one shot at this. Bethany's arm throbbed, an uncomfortable reminder of everything they'd been through to get to this point.

She didn't know what they would walk into once they wrenched open a portal. She didn't know who—if anyone—would be waiting for them when they emerged, and, above all, she didn't know what she would say to Emma.

She wished she still had the journal linked to Luke's. She wished she could write him a note to tell him they were alive and on their way. That she had some way to warn them that no matter what King Aragon told them, his only goal was to keep the throne. And even so, after everything, Bethany knew that Igraine would do anything to end the Pendragons—all of them—if given the chance.

Bethany and Kenna pushed through the crowd swelling around Igraine.

"It's time," the ancient witch said, jutting her chin to the sky where the red accretion disk hung ominously over the planet. She reached into the folds of her dress and withdrew the gaudy necklace with Mountains' severed claw. She beckoned to Bethany. "Wrap your hand around my wrist."

Despite knowing this was coming, Bethany shuddered. The very idea of sharing her powers with the woman who had imprisoned and tortured her—not just physically, but mentally—was abhorrent. Getting far too close to Igraine for comfort, Bethany took hold of Igraine's wrist. Behind them, the Emrys and the Fifth Travelers huddled together in a semicircle.

Igraine raised the claw high in the air, stretching their arms out. Bethany focused on channeling power into Igraine's hand, loath to admit the process was probably easier thanks to the fact that Igraine had stolen her blood in Valona. She felt the claw catch on the air, as if it had found a tiny aberration in the smooth fabric of space and time. Igraine capitalized on it, and a surge of energy poured out of them and into the claw. Igraine dragged it down, and the now familiar sound of a portal opening filling the air.

The scar pulsed with Bethany's heartbeat, somehow now in time with Igraine's.

One of the Fifth Travelers behind them made a strangled sound, and Bethany risked a glance over her shoulder. The wave had crashed against the cliffs, and Bethany belatedly realized the only reason they hadn't heard it was because sound had slowed. A few seconds later, the whoosh and crash of the wave reached them, causing more of the Fifth Travelers to crane their necks.

"Hurry!" Kenna urged, the whites of her eyes revealing her panic.

"Silence," Igraine wheezed, clearly taxed by the effort of creating the portal. Bethany felt drained too. When they reached the bottom of the tear, Igraine pulled the claw away. "Now comes the hard part," she panted.

"There's a harder part?" Bethany exclaimed, her heart speeding up as the water poured toward them, washing away the remnants of the settlement. It would reach them in moments.

"Dig your fingers into the center and open it," Igraine commanded.

The Night's Empress did the same with the Olis claw, wiggling its point into the void and yanking right while Bethany yanked left.

And it *burned*. Bethany suddenly understood the vast pain Igraine had suffered trying to keep herself from falling through—why the edges of portals were only meant for Olis claws to touch—but she forced herself to keep subjecting her skin to the cold fire of the open universe.

Tears pricked the corners of her eyes, the pain mounting to a crescendo. Igraine illuminated the portal like she had all the others, showing a quiet field of snow with a dark edge of trees in the distance.

"Go!" Igraine gasped to the people behind them.

Kenna urged her people through, and one by one, the collection of lost scouts jumped into the void, followed by the Emrys, Hela, Rissy, and Harlow. Kenna was the last to jump through, briefly touching Bethany's arm as she passed.

"You as well!" Igraine panted to Bethany. The Olis claw shook in her hand with the effort of holding their escape open.

Startled, Bethany let go of her side of the portal and squeezed through the gap just as the water from the massive ocean reached their feet.

After a brief sensation of falling, she landed in a crouch on the cold snow of Talahm, feeling lighter than she ever had in her life. A surge of magic filled her, evidence of how much the black hole had taken from not just her, but from every Fifth Traveler trapped there.

"Help me close it!" Igraine commanded as she stumbled through, twisting behind the portal and away from its increased gravity.

Bethany sprang to her feet and physically pushed on the other side of the portal's edge. Before it could completely close, a jet of water shot through the portal, drenching all the survivors in its path and washing away the snow to reveal old, pockmarked flagstones.

Inch by agonizing inch, the portal finally sealed, cutting off the stream. Bethany sagged, exhausted, but scanned the tree line for any sign of Luke or the others.

But there was nothing.

"Ah," Igraine said, sounding pleased but pained. "We're early."

The sound of crunching snow drew their attention, and Bethany called fire to her hand just in case. From the ethereal gloom at the edge of the forest, thirty men appeared, all of them wearing armor Bethany had never seen before.

"Good thing, too," an older man at the front said in a deep, sinister voice that made goosebumps erupt across Bethany's skin. He seemed unnaturally tall, and his skin stretched taut over his face, like there wasn't enough left to cover him. "Pendragon is on his way."

"Well then," Igraine replied, wrinkling her nose. "You certainly look like you need a new body before facing him. What happened to the one offered up on a silver platter?"

The cold started to re-freeze the ocean water that had seeped across the clearing. Thick flakes of snow stuck fast to the new ice, and Bethany sensed it wouldn't be long until the evidence of their arrival disappeared.

"I secured a much greater victory in the moment," the creepy old guy continued. The men with him looked ready for battle.

"You know him?" Bethany asked warily as Kenna began shepherding her people behind the long, broken pillars on the other side of the Titan Obelisk. Among them were Lincoln and Penny, both shell shocked.

"Cleopas Rhakmar, King of Keldvaar," Igraine said, sounding bored and annoyed at the same time. "Did you really let him slip through your fingers so easily?"

But before Rhakmar could answer, a steady *thumping* above the clouds made them all fall silent.

"Follow me," Rhakmar said sharply, striding past Igraine toward where Kenna had sequestered her people. His men marched after him. "I know a place we can hide until Pendragon catches up."

Bethany's heart thundered at the thought of facing the King after what Igraine had told her. Distracting herself, she made sure everyone was out of the clearing before she followed, concealing the rear of their strange group in magic.

Lincoln and Penny waited for her, their faces drawn as they held the thin blankets from Langoth around their shivering bodies. Bethany took one look at them and tapped their shoulders, giving them some warmth with her abilities.

The thumping grew louder, and Bethany hung back to find out what it was.

"Something tells me we walked into something just as bad as Langoth," Lincoln whispered, crouching behind the pillar.

"What are you doing?"

"Watching the skies. That is my profession, remember?"

Penny snort-laughed next to him, and Bethany let out an exasperated sigh. She sucked the breath back in when ten massive creatures descended, as large and fluffy as snow leopards. They landed with force, making the ruins shake.

"What are *those*?" Penny breathed in shock.

Stunned, Bethany watched as they stretched, their wings fluttering a few more times before retracting against their sides. Most of them sat on their haunches at the edge of the courtyard, but two chose to roll in the snow like dogs.

Bethany struggled to find her voice. "They're the Olii. Magic flying cats. I've met the ones you'd know as Merlin and Morgan Le Fay... but these must be the rest of them. And I have no idea why they're here."

She seized Penny's shoulder and shoved her away from the pillar, doing the same to Lincoln before forcing them to run with her after the retreating survivors.

As they ran, she cast as much concealing magic as she could. If the Olii were here for Igraine, they'd probably kill everyone with her.

Rhakmar led them into a large, boxy room deep within the destroyed temple complex. It already looked lived in, complete with crates of food, stacks of firewood, and a huge pile of folded blankets in the corner. An almost-dead fire in the center of the room had a ring of snow around it, and when Bethany looked up, she saw an opening in the stone ceiling to let the smoke out. Two of Rhakmar's soldiers tended to the embers, and the fire caught again.

"Guys, I counted ten Olii landing back there," Bethany said over the muttering among both the Fifth Travelers and Rhakmar's men.

Igraine whirled around. "Did they smell you?"

Bethany shook her head. "I don't think so. I covered our tracks with magic."

Igraine relaxed. "No need to worry about them for the time being, then. They can wait."

Rhakmar loomed over them, invading Igraine's personal space until she stepped back and glared up at him.

"Can I help you?" Igraine asked in the snarkiest voice Bethany had ever heard.

"You haven't forgotten what I taught you, have you?"

Igraine shoved his shoulder with her good hand and laughed. "On the contrary, my friend! I've *perfected* your Blacksoul Rituals. Are you worried they won't work on that twig Argent?"

Bethany froze, remembering what had happened between Igraine and the Prince back in Valona. Igraine had wanted him dead, and she'd tried to strangle him before Emma had zapped her with overpowered lightning.

Rhakmar chuckled. "He's not a twig. He's a sapling. And saplings can grow strong."

Bethany retreated slowly from the confrontation and over to the corner of the room where Lincoln and Penny huddled against the wall, looking just as scared as she felt. From the edges of the crowded room, Hela, Harlow, and Rissy crept over to Bethany and the Emrys.

"Do you know what this is about?" Hela asked, crouching next to Bethany. "Why would he want the Prince? I've never heard of Blacksoul Rituals before."

Bethany shook her head and shrugged, her arm protesting. Rissy laid a hand on her bicep to refresh the numbing.

"This body won't last much longer," Rhakmar said, his voice thin and raspy.

Igraine arched her eyebrow. "Hopefully you're not so deluded to think I can just wave my hand and complete the Rituals willy-nilly. You know it takes time, especially if he's not willing."

A wide, sinister grin stretched across Rhakmar's face. "I know just how to break him. I tricked his wench into taking down Raphael's shield in exchange for his soul... and the Khozek."

Igraine's eyes widened. "She released *all* of the Nephilim?"

Rhakmar laughed. "She caved the moment I threatened to take him. Who's to say he wouldn't do the same for her?"

Thoroughly confused now, Bethany listened with rapt attention in case she could make sense of it.

Beside her, Lincoln twitched violently, as if throwing something off his chest, but there was nothing there. He squeezed his eyes shut and started muttering under his breath, Penny's hands tight in his.

Rhakmar carried on, clearly excited to have someone else hear his story. "And then I chased them until their ship disappeared and reappeared further north. They took a little detour and wrecked at Sapphire Falls, but they never noticed when we sailed right past them."

*That must've been when the figurehead came through!*

"You know," Igraine said slowly, talking like he was a particularly dimwitted child, "if you want the Rituals to go faster, I need the Khozek to do it."

Rhakmar cocked his head, and Igraine walked around the room, dragging her intact fingertips along the rough stone walls. "So, we take the Khozek, kill the girl, and settle our accounts with the Pendragons."

Bethany's heart stuttered. Emma was in even more danger than she realized.

But Igraine shook her head, still running her nails over the walls, boxes, and blankets as she circled the room. Apparently, she wasn't concerned that the Fifth Travelers were listening in. "Kill her? No, her future is set by prophecy. There are other ways to...." She trailed off, tapping her chin in thought. "Break him, take him, and remake him," she listed as if they were ingredients for a cake.

Rhakmar's shadow moved by itself, his eyes as black as the monster about to consume Langoth, and Bethany's horror intensified. "What do you suggest?"

Igraine smiled. "Divide and conquer. She can't protect her Prince and the Khozek at the same time."

Rhakmar's grin grew impossibly large. "Marvelous. I've always admired your ingenuity."

Something unseen shrieked next to Lincoln, and Bethany instinctively erected a bright gold shield around them. Fear spiked in her chest, and she couldn't breathe.

"Naamah, leave him alone," Rhakmar snapped, turning his attention to the corner.

The shrieking stopped, and Lincoln sagged. Bethany propped him back up with her right shoulder, dropping her shield. Lincoln's breathing came in short gasps.

"Sorry about that. She's been trapped in the jungle for so long she forgot proper possession etiquette."

Bethany's world screeched to a halt, her terror a suffocating wave she saw reflected in the eyes of her battle sisters and the rest of the Fifth Travelers.

"Don't worry, pet," Igraine cooed at Bethany, the smile not quite reaching her eyes. "I won't let any of my witches be possessed... unless they step out of line."

It didn't take Bethany long to re-acclimate to Talahm, though she could have done without the chill. The demon army prowled, and without her journal or connection to Emma, Bethany felt even more isolated than she had on Langoth. Her only consolation was that she was in good company with Hela, Rissy, Harlow, and the Emrys.

Rissy had also taken the time to look at the hand Bethany had used to grab the edge of the universe. It had left a long, angry burn, but with Rissy treating it every day, the injury had slowly gotten to the point where she could make a fist without her palm hurting.

Another thing for Luke to heal later. If they survived that long.

Though no one was allowed to leave without an escort, the Fifth Travelers kept to themselves.

Bethany felt like she was losing her mind until three Nephilim guards entered from a rear passageway a week after the Olii had arrived.

"They're on their way," one of them said. "We forced Pendragon's people up the path to the outskirts."

Bethany shot to her feet.

So did Igraine, and she held up her intact hand. "We must be silent and unseen. Let Pendragon show us whose side he is really on. Yours, or his own."

Behind Igraine, Rhakmar smiled that creepy smile again.

Bethany found it hard to stand still. If King Aragon was here, that meant Luke, Emma, and Argent were too, and those were the people she wanted most to see. She wanted to scream that Igraine and Rhakmar had plans for them. And she wanted to tell Emma what Igraine had finally revealed about her true fate.

That the Prophecy of the World's End had more to it.

And Emma's life could depend on Igraine if Rhakmar didn't kill her first.

"Conceal us all," Igraine told Bethany. She'd regained enough strength to reinforce her glamour, and she didn't look half as haggard as when they'd left Langoth.

Bethany looked at the survivors. They would all have to come, whether as Igraine's allies or Rhakmar's hostages. She obeyed without question, not wanting to risk one of the demons thinking she was stepping out of line.

Six minutes and half a mile later, Bethany crouched behind one of the large broken stones along the edge of the temple ruins. Her bum arm still strapped against her chest, she forced herself to breathe long and slow, calming her racing heartbeat. Even though she'd made them all invisible, she still felt exposed when she peeked over the top of the stone slab.

Her heart clenched with relief at the sight of Luke and Emma and the others coming into view. Sargateth, who took position at the vanguard, called out to the Olii, who had done nothing but laze about since they arrived.

"Trust me, Bethany Celeste. Let him show his true colors," Igraine whispered next to her.

Rhakmar squatted behind them, his sinister presence overwhelmingly dark.

Bethany swallowed her guilt over watching events unfold, but if Igraine was right... King Aragon would stop at nothing to protect his throne, even if it meant condemning her.

She almost cast her mind out toward Emma's, but she squashed the thought before she could accidentally give them away. Even though Igraine had committed horrible atrocities in her pursuit to end the Pendragons, she *had* saved the Fifth Travelers and made Bethany leave Langoth before she did.

Even if they'd walked right into Rhakmar's waiting hands.

Luke darted in front of the King, erecting a shield, and all hell broke loose.

*Igraine was right,* her rational brain said, sounding scandalized.

Even if the King succeeded in whatever plan he'd cooked up to keep them from coming back, he was too late. An unexpected wave of gratitude for Igraine getting them back *early* swept through her.

Bethany almost cheered out loud when Luke tackled Sargateth, but she stuffed her fist in her mouth when the Olis immobilized him to mess with the Titan Obelisk.

"What have you done?" Luke yelled, his emotion shooting through Bethany like an arrow.

"Now," Igraine whispered.

Heart pounding, Bethany stood and released her invisibility spell.

# CHAPTER TWENTY-ONE
# WHOSE SIDE?

Emma rushed to Luke's side, sliding a little on the icy ground as she helped him to his feet. She burned with anger, a hair's breadth away from blasting King Aragon into smithereens. She might have, if not for the fact that Argent would never forgive her.

"I did my duty," Sargateth answered with none of his usual bravado. He fixed his sad, disappointed gaze past Emma and onto the King. "Even if I didn't want to."

"Don't you understand?" King Aragon insisted, sagging with relief. "We stopped Igraine! We just thwarted prophecy!"

Movement on the edge of the temple grounds caught Emma's attention.

"On the contrary, *Your Majesty*, I believe you played right into it."

That voice lived in Emma's nightmares. She could hardly breathe as she watched Igraine Pendragon come into view with a cloak over her shoulders and arms. A familiar blonde stood behind her.

*Is that Bethany?*

Luke tensed at her side, but Emma clamped her hand down on his arm. "Bethie!" he yelled, his voice cracking. "Emma, connect her back to us!"

Emma remembered Argent's worries from Sapphire Falls. "No! What if Igraine is controlling her? She'd get into our heads, too!"

Bethany waved with the hand not strapped to her chest, but she didn't break rank with Igraine. Chills that had nothing to do with the winter climate raced down Emma's back.

Mountains, Eternal Winds, and the other three Olii in the center of the field turned around to face the newcomers. The six on the sidelines got to their feet, stamping their paws in the snow.

A third figure appeared, and Emma's heart dropped like a stone to the icy ground.

*Atlas.*

Then she saw what could only be described as a horde of men and women follow out from behind the broken pillars, some in armor, some in rags.

"What is this?" King Aragon said, as pale as a sheet. "How—"

"I think it's clear how," Tomás interjected sharply, coming to Emma's other side. "We got here too late."

The part of Emma that was unbelievably relieved that Bethany hadn't been sentenced to die in a black hole warred with the fact that Bethany stood with Igraine like allies.

Just like Argent had seen through the portal.

"What do we do, Dad?" Luke muttered.

"We fight," he answered, sounding unusually calm as he ushered them back toward the rest of their group. "All of us. We cannot be divided now on their account."

Emma kept her hand firmly around Luke's arm and took her place near Argent, who looked pale as he stared at Atlas. The Prince's fingers tightened around the yoke of the Elvara Bow.

Mountains slunk away from the Titan Obelisk, back to the Pendragon side of the field.

"Bethie!" Luke shouted again, straining to escape Emma's grasp.

"Witch!" a deep, echoing voice boomed. The sound of it startled Emma, but she managed to hide her flinch. Eternal Winds took a step toward Igraine, the other three Olii at his flanks. "Declare yourself, for you are subject to Catigern."

Igraine frowned, glancing at Eternal Winds as if he were merely a fly buzzing around her chambers. "I've heard of you," she said, her unconcerned expression causing anxiety to wind around Emma's gut. "But you haven't known about me for long, have you?"

"I said declare yourself!"

Igraine pushed her shoulders back, her stance full of power. "I am your worst nightmare, your future queen, the bane of all Pendragons. I am Igraine, the Night's Empress, and you will soon *bow* to me!"

"I see no need for a trial. You are charged with treason," Eternal Winds snarled, his claws digging tracts into what had once been the temple floors.

"Good luck with that," Atlas said, his gaze sweeping across the courtyard. His armored Nephilim had formed rank behind them. And the people in rags, who Emma assumed were the Fifth Travelers, huddled near the back. Atlas's eyes lingered on Argent, and Emma stepped in front of him. Even if he'd chosen wrong in regard to Bethany, Emma wouldn't let the Nephilim King touch him.

Eternal Winds' ears twitched. "And who are you to interfere?"

Atlas bowed. "Do you not recognize me? I have treated with many of you over the centuries, from my palace in Keldvaar."

Eternal Winds cocked his head, glancing at the other Olii and then over his shoulder at Sargateth and Morgan.

"The Nephilim were released," Sargateth called out, sounding reluctant to share the news.

Emma's stomach twisted with continued guilt.

Their ears flattened, the Olii hissed at Atlas and his army. Igraine stood with one hip cocked, as if without a care in the world.

But Emma knew better. This woman wanted to erase the Pendragons and the Artairs from this planet, and they'd lost their chance to avoid facing her.

Luke nudged her with his shoulder. She followed his gaze across the divide toward Bethany, who had started to inch away from Igraine. Behind the ranks of soldiers, five other heads moved, three of which Emma recognized as witches from Bethany's coven.

"All of them?" Eternal Winds shouted, fear lacing his words for the first time. "Since when?"

"Since I let them out to save Argent's soul," Emma said before she could stop herself, trying to keep the attention on them.

"And I'm here to claim him anyway," Atlas drawled. "He just needs a little breaking first. Then I can have what Igraine promised me in return for her vendetta against her offspring.... Ultimate control over flesh and spirit, man and magic."

"Together," Igraine interjected.

"Together," Atlas repeated, as if only indulging the woman who could wipe the floor with him if she wanted to.

"By the grace of the Creator," King Aragon said under his breath, but still loud enough for Emma to hear. "I hereby renounce the throne and relinquish all rights, powers, oaths, and responsibilities vested in me as King of Renova. By the laws and customs of our land, the authority of my crown is hereby placed upon Argent Arthur Pendragon, who has been duly prepared to reign with wisdom and justice."

Emma couldn't believe what she was hearing and risked a glance toward Argent.

The Prince wore a solemn but determined expression as he answered his father, equally quiet. "I, Argent Arthur Pendragon, swear to uphold the laws, traditions, and well-being of Renova and to serve my people with honor and integrity."

Aragon's next words were firm. "Long live the King."

For the first time in what felt like weeks, Argent's presence pressed against the link they shared in Emma's mind. She hesitated before letting him in, still angry about his decision to side with his father. But they couldn't let anything distract from the looming battle—not even this unexpected transfer of power.

*You stop Igraine. My father and I will handle Atlas.*

Emma didn't answer him, but she discreetly nodded. She knew how to fight against magic better than she knew how to fight against demons.

"The only ones who will be broken today are you all," Eternal Winds spat, his hackles raised. "Talahm is not under your dominion or command, nor shall it ever be."

"Oh, and it's under yours?" Igraine snapped. "You don't even know your own kin for what they truly are." She scanned the rest of the people who had gathered to meet her, her eyes stopping on someone behind Emma. "Your mountain crumbled because of *his* claws."

A sudden impact sent Emma tumbling. Luke caught her before she hit the ground, and she floated weightless in his arms until he set her back on her feet.

Her heart stuttered. A tall, rugged man with short, choppy chocolate hair forced Tomás across the gap.

"Mountains!" Morgan shrieked behind Emma.

Atlas laughed, his booming guffaw shaking the snow from the trees at the edge of the forest.

By the time Emma understood her father's captor was *Mountains* of all people, they'd already made it to Igraine. Mountains had curled his intact hand into Tomás's hair, yanking his head back to expose his throat. Disgust bubbled in her chest when *Mountains Crumble Beneath His Claws* pressed a demanding kiss to Igraine's lips. The cloak slipped from her shoulders and pooled on the ground behind her.

Sargateth *roared*. "Mountains, what are you doing? You're with her?"

"I've been with her since she escaped Uther," Mountains shouted across at them. His golden eyes shone even as a human, a form Emma never thought she'd see the Olis take. "I found her. I saved her. I cared for her like no one else did," Mountains continued, venom dripping from his words. "For well over seven hundred years! When she told me what Firstborn and Purifying Fire did to her—how far they had fallen from their promise to protect humanity, catering to the whims of a foolish monarch—I knew I had to keep her safe. It was with *my* help she found immortality; with *my* help she planted the seeds against you when our so-called leaders brought Arthur here and revealed the depths to which they had stooped—eternal fealty to a monster!"

"You lied to us," snarled Eternal Winds. The leader of the Olis Catigern took a few steps toward the enemy, yanking back a paw when met with a sharp strike of magic from Mountains. "You lied to us all for seven centuries?"

Mountains spat on the ground. "You deserved it."

"You knew they were already here," Emma realized. Out of the corner of her eye, she watched Bethany and her five companions continue to edge away from their enemies, but then they were all detained by Nephilim soldiers. "What else have you known all along?"

"Every piece of the puzzle, stupid girl. I helped her orchestrate the rise and fall of kingdoms long before your great-grandparents were born. I introduced her to Atlas, and yes, *I* was the one who told him all about your plans."

Mountains glanced back at Igraine and did a double-take at the stump ending where her left hand should have been. His eyes bulged in surprise, filling with righteous fury. His unmarred hand reached into Tomás's hair and yanked the prophet's head backward.

"Who did this?" Mountains hissed, pointing at Igraine's missing hand.

Emma immediately pictured her mother waving at them from the shore as *The Sea Wolf* sailed away from Sapphire

Falls. Emma had lived with a constant underlying terror of losing her father since Luke's frightening Vision when she'd first come to Talahm. And even though her own precipitate Prophecy had once altered the outcome of her father's prophesied death, Emma couldn't help but wonder if Tomás had been living on borrowed time.

"Who did this?" Mountains screamed, pulling Tomás's head back even further. All the Prophet could do was scrabble at his captor, since the enchanted exoskeleton had not been designed to support its occupant bending backward.

A cry escaped Tomás's throat, and Emma frantically thought back to the battle in Igraine's chambers. *How did Mountains miss when Mom shot Igraine's hand? He was right there. He was—he was behind the portal! He didn't see the bullet hit her hand!*

Emma stepped away from Luke and Argent. "*You* did that to her, Mountains!" She yelled, keeping attention on her while Argent—now *King*—retreated to the edge of the battlefield and nocked an arrow on the bow. "You opened the portal that took her to Langoth, don't you remember?"

"The portal would not have done this!" Mountains screamed, pointing at Igraine's stump. Igraine seemed unbothered by her lover's outburst. In fact, she appeared to revel in it. The Olis in human form now took the brunt of Tomás's weight, his hand still curled tightly around the other man's hair. Clearly in pain, the elder Prophet could not do much, immobilized as he was.

Emma's heart twisted. Hate for Igraine flowed through her veins. "We didn't need magic to permanently relieve her of that appendage," Emma snarled. "You want to know who it was? It was me. It was Bethany. It was my brother. My mother. My *Prince*." She didn't think it was her place to reveal what had taken place between the two royals. "All of us who were in that room that day, Mountains, are responsible for what happened to her. And you know what?" Magic crackled up and down her arms and filled her personal space, the ends of her hair sparking. "We should have aimed at you instead."

Mountains transformed, raking his claws down Tomás's back and wrenching an agonizing cry of pain from him. The claws came away bloody, and with a crazed gleam in his eyes, Mountains let Tomás crumple to the ground in favor of pacing back and forth before Igraine, as if protecting her from further harm.

"Dad!" Emma and Luke both cried.

"Olii, attack!" Sargateth roared at the top of his lungs, his authority as firstborn of his kind spurring the ten others into action.

Mountains snarled, readying a pounce.

Sargateth and Morgan transformed into their Olis forms, meeting him halfway. *Forever in a Day's First Hour* and *Nightbows Sweep Past Timeless Stars* joined them. The great flapping of their wings drowned out all other noise, and Igraine used the chaos to start firing bolts of magic into the defenders. Blocks of rubble exploded on impact, sending clouds of fine dust into the cold northern air.

Bethany and her coven sisters freed themselves with a whirlwind of fire and ice, and they sprinted across the slick courtyard to the Pendragon side.

Then Igraine turned her attention on the Khozek planted at the base of the Titan Obelisk.

*We played right into her hands!*

Dread flooded Emma's body, torn between stopping Igraine and helping Luke get to their father. The runes of his exoskeleton flickered through the dust and blood pooled around him, melting the snow and ice into a slurry. Tomás's hands clenched and unclenched at his sides, his paralysis keeping him from helping himself.

Panic overtook her when one of the Olii, *Sharpest Edge of Diamond Skies*, flapped from the chaos to crouch over Tomás.

"Dad!" Emma screamed. But instead of injuring him further, Diamond Skies forced Tomás to roll over with both paws and started healing the gashes down his back.

*Cover me*, Luke said clearly in her mind. She quickly changed tactics, defending Luke as he attempted to cross the no-man's land to his father. Igraine kept trying to advance toward the Khozek, but the Olii drove her back.

Atlas charged across the field, drawing his massive sword as he ran straight for Argent. Most of his soldiers dutifully followed, the rest guarding the now captive Fifth Travelers.

Argent shot one of the Elvara Bow's special arrows at Atlas, who knocked it out of the air with his sword. He tried again, but Atlas blocked the second one too, his supernatural speed more than a match for Argent's skill as an archer.

Dakota, Evie, and Cara darted in front of the royals, fighting with staffs in one hand and blades in the other. The clang of steel on steel pierced the air, and Atlas crossed swords with Aragon, who had moved in front of Argent so he could regroup further away.

Argent started shooting Elvara arrows, releasing them faster than Emma thought possible. Two soldiers went down. Then three. Then five. But then they got too close, and he finally had to trade his bow for steel.

Eternal Winds, Secrets Buried, Scattered Sands, and two others Emma didn't know all jumped into the fray against the Nephilim, crushing armor and bodies beneath their massive paws. Their wings stirred up the air and snow, blinding their enemies. Initially, Emma was relieved to see the five Olii fighting against the Nephilim troops, but their unnatural strength evened the playing field.

"Stop fighting!" Bethany screamed at the top of her lungs. For an impossible moment, time stood still and the dust settled, all eyes on the Firewhip. "If you kill Igraine, we're all doomed."

"If we don't, this world will never be the same," Aragon called out.

"She can *help*!" Bethany insisted. Even her coven sisters behind her all seemed to agree.

But no one listened. Time sped up again, and the noises of battle overpowered everything. Her attention split between Igraine, who kept trying to get past the Olii guarding the Khozek, and Bethany, who had finally started to fight her way across the battlefield.

Emma's mind raced. Would she have to fight her best friend?

Sargateth, Morgan, and the other two Olii refocused their magical attacks on Igraine and Mountains, who now fought together as if they'd trained their whole lives for this moment.

"Cordelia, are you going to help us or not?" Morgan yelled through the swirling dust, her voice loud over the clash of swords.

The sea captain sat on the edge of the temple grounds. She took a dainty sip from her bottle.

"Why in the Lord's name did you bring wine? This is not the time to get drunk!"

Captain Roque set the bottle in the snow next to her, then crossed her arms. "I have no stakes in this stupid battle. I came to see if the Pendragons will die."

While Mountains was otherwise occupied with his kin, Emma tracked Igraine, blocking the old witch from the Titan Obelisk. She ignored any banter as she tried to land a hit on Igraine, but all she could do was desperately defend against Igraine's attacks. Luke had gotten pinned down in the fight, holding a shield over himself while three Nephilim struck it from all sides with their swords.

And then *Fairest Breeze Between the Trees* and *Ever Seeking Moonlight's Touch*, the Olii from Korad, broke ranks, raking their claws across Morgan's wing.

The second-born Olis screamed in pain, twisting her body around to counter the move. Not having expected the betrayal from her kin, she hesitated, apparently not wanting to inflict permanent damage. But the decision was yanked from her hands when they attacked again, magic now thundering around them.

Sargateth roared in righteous fury, batting Mountains across the face and leaving a long, bloody gash from his cheek to his throat.

The Archmage then reared onto his hind legs and clapped his paws together. The same bright light with which he'd held Fairest Breeze in contempt rocketed outward, and when it hit the Fairest Breeze in the chest she collapsed to the flagstones, unmoving but for the rise and fall of her chest.

Emma's heart nearly stopped in fear, watching the incredible battle unfold before her. Olii fought each other with deadly force; brother had turned against brother. And the utter chaos still blocked Luke in his attempt to reach their father.

"Think, Emma, think," she muttered to herself, trying to slow her heart rate.

"Don't panic," Bethany said breathlessly, appearing at Emma's side.

Emma brought both hands up, ready to attack with blue-black energy, but Bethany forced her them down.

"You can't kill Igraine," Bethany said, tripping over her words. "If she dies, so do you! The King knows the full Prophecy!"

"What full Prophecy?" Emma racked her brain, still on guard. In the periphery, she tracked Hela Tanberg, Rissy

Clement, and Harlow Barnes as they seamlessly integrated with the Royal Coven fighting the Nephilim. The two others from their party, a man and a woman, had crouched behind tree trunks lining the forest's edge.

In the back of her head, she felt Argent's determination mixed with his fear. Atlas traded equal blows with Aragon, ever pressing toward his prize.

"The one about you and Luke!" Bethany said, grabbing Emma by both shoulders and forcing her to duck. A jet of fire speared overhead.

"The World's End? Me being the Seventh Sorceress?" Emma said, shooting an ice spike at Igraine's back. It turned to water on contact, dripping harmlessly to the snow. "We have bigger problems right now! Help me free Luke!"

In the precious minute it took them to take out the Nephilim hammering against Luke's shield, Igraine had started issuing commands to the remaining soldiers who had stayed behind to guard the Fifth Travelers. An older woman with graying hair seized the opportunity and started to direct the captives to run to safety. They fled to where the other man and woman had already hidden themselves, now waving for the others to join them. Emma threw ice bolt after ice bolt, bolstered by Bethany's magic.

The Royal Coven—or, what little of it had come with them—ferociously defended the royals from Atlas and his minions. The rest of the Olii split between battling Nephilim and fanning out to flank Sargateth and a limping, bleeding Morgan against Igraine and Mountains. Cordelia sat by herself at edge of the battle, watching the chaos with narrowed eyes.

Luke finally finished his long scramble toward Tomás, immediately raising a shield around him, his father, and Diamond Skies.

Emma breathed a sigh of relief.

"Emma, listen! King Aragon and Sargateth have lied to you—to all of us— since the beginning!"

Emma's next lance of ice missed its mark by several inches. Panic squeezed like a vice around her heart. "Are you with her or against her?"

Bethany let out a cry of frustration. "Against? Neither? She's the reason we got back at all!"

"So she fed you lies to get you to believe her, is that it?" Emma put space between them again, then slipped right to avoid a jet of fire from Igraine. "She sure seems like she's trying to kill me right now, not save me!"

"Am I, darling, or am I just seeing what you're really made of?" Igraine asked, lifting several of the stones behind her with earth magic and hurling them across the divide. The defenders dropped to the ground or dodged, but Emma cracked the temple covering in half before it reached her. "Your true enemies are the ones who led you here."

Atlas finally knocked Excalibur from Aragon's hands, and Argent rolled, taking the next strike against his bracer. The impact made him cry out in pain, and Emma could feel it through their renewed mental link.

Hela Tanberg surged forward, snapping energy whips at Atlas to drive him backward, but he caught them around his sword and yanked her toward him. He grabbed her by the throat and squeezed.

"Don't listen to her," Sargateth barked, his deep voice booming across the chaos.

But Emma heard the fear in his voice. She knew Sargateth, knew his tendency to be cryptic—to hold information back. Sometimes he did it on purpose, but for such an old creature, he was just as fallen as the rest of them.

Aragon had prevented Sargateth from going after Magdalin when she'd gone missing, had commanded Sargateth to stitch shut the Titan Obelisk. What if he'd also commanded Sargateth to keep this new secret buried?

"Tell me, Bethany," Emma demanded.

Her best friend's face fell. "I don't remember the exact words, just that it really ends with you dying. She has the power to stop that from happening—"

"Come to me to hear the truth," Igraine cackled.

"She's baiting you!" Morgan cried out.

Igraine's face turned so ugly Emma thought the refreshed glamour had dropped for a moment. "Am I, *Mistress* Le Fay? Am I baiting her, or am I giving her the truth you and your wretched twin have kept from her since the beginning?"

"Emma, don't listen to her!" Morgan begged.

Sweat trickled down the small of her back, her skin tingling with the bite of cold warring against the heat of battle. Dakota used earth magic to send a flurry of stone shrapnel at Atlas's face, and he let go of Hela, who fell to her knees, gasping for breath. Evie dragged her backward and, together with Cara and two Olii, planted themselves between Atlas and the royals. Blood trickled down Atlas's face, his skin peeling away from his cheekbones where the stones had struck him. Protected by the witches and Olii, Aragon and Argent helped each other to their feet. Argent picked up the Elvara Bow again, nocking another special arrow on the string only to loose it into an approaching soldier, who let out an ethereal scream when it struck.

He only had four of those arrows left.

From the trees, the older woman emerged, her hands filled with bright purple magic as she walked toward the Nephilim like this fight might be her last. Three others followed her, only one of whom had a staff.

"Tell me," Emma said, wanting it all to end but unsure of how to do it.

Igraine looked like she wanted to rub her hands together but lacked one half of the equation.

"Igraine, don't—" Sargateth attempted to interfere again, but Igraine chose to ignore him.

"'The world plunges into darkness,'" Igraine started, her voice carrying across the entire battlefield. The Olii still tussled with Mountains and the Nephilim, but Igraine's side was winning. "'The end of it all approaches, the last untouched havens of light a beacon to those who survive.'" Igraine took a step forward, her sharp eyes locked on Emma's. "'As the universe splits—'" Igraine gestured all around them— "'and the fabric of reality itself unravels, only the Seventh Sorceress and her Sentinel can seal out the forces of evil.'"

The Night's Empress closed in, and Emma contemplated striking her with another blast of magic before dismissing the idea. "'You will know her by the heavens upon her hand,'" Igraine's eyes flickered first to Emma's right palm, then to the tesseract imprints on her pauldrons, "'the mark of power beyond anything imaginable.'" Emma knew the witch was drawing her in, luring her closer, but she couldn't help but hold off, even as Igraine took yet another step toward her.

"Don't say another word," Morgan commanded with pained panic, but given the gleam in Igraine's eye, it only encouraged her more.

"'When she comes, the horizon draws near to the woven realms of men and magic, hungry to draw it all into the void.'"

Emma's heart skipped a beat. *This was left unsaid. Sargateth knew about the black hole!*

"'Beneath the swimming stars, she spends herself to sever the worlds—payment to balance chaos with order.'"

Emma's world dropped beneath her feet. "What?" The chill cut her to the bone, as if someone had dumped a bucket of ice water over her head. She couldn't move when Igraine took a final step, reaching up with her intact hand to stroke Emma's cheek in mock concern.

"Born to save," Igraine whispered, "yet raised to die. It's no wonder Merlin kept those last lines to himself."

"Don't listen to her," Sargateth growled between swipes at Mountains and *Ever Seeking Moonlight's Touch*, twin of Fairest Breeze.

"Did she lie?" Emma demanded, searching Igraine's face for any hint of deception. "Sargateth, *did she lie?*"

His silence answered her just as much as the smirk on Igraine's wrinkled face. Triumph glittered in her eyes. "I wouldn't lie about something like that." Igraine leaned in, putting her lips to Emma's ear. "I protect, reward, and cherish my witches instead of lying to them. And I can offer you a way to survive the fate they hid from you."

# CHAPTER TWENTY-TWO
# THE SCALES TIP

"No!" Aragon's deep, strangled scream echoed across the battlefield.

Emma pushed Igraine away and whirled around, only to choke on the frigid air.

The Nephilim King had Argent by the throat again, the Elvara Bow out of reach and useless.

Argent's eyes were squeezed shut, his mouth moving as if muttering something under his breath.

Atlas frowned, his fingers tightening. "Who's protecting you?" His sibilant hiss carried across the snow. "If I can't take you, I'll kill you instead—"

"Take me!" Aragon cried out, dropping Excalibur with a clang and taking tentative steps toward his son. "Don't kill him. Take me in his place."

Atlas only hesitated for a moment before shoving Argent away and seizing the former King's head with both hands. "It's a pity Igraine never tried the Blacksoul Rituals on her own children. It would have made my life much easier."

Sheer horror filled every cell of Emma's body as she watched Atlas's host collapse like a puppet whose strings had been cut. At the same time, Aragon fell to his knees, groaning, his head in his hands.

A moment later, he stilled, lifting his head to blink.

His eyes were as black as night.

Atlas had taken him.

After a long, infinite moment, the roar of the battle rose again. The older woman from the Fifth Travelers started to magically pummel Atlas—now in control of Aragon's body—with Bethany and the other surviving witches.

Cara and Harlow lay sprawled on the ground, unmoving. The Olis fighters continued to war against the Nephilim soldiers, now dwindled to less than ten, and the bodies of the others were strewn across the battlefield, their blood mixed with the snow. All around them were the whispers and shrieks of disembodied spirits.

*Emma, stop Igraine!* Argent's frantic voice exploded inside her head. He'd crawled to retrieve the Elvara Bow, but he didn't look like he wanted to shoot his father with it.

Emma spun around, spotting Igraine nimbly darting through the chaos toward the Titan Obelisk.

But before Emma could take a single step, a jet of crackling orange magic struck her full in the chest.

It *burned*. Not like fire, but like a deep, bone-shattering cold that soaked every fiber of Emma's soul. In her daze, she barely made out the Olii rising up as one to subdue *Ever Seeking Moonlight's Touch*. An arrow with blue runes on the shaft whizzed through the air, missing Igraine's head by less than an inch, its fletching catching some of her hair.

Struggling to draw breath, Emma tried rolling on her side to find her brother, her Sentinel, and in one wild moment Emma's eyes locked with Luke's behind the shield where he and Diamond Skies worked together to heal the claw marks left on their father by Mountains.

No thoughts passed between them.

Only mutual dread.

The sounds dulled to a low roar and the fighters around her blurred, the deep, agonizing cold slowing her thoughts to a near standstill.

*Am I going to die here?*

And then, a familiar face bent in front of hers. Furrier than he normally appeared, the deep lines of concern around Sargateth's eyes spoke volumes.

Sitting on his haunches, he gathered a bright white ball of energy between his paws, breathed into it, and then slammed it against the very spot where the orange magic had struck.

Warmth returned to her limbs, and breathing became easier. But she felt like her every nerve had been exposed to a thousand volts of electricity. *Was this how Bethany felt when I accidentally electrified her?* Sargateth maneuvered her onto his back, but whatever instructions he spoke never made it through the dull roar in her ears. She curled her fists into his fur, holding on with the strength she had left. As soon as she did, Sargateth loped away, carrying her behind the rubble protecting the rest of Camelot's fighters.

"The King," Emma rasped, unable to hear herself. She looked frantically past Sargateth. Even though he'd tried to sentence Bethany to death, he didn't deserve to be possessed.

Argent didn't deserve to lose his father.

She rolled onto the stones, her body like a ragdoll.

"I know Argent is King now. But there's nothing I can do for Aragon."

The words barely registered before she remembered that Sargateth had lied to them—to her—about the Prophecy that brought her to Talahm to begin with. How could she trust him now? Could Igraine really have the answer?

"We are losing," Sargateth continued.

She struggled to speak. "But Luke's Vision! This is the way we win!" But she wasn't sure if she believed it now. What if Luke's memory of the Khozek had been planted by Igraine all along? What if they were now beyond the scope of prophecy?

"Emma, we are *losing*." He generated another ball of light and pressed it into her chest again. The warmth spread to every fingertip, and her nerves stopped feeling like she'd stuck her fingers into an outlet and didn't let go. "I have failed you in many ways, the worst of which you discovered today." Fluidly, he transformed back into his human self, lifting her to her knees with both arms. "But Moonlight's Touch stooped to dark magic with that spell, and it would have killed you in a few more seconds. I don't know how to stop Igraine, but I have faith that you can. Atlas will have to wait."

"Can she stop Lancelot's Prophecy from killing me?" she croaked, limbs tingling. She still couldn't move her fingers.

Sargateth's breath hitched. "Even if she could, I can't imagine the price she'd make you pay for it. You've seen her brand of magic, Emma. If anything, she'd own you like she owned Septim. Like Atlas now owns Aragon."

Emma gritted her teeth. "I'd rather die."

She leaned forward, and Sargateth encased her in a hug that felt incredibly comforting yet filled with his shame. He smelled like sweat, dust, blood, and a deep, ancient magic that defied description. His muscles trembled with exertion, and Emma realized that despite their power, the Olii were just as chained to the laws of magic as she and Igraine were. Even if Emma was the Seventh Sorceress, Igraine had centuries of skill, endurance, power, and practice to hone her fighting skills. The only way they'd managed to overcome her in Valona was by tricking her into the portal.

Emma's hands curled into Sargateth's back, dutifully shoving her anger at his lie of omission into the deepest recesses of her mind. She could deal with that later. "I have an idea, but I need Luke for it," she whispered.

"Consider it done," Sargateth answered without hesitating.

"I'll thank you after you've followed through, not before." Emma clenched her jaw.

She peeked around the stone slab. *Eternal Winds Obey His Call* wrestled Atlas. The four other Olii who had been fighting against Atlas struggled to subdue *Ever Seeking Moonlight's Touch*, putting Morgan, Nightbows Sweep, and Day's First Hour at a disadvantage against Mountains and Igraine.

A few of the surviving witches faced off against the last of the Nephilim soldiers, but it was now five against ten, and Emma could see the fatigue in the coven's slow reactions.

And King Argent—he'd picked up the Elvara Bow and nocked one of the special arrows, stalking the edge of the battlefield toward Mountains and Igraine. Bethany went with him, defending him even as she appeared to be desperately talking him down from his clear target.

Igraine.

Fury painted his cheeks red, and the scars on his face stood out.

Emma sucked in a deep breath. "Get me to Luke."

Sargateth laid a hand on her shoulder. "Time to end this."

Emma made herself invisible, and he raised both eyebrows until she made it so he could see her. Then she burst from behind the stone like a rabbit, bounding across the battlefield now slick with blood and melted snow. Sargateth followed, intercepting any stray shots that veered too close. Emma dodged and weaved, breathing hard, until she slid right through Luke's shield.

Luke looked close to tears, his hands trembling as he continued the tandem healing of their father with Diamond Skies. Another spell hit the shield protecting them, its gong reverberating across the battlefield. Tomás was still on his front with five deep tracts in his back from Mountains' claws. Diamond Skies had stopped the bleeding, but the wounds were still fresh and raw. Each pass of the Olis's paws generated a thin new layer of skin. Only sheer luck and his thick leather jerkin had protected Tomás's spine from being severed.

*Luke, Dad,* Emma reached out, *I'm right next to you.*

*Mountains did a number on him,* Luke replied, his mental voice shaking. *I can't do much except keep him from going into shock.*

Emma scanned the battle until she spotted Sargateth, now veering around to Atlas, who had just punched Eternal Winds in the throat.

*I need you to help me take down Igraine.*

Luke nodded without question. "I have to go for a few minutes," he said out loud to Diamond Skies, who hadn't noticed Emma. "Keep him stable, okay?"

"Waste no time," Diamond Skies replied without looking at him.

Emma crouched at the ready. Dust choked the air as spells and magic hit the remnants of the temple. Bitter cold pressed against them, their breath raising in chilly puffs.

Her heart clenched with renewed panic, but she forced it down and sent her brother her plan in a barrage of mental images.

*Get ready,* Emma said as she turned Luke invisible. She laid a hand on the back of her father's knee, hoping to give him comfort while she drew the same from him. *We don't have much time.*

She and Luke darted, unseen, through the fighting until they were within spitting distance of Igraine and Mountains.

Even though the Olis had re-taken his natural form, he and Igraine moved like dancers, their attacks so coordinated they must have been mentally connected.

Morgan, wing dragging, had fallen back to shield the Khozek against Igraine's relentless magic. *Forever in a Day's First Hour* and *Nightbows Sweep Past Timeless Stars* alternated between defending and attacking, though they didn't appear to send anything deadly at Mountains.

As if they were afraid of killing him.

Bethany placed herself between Argent and the fighters, her back to Igraine as she argued with him.

Sweat collected at the small of Emma's back, and every breath felt like a struggle. Running on adrenaline, instinct, and the connection to Luke, Emma counted down from three.

Luke tensed beside her, both hands already up.

*Now!*

Emma sprinted the last few feet until she entered the space between Igraine and Mountains. Luke erected a tight shield around the three of them, and Emma made herself visible, unsheathing one of her daggers at the same time. She tore it through the fabric of Igraine's sleeve.

"No!" Bethany shouted from outside the shield, her voice muffled and far away. "Emma, no!"

"Your magic is useless against me, child," Igraine spat, backing up.

Mountains swiped a massive paw toward Emma, but she ducked and rolled—Luke's cue to fill the tiny space with smoke. Igraine and Mountains stumbled, coughing and swiping to clear the air, but it was too thick.

Emma capitalized on their confusion and performed some of the hardest magic she'd ever done. Igraine's flowing purple dress, slashed sleeve and all, coalesced around Emma. Her hair turned long and silver, and her left hand disappeared at the wrist. Across from her, Igraine shrank to match Emma's height, a leather cuirass and battle witch skirts replacing her dress. Her hair turned jet-black, and Emma was struck by the odd sensation of looking into her own confused eyes.

She sprang forward, seizing Igraine with both hands and using the momentum to shove Igraine into the space she had just occupied.

Seconds later, Mountains blew out a deep breath of air magic, clearing the bubble.

A deep roar of rage exploded from the Olis, and without hesitation he pounced on Igraine—who now looked just like Emma.

All five of his claws sank deep into the flesh over Igraine's heart.

Emma held her breath, pulse racing. She kept both of her eyes fixed on Mountains as he twisted his paw, blood staining the fur around the ends of his claws.

But then he froze, and his next breath rattled. "No," he whispered.

Emma let the illusion ripple away, and Igraine turned back into herself. Streaked with blood still seeping from the deadly wounds, her chest stilled. Her long silver hair puddled around her head, her eyes open but unseeing.

"No!" Mountains roared, getting to his feet and turning to face Emma with hatred and fury in his wide, golden eyes.

Luke dropped the shield, and then an arrow hit Mountains at the juncture between his neck and shoulder, the blue runes on its shaft shimmering in the shadow of his fur. It took Emma a second to register the *twang* and *thwack* of the Elvara Bow.

Mountains stumbled, his face turning back to Igraine's still form. "My Queen—" Mountains croaked, fully collapsing and falling to his side. His barreled chest heaved twice. The ancient's body stilled, only rustled by the wind stirring his fur.

In the air, Emma felt a charge of magic building like electricity. She scrambled backward. A great crack rent the air, and every fighter still left standing was knocked off their feet. Emma lifted her head, brushing hair out of her eyes.

Luke crawled forward. "Are they both—"

"Wasn't there a way to stop her without killing her?" Bethany cried as she struggled into a crouch, her left hand splayed for balance against the fragmented flagstones. Argent sat up behind her and sprang to his feet.

Emma breathed hard through her nose, the elation of victory ebbing at her best friend's words. "If there was a way, wouldn't you have taken it on Langoth?"

"She could have saved you," Bethany whispered. "You shouldn't have done this."

Morgan, still in her Olis form, rushed forward, crouching at Mountains' side. "This was your plan?" she cried out as she conjured a healing projection. The bright winter landscape made its dullness obvious.

"I only tricked him into killing her," Emma said, still sitting on the cold flagstones.

"*I* killed him," King Argent said firmly, offering his hand to Emma. She accepted it, and he helped her to her feet.

Morgan turned her wide, shocked gaze up at them, despair on her blood-spattered fur. "No Olis has died before," she whispered. "We don't know what that will do to the balance!"

A grunt from behind them drew their attention to where Sargateth had Atlas in a headlock. He reached into his pocket and withdrew the wardstone Emma had neglected to leave behind in Keldvaar, slamming it between Atlas's shoulder blades. The Nephilim King stiffened, now trapped in a miniature shield. Sargateth struggled to his feet and bent over, breathing hard.

At their leader's capture, the four surviving Nephilim soldiers laid down their swords and put their hands in the air. Hela and Evie held them at staff and sword-point.

Two of the witches who had followed the old woman into the fray had not survived, but the woman herself knelt at Atlas's head. With her hands splayed against both sides of his face, she closed her eyes and spoke silent words that Emma couldn't decipher. A strange half-moon tattoo on her cheek glowed as if exuding magic.

Rissy knelt at Tomás's side, her face streaked with blood, a healing projection hanging in the air next to them.

Argent left Emma to walk across the carnage to his father, but he halted a few feet away when the old woman looked up at him and shook her head.

Tears cut through the dust caking Sargateth's face, and he limped over to the Titan Obelisk and knelt. He pressed both hands against the Khozek and the black threads unwound themselves, retreating back into their source.

Eternal Winds, who had recovered from his throat-punch, dragged himself next to Sargateth. Together, they chanted in their native tongue until thirty-seven golden threads emerged from the Khozek, hovering in the air like tiny snakes. A second later, they all shot in different directions, and the shrieks and screams of the disembodied Nephilim—most of them near the hiding Fifth Travelers—intensified as the Khozek's threads latched onto them, reeling them back toward Sargateth and Eternal Winds. The four Nephilim soldiers collapsed, the Khozek having yanked the foreign spirits from their bodies.

It didn't take a genius to realize the hosts were dead.

Only Atlas remained, inside Aragon's body and trapped by the wardstone.

A tearing sound filled the clearing, so loud that everyone able clapped their hands over their ears. The jagged purple line hung for a moment over the Titan Obelisk before it pulled itself inward, bubbling at the edge without a second force to truly open it. Emma watched in horror as gravity increased, drawing small pebbles and remnants of the fight toward it. A second later, the edge burst inward, exposing the thin black void.

Right where the Khozek had sealed it.

Sargateth snatched the Khozek before the portal could swallow it, but then struggled to retreat, teetering from the gravity well. Eternal Winds leaped forward, tackling his elder with enough momentum that they tumbled out of range, the Khozek tucked between them. They both sat up, breathing hard as they stared at the portal.

Tremors rocked the remaining temple towers until they fell, sending shards of stone flying through the air. Emma flinched, turning her back to the shrapnel.

"No," Morgan wheezed, her eyes wide with fear. The whites of her eyes contrasted starkly against her deep purple irises. "No, this is impossible—"

"It's not," Sargateth said with clear anguish. "This is but the continuation of what Lancelot Saw. And if we do not leave this place, more of us will die before our times truly come."

"Can't I just fulfill Lancelot's Prophecy now? Cut off Langoth completely, right here?" Emma asked, glancing sideways at Sargateth.

But before the Archmage could answer, a sharp crack of breaking rock rent the air, and the portal tore the Titan Obelisk away at its base.

Eyes wide and terrified, Sargateth handed the Khozek to Eternal Winds, who cradled the object against his chest with one paw. The golden threads trapping the spirits now looked like pustules against the blue-black stone.

Sargateth hurriedly limped over to where Atlas lay immobilized. He commanded four Olii to hold the Nephilim King down, and Sargateth peeled the wardstone away. Hurrying back to the broken base of the Titan Obelisk, he created a shield around the open void. His face was still covered with marred dust and blood, the tracts from his tears still fresh.

While the wardstone shield kept the detritus of the battle from tumbling toward the rift, Emma still felt the draw.

"Even if that had not just happened," Sargateth said through heaving breaths, "Lancelot Saw you beneath the swimming stars. The Sal Dorhana of Skypoint." He pointed at the Khozek. "Where I made that."

Emma's heart sank, and her sense of approaching doom increased.

She knew the full Prophecy now.

To save Talahm and Earth, she had to completely sever their ties with Langoth—and each other.

Even if it cost her life.

# CHAPTER TWENTY-THREE
# HEART AND SOUL

"Bethie!" While the others mobilized the injured, captives, and survivors to return to the ship, Luke almost tripped over his own feet as he made a beeline for his girlfriend.

She looked up from where Igraine and Mountains lay in silent death, her eyes filled with fire when they met his. "You are a scrumptious sight for these very sore eyes," she said, wincing as she struggled to her feet.

Luke cast the medical projection, but before he could take a good look at it, she fisted the collar of his robes with her good hand and yanked his head down into their first kiss in what felt like forever.

He moaned, cupping her cheeks with both hands, fervently kissing her back as a man long separated from his love. She was a breath of fresh air and rekindled his spirit after months of dread and despair.

"I'm so sorry," he said between kisses. "I never should have dropped that shield."

"Shut up, you wonderful man." Bethie peppered his face with kisses, but when he tightened his arms around her, she let out a cry of pain.

"Let me look," he insisted, pressing one last kiss to her forehead and studying the medical projection. "Is this still broken from Valona?"

Bethie scowled. "Yeah. Rissy's better with skin than bones. All she could do was numb it—said fixing it was above her pay grade."

Luke rubbed a hand against his beard, frowning at the injury. "It's off by four millimeters, and it still looks pretty fresh. I'll have to re-break it."

"That's what Rissy said." She chewed on her bottom lip. "Can it wait until we're on the ship? I'm assuming you still have a ship."

Luke nodded, brushing his fingers against her upper arm and casting an overpowered numbing charm. She visibly relaxed when it took hold. "It's a difficult path down through the caverns. I can levitate you in some places, though—"

"Levitate me the whole way if it means I'm close to you," Bethie interrupted, kissing him again.

Luke felt like he could float, but it wasn't long before the activity around them brought him back to reality. With their mission complete, they now had to get everyone safely down to the ship and back to Sapphire Falls.

Including Aragon, now possessed by Atlas.

Wrapping an arm around Bethie's shoulders, Luke took in the devastation. Diamond Skies and Emma had gotten their father on a stretcher. The surviving members of Renova's Royal Coven escorted the Fifth Travelers down the path toward the caverns. Eternal Winds and Sargateth were debating what to do about Atlas, still pinned down by the four Olii.

Not only did he have crimes to answer for, but they needed to figure out if Aragon was still in there somewhere.

If they could save him.

But aside from counting the dead, they had time for little else.

Emma rose from her crouch beside their father and walked over to them. Luke could see the exhaustion in her face, feeling it across their bond.

"Are you yourself now?" Emma asked, still a little wary.

"I never stopped being me," Bethie answered firmly.

"But Igraine—"

Bethie shook her head. "She said she had a way around Lancelot's Prophecy. She could have saved you since Pendragon didn't care enough to share the whole truth."

Luke glanced down at her. "But now she's dead."

Bethany took a deep breath. "As a doornail. And now it's up to us to figure out how to keep Emma alive."

Luke caught his sister's eyes. *We're in this together until the end. Reconnect her to us.*

It was a testament to the rebuilt trust between Sorceress and Sentinel that Emma didn't hesitate.

Bethie gasped next to him, and Luke felt her presence blossom to life in his head.

*I didn't have time to get used to this in Valona,* Bethie's voice echoed through Luke's mind. *This is amazing!*

He felt Emma withdraw, her presence just a pinprick on the edges of his awareness. Then, he imagined scooping Bethie into his arms and flooded their connection with love and relief. Next to him in the real world, she leaned into his side, and he could feel her tension melt away. He pressed a kiss to the top of her head. Out of the corner of his eye, he watched Morgan, now back in her human form, levitate the litter carrying the elder Prophet.

Argent, who had been talking with Sargateth and Eternal Winds, excused himself from the conversation and unstrung the Elvara Bow. He secured it across his back, then knelt to retrieve Excalibur from where Atlas had dropped it, lifting the legendary sword to rest against his shoulder. His own sword was back in the sheath at his side. He called out to Evie, and she followed him as he walked across the snowy grounds to where Cordelia still sat, mixed displeasure and delight on her wrinkled face.

"Mage Watson, take her into custody."

"Gladly," Evie replied darkly, seizing Cordelia by the wrist and dragging her to her feet before she could protest. She formed handcuffs with strands of restraining magic, much like how Ebony Reva had caught the assassin who set off Septim's curse.

"Unhand me, you lousy squids," Cordelia snarled, but Evie had been too fast. "What gives you the right—"

"Muzzle her, too," Argent commanded.

Evie produced a rag and stuffed it into Cordelia's mouth. Then she forced her toward the train of people heading to the caverns.

Argent followed at a distance, weariness etched into his young face. When he passed Emma, she fell into step with him. Close enough to talk but not touch.

Luke wondered how she would process everything.

Finally, Sargateth and Eternal Winds came to an agreement. Diamond Skies and an Olis named *Hallowed Strength of Stone and Flame*, would escort Atlas to *The Sea Wolf* and remain as his guards for the voyage. Eternal Winds would coordinate with the rest of the Olis Council to take the traitors and Mountains' body back to Skypoint.

Cara Fletcher, Dakota Pack, and Harlow Barnes still lay where they'd fallen on the temple grounds. The three witches from the Fifth Travelers lay beside them, together in death. The older woman who had helped fight Atlas stood in front of the dead, leaning heavily on a short, squat man with a waning crescent moon tattooed on the left side of his face.

Luke and Bethany started after the rest of Camelot's delegation, picking their way through the exploded stones, toppled trees, and burnt shrubs covered with a fine layer of snow. The flakes continued to fall, slowly hiding all evidence of the battle, including the dead.

When they reached the entrance to the caverns a few minutes later, Hela Tanberg waited for them, her throat bruised. Oren had already left, leading the survivors through the treacherous path inside the Dragontooth Caverns.

Luke had never seen any of Renova's Royal Coven cry, but he saw the evidence of Hela's tears. They hadn't had the time to bury anyone, let alone perform the funeral rites that every fallen coven witch had received during the Valon War.

Hela didn't speak, merely nodded at them both before disappearing into the darkness after Emma and Argent.

Bethie began humming a tune Luke didn't recognize, but it soothed his frayed nerves as they left the eerie whiteness behind and entered the abyss.

When they reached the mouth of the caverns, Luke and Sargateth secured his father in the center of the longboat. Oren, Bethie, and Argent clambered aboard after them, and Evie, still detaining Cordelia with magic, took control of the rudder.

Emma stayed behind with Morgan, and Luke wondered how much of it had to do with needing some space from Argent.

As they zipped away from the massive island, Bethie kept looking back at the caverns, her messy fishtail braid coming even more undone in the wind.

*Did you forget something?* Luke asked in his mind.

It took her a long moment to answer. *No. I just hate leaving my sisters behind.*

Luke tightened his hold on her, careful not to agitate her broken arm. In front of them, his father lay in repose, looking far too close to death. Sargateth held stabilizing magic over him, but the eldest Olis looked like he was hanging on by a thread himself.

When the longboat bumped against the side of *The Sea Wolf*, the crew threw over a ladder. Luke climbed up first and then levitated Bethie without a word.

A hive of activity greeted them. Luke gave his father his full attention, his magic working in tandem with Sargateth's to bring the litter up.

He started toward the shipboard infirmary with Bethany when a commotion from the railing caught his attention.

Cordelia struggled as Evie levitated her aboard. When her feet touched the deck, she tripped and fell, her hat falling at the feet of William Pendragon.

Argent's voice rose over the hubbub of the ship, loud enough for the crew to hear him. "Cordelia Roque, you are hereby stripped of your rank, and you will spend the remainder of this voyage confined to the brig."

Cordelia's eyes bugged out, and her hands, still secured by Evie's magic, curled into fists. She tried to spit out the balled-up rag but couldn't.

"My father passed the rights and responsibilities of the crown to me before the battle started. I am now your King, whether you like it or not, and you said yourself that you were not there to help, but rather to watch your rulers die."

Evie lifted Cordelia and shoved her forward, seizing one elbow to lead her away before she could protest.

"First Officer Pendragon," Argent said, audibly weary, "are you able and willing to take command of this ship and steer her homeward?"

"Aye, Your Majesty," William responded, his bushy salt-and-pepper beard twitching.

"Then congratulations on the long-overdue promotion, Captain. The ship is yours." Without another word, Argent walked toward Luke, his hand brushing against the edge of Tomás's litter as he led the way below decks to the infirmary.

Bethie caught Luke's sleeve. "I can stay up here and give you guys space to work."

Luke twisted his hand, threading their fingers together. "I wouldn't dream of making you suffer any longer. The Olii did what they could for Dad on the battlefield." And it was true. He didn't know what else they could do to improve his father's condition. At this point, Luke could only defer to Sargateth's expertise.

Bethie didn't respond, but he could feel her anxiety lessen through their bond. He tugged her hand, leading her down a set of stairs in the middle of the sterncastle deck.

The door at the bottom opened into the small shipboard infirmary.

Five twin-sized beds were crammed together on one side, while the other had a full wall of cabinets and drawers stuffed with medical supplies and potions.

Sargateth had already moved Tomás to lay on the second bed from the end.

Argent, his hair a mess and armor still covered with dirt and blood, sat on the edge of the bed shoved against the wall. He leaned over, his elbows resting against his knees. He hung his head.

The King—no longer a Prince—did not move, not even to acknowledge their presence.

Luke swallowed, not sure what to think now that Argent technically wore the crown, even if it had not touched his brow yet.

Luke's gaze strayed to his father and his heart seized. "I'm going to fix up Bethie," he said, his voice hollow.

Bethie squeezed Luke's hand.

Sargateth, standing awkwardly at the foot of Tomás's bed, nodded stiffly and left. The stasis charm glowed softly in the low light.

Luke instructed Bethie to take the bed closest to the door, leaving two empty mattresses between them and his unconscious father.

As she leaned back against the pillow, a hint of a smile tugged at her lips.

Luke furrowed his brow, tipping his head to one side. *What is it?*

*Just remembering the last time I was in a hospital bed with you watching over me.*

*Feels like forever ago.* He cleared his throat. "I'm putting you to sleep. When you wake up, you'll be as good as new."

"Wait." She sat back up and kissed him once more.

Luke wrapped an arm around her upper back and eased her down, savoring the combined physical and mental connection. He pulled away, his face flushing at the thoughts of what he wanted to do with her. Then he pressed his scarred palm against her cool forehead, and she tipped into magical slumber.

It didn't take him long to fix her arm. The hardest part was aligning the bone again after re-breaking it. He forced himself to stay focused on Bethany, even though his father lay a few feet away in a dead sleep. Much like he'd done with Emma after Keldvaar, he wrapped both hands around her arm where the break had been and sent pulses of powerful healing magic through the bone. On the medical projection next to them, he watched as the crack faded with each successive burst of magic until it disappeared completely.

He couldn't help but be glad that her injury had not been caused by an Olis's claws, which seemed to need an Olis to heal.

Luke dismissed the projection and gently brushed a lock of Bethie's hair away from her face. Still in deep, magical sleep, she didn't react, and Luke decided to leave her that way. He doubted she'd gotten any meaningful rest since before setting out to Valona all those months ago.

His own weariness hit him like a wave. He stretched out beside Bethany on the bed, tucking her into his side, and he fell into his first restful sleep in months.

Luke woke to the gentle swaying of the ship carving through the ocean. Bethie had shifted in her sleep, her newly healed arm thrown over his stomach and the full length of her body pressed against his side. Cracking an eye open, he met Bethie's half-lidded gaze.

*I'd forgotten what it's like to not have a broken arm,* she whispered in his head. *I could get used to waking up like this.*

*Me too.*

She grabbed his hand and brought it to her face, kissing the scar. *You'll have to tell me how you got this sometime.*

Luke smiled and rolled to take stock of the infirmary. When his eyes adjusted, he saw King Argent hadn't moved. Luke heard a soft murmuring weaving through the rhythmic rise and fall of the waves, and after a moment realized Argent was praying over Tomás.

Luke wondered why the King was still down here. Then he realized that Tomás may have been as much of a father to Argent as his own. The thought sent a little twist of guilt through him.

Luke and Bethie both sat up, swinging their legs over the edge of the bed. Bethie leaned to grab her boots, and the bed creaked.

Argent finally looked up.

Even in the low light, his eyes were bloodshot. His face was stained with tears, and hair stuck out at odd angles across his face, held up by dried sweat.

A quick glance at Tomás's chest told him he still lived, but Argent had kept vigil for hours.

Perhaps it had been to avoid who waited for him in the brig.

"Hi," Bethie said. "I never said thanks for coming to rescue me. In Valona, I mean."

A myriad of emotions flitted through the King's green eyes. "I could not have borne staying behind," he answered, his voice like gravel.

Footsteps sounded on the staircase outside, and Emma entered a moment later, bringing a fresh burst of ocean air and a tray full of food with her. She set the tray down at the end of the bed across from Luke and Bethie and went to Argent, who looked at her and stiffened. Emma hesitated at the end of her father's bed.

Luke had the vague sense that Emma and Argent were having a mental conversation, but he couldn't hear any of it.

Finally, Emma's face relaxed a bit. She helped Argent to his feet, then assisted him with his armor, piling it on the bed. After another beat of silence, Emma hugged Argent so close that Luke turned his face into Bethie's hair.

After a minute, Emma and Argent came over to sit on the other empty bed, and all four of them faced each other for the first time since Valona. Bethie shuddered and leaned into Luke's side, and he wrapped an arm around her shoulder.

Finally, Bethie reached for some food and broke the silence.

"I'll tell you about the tidal waves and the wendigo if you tell me what the heck happened in the last—" she held up her blank wrist as if checking the time, "—three-ish months. Oh, and this ship's original figurehead is hurtling into a black hole, if anyone cares."

Argent was the first to react, and it was exactly how Luke expected.

"Bethany. I don't know how much you heard or saw while hiding—"

"Oh, enough to know you did something you probably regret," Bethany interrupted. "What I don't know is *why* you'd even care if I'm possibly a descendant of Arthur from Earth. It's not like I'm queen material. And even if I was, I wouldn't want the throne."

Argent stared at her, mouth hanging open. "But how did you know that was even a question?"

Luke reeled as Bethany told him about how Igraine illuminated the portals and how they'd both seen Davan Ender bringing Bethany's parents to Talahm. If age had given Igraine anything, her ability to connect dots was unmatched.

"I'm pretty sure we'd know if we had English roots," Bethany finished with one cheek squashed against Luke's shoulder. Their hands entwined over his thigh. "Mom wheedled Dad into doing one of those genealogy DNA things a few years ago, and it came back mostly Germanic and Scandinavian on both sides, but nothing from Britain." She tucked a leg under her. "Unless Renault sends another letter—I'd still like to give him a piece of my mind—we have to wait until we reach Camelot to hear what Davan found."

"I'm sure there's some kind of magic to determine your ancestry, if you are indeed curious enough to verify." Argent closed his eyes, pinching the bridge of his nose as he drew in a deep breath and sighed. "But what we did was never about your ancestry. It was about facing Igraine. He—and I—did not want to face such high costs."

Bethany stilled, and Luke could feel her conflicted emotions beat through their bond like a drum.

They'd ended up paying a steep cost regardless.

Finally, Bethany nodded grimly as if coming to terms with how close to death she'd been. A mental image of the tidal wave flashed through Luke's mind. "I didn't want to either."

They all fell quiet for several moments, but Bethany broke it once again.

"So.... Did you leave your mom in Camelot?"

Luke's heart dropped like a stone. He shot to his feet and hurried to the end of his father's bed to rifle through the bunched-up robes on the floor. His hands trembled as he plucked the journal from deep pockets.

Grimacing, he flipped to the last page with handwriting, soaked with far too much blood.

There, in shaky script, his mother's words.

*Don't be dead, Tom. I could not bear losing you twice.*

"I need a pen," Luke said thickly.

Emma shoved one into his hand, and he scribbled out a quick sentence reassuring his mother that his father was alive, but injured and unconscious.

He sagged back onto the bed beside Bethany, handing Emma the journal to talk to their mom.

But their tribulations were far from over.

With the death of an Olis, the release of the Nephilim, Atlas as their captive inside Aragon, and Lancelot's full Prophecy looming, they had one last mission.

To cut off Langoth for good and keep Emma alive.

# FINISH THE STORY
## THE LAST HORIZON

Die to save the universe, or die with it.

Confronted with a horrible truth kept secret for centuries, Seventh Sorceress Emma Artair has no choice. She can only save the world by sacrificing herself, but accepting it isn't easy… and neither is her final journey.

To reach the swimming stars beneath Skypoint, *The Sea Wolf* must sail through waters fraught with danger and the bloody consequences of Emma freeing the Nephilim. As the last horizon looms, Emma and her friends face deception, possessions, betrayal, death, and thousands of rogue portals—each obstacle dashing hope and cinching Emma's fate.

With secret bloodlines, an imprisoned king, and a demon working against them, the heroes face their hardest battle yet: make it to Skypoint before the Nephilim overrun the world, before the black hole consumes Langoth, and before Emma loses her nerve.

After all, how does one walk into eternity's arms?

Get Book 4 at **https://talahm.com/the-last-horizon** or by scanning the code below:

# ALSO BY COLLEEN MITCHELL

## THE CHRONICLES OF TALAHM

### Main Series

Book 1: *Mark of Stars*

Book 2: *The Prophet's Ruin*

Book 3: *Tides of Fate*

Book 4: *The Last Horizon*

### Companion Stories

*The Orphan's Gambit*

Visit talahm.com for the latest reading order and available books in the Talahm universe.

# ACKNOWLEDGEMENTS

All praise, honor, and glory belong to my King of Kings and Lord of Lords, Jesus Christ. It's only through the gifts He's given me that I've been able to write a single word, let alone string together enough to make a book (or three).

My husband Tim, thank you for your unwavering support and encouragement, and for being a masterful sounding board for ideas.

My best friend Jeannie Sweeney, I wished we lived closer. I miss our day-long writing sessions at your house that got interrupted by giggling over our characters. Thank you for being an awesome human.

To my parents, thank you for all your support and encouragement. The first book in this series was dedicated in part to my dad, who passed in November 2019. And the second book was dedicated in part to my mom. I love you!

I could not have finished any of my books without Tally Ink or the constantly encouraging community fostered by our Professional Premium members. So this is a big fat thank you to every single person who joined our calls, offered feedback on blurbs and brainstorming, and became a friend.

Special thanks goes to Karilyn Turner, the absolute best critique partner imaginable, whose comments never cease to make me howl with laughter (or snort), and whose reader brain helped fix some pretty major issues. My proudest moment with Karilyn was rewriting King Aragon across three drafts such that I made her go from wanting to yeet him into the abyss to actually liking him enough that his fate made her sad! And yes, I promise you'll get more of Igraine and Mountains in her villain backstory book.

My coach Dave Moreno, thank you for your strategy, wisdom, and suggestions on the business side of this writing adventure.

My incredible editing team: Halie Fewkes Damewood, Lauren Loftis, and Shanna P. Lowe, thank you for your endless pushing to *make the story better* whether through repeatedly blowing things up, streamlining and deleting unnecessary words, or helping me find the perfect balance between commas and em dashes.

Thank you to my artists! Angelique Modin never ceases to amaze me with her cover art skills. I know it took a while to get the wolf head right, but gosh does it look fabulous! And LeighAnn Lopez, I don't think I can thank you enough for the gorgeous chapter illustrations—not just in this book, but ALL of them! And the full world map! So pretty.

And lastly, to YOU, my reader! Thank you for trusting me to continue the series and reading all the way to the end. The home stretch is in view.

To sign up for updates on future books (whether in this series or another), visit www.talahm.com.

See you in Book 4!

# ABOUT THE AUTHOR

Colleen Mitchell finds it oddly satisfying to tug on reader heart strings, which started in Fanfiction and bled into her original works. She's been writing since age twelve and spent a good chunk of choir class ignoring the teacher to trade stories with her best friend in the back row.

She lives in Montana with her husband Tim and their cat Luna.

You can visit Colleen online at talahm.com, or on Instagram @colleenmitchellwrites.